The Worst of Us
A novel by Jason Dias

Acknowledgements and Dedications

Thanks to Kim Hsin for always being encouraging. To the Colorado Springs Fiction Writers Group for putting up with me and giving away their time. To Louis Hoffman and Bliss Dijulio who keep me working – when the bills are paid, I get to write. And to Mark Yang who taught me to be OK.

One

"Crash call, two one four a hundred twenty-second street." The voice on the radio was all treble. Lisa cracked an eye to look at it as if looking at the speaker would make it more intelligible.

The white van edged away from the curb. The driver, a middle-aged man in a paramedic uniform, touched a button on the radio. "Copy that. We're *en route*. Got any more information for me, Susan?"

"Black male, mid-seventies, hundred fifty pounds, five-ten. Witness says the guy was high on something. Ranting about ghosts. Then he had a seizure and dropped."

"Roger." Then, to Lisa in the passenger seat, "Looks like you're up, doc."

The van didn't have any special markings, just a state government plate. Lisa Jayne, likewise, was not in paramedic regalia. "I didn't sign up to run the crash cart, John," she said.

"You know how it is," John said. They were rolling fast now, too fast. Along dim night-time streets it seemed even faster. "You got the MD, you're on duty. Slow night in MH anyway."

MH for mental health. "Whatever," Lisa said, then tried to shut her eyes and relax through the ride. It was going to get hairy when they got where they were going. Which might as well be the moon for all she ever got into the neighborhoods with streets in the hundreds. At least it would keep her certs up.

Sooner than she wanted, John pulled the anonymous white van over against another curb and she tumbled out, bag in hand, the stethoscope around her neck her only badge of rank. She pulled med gloves out of a baggie in her pocket as she went. There was the victim, face-down across a curb outside an all-night McDonalds. A crowd of people melted away at the sight of Lisa and her partner. Like roaches when the lights come on, like ghosts in the night.

The victim was clearly part of New York's burgeoning homeless population. He had on a long tan trench coat despite the season, fingerless gloves, slacks that had seen better days. A shirt whose color was hard to discern in the uncertain light from the windows all around, maybe navy, maybe black, but certainly dirty.

Lisa crouched by him to feel for a pulse. John brought around the crash cart – really just a bag with more portable versions of the stuff she was used to at the hospital – and set it next to her.

"Pulse is thready but acceptable," she said, and scanned for wounds. No obvious cuts or bleeding, not on this side. Neck injury was always a possibility and she wasn't supposed to gamble but she did. "Let's roll him over, get a look at his face." John helped and they got the guy over onto his back, no problem. He was light. Too thin. Contusions on his face, most likely from falling. Bad teeth. He had patchy hair, uncut and uncombed, sticking out like clumps of weeds in an unkempt field. She put her ear near his mouth. "Breathing is fine. We won't need to crash him. Breath stinks, probably some untreated diabetes."

"Wrist," John said.

Lisa looked at the wrist she hadn't checked for a pulse. The victim had a bracelet on. Metal, solid, shaped like a flattened out C wrapped around his arm just above the hand. A medic-alert bracelet. "What have we here?" Lisa said, and read the notations. "Well, maybe not such a slow night after all, John."

"Psycho?"

"Yeah, he's a schizophrenic. So maybe not a drug problem after all."

"Not illegal, anyway."

"Yeah," Lisa said. "Let's get him up on a stretcher. We'll take him down to County."

They shouldn't have come out on a run like this, just the two of them. Getting a dropped body onto a stretcher was usually work for more than one retired firefighter working part-time and one wiry little psychiatrist. But the guy was underfed enough they managed without too much trouble.

The back of the ambulance was primitive, none of the high-tech life-saving gear in a modern unit. Lisa's job wasn't, primarily, dealing with injuries and serious medical crises but mental health ones. Still, she found what she needed in back while John got the van rolling. "Pulse-ox is low," she said, more for the recorder on her collar than for John, who wasn't listening. "Ninety-six, not critical. Applying oxygen. Patient seems to be in fair health. Facial contusions, some bruising to the arm indicative of intravenous drug use. Doesn't look very recent, maybe forty-eight hours. Dentition isn't good. John, alert County we're going to want blood work, right away."

She strapped sensors around the man's chest, watched a portable display flicker to life. Green lines bounced and jagged across it, peaks and valleys.

"EKG looks pretty clean, for a man his age. No obvious cause for unconsciousness. I wonder if..."

The man's eyes opened. His voice was muffled and distorted by the oxygen mask on his face. He said, "You've got one on you."

"Good," Lisa said. "Consciousness evident at..." She glanced at her watch. "Nineteen-thirty-one. Sir, can you tell me your name?"

"MacAvoy, Elbert T., private first class, United States Army." He rattled off a long number.

"Nice to meet you, Elbert," Lisa said. "Do you know what year it is right now?"

"Two thousand and some," he said. "Fourteen, maybe, or fifteen. I lost track. Barack Obama is the president, and I guess I'm in an ambulance. You're too pretty to be a cop and I guess I'm too old to abduct for fun."

"Patient seems lucid," she said into her collar. "Continuing oxygen as a precaution."

"You talking to that thing?" Elbert said.

Lisa looked automatically at the microphone. "Does it bother you?"

"Yes it does, some. Never seen anyone talk to them before. You taking me to the hospital? I don't really want to go to the hospital. Reagan said I couldn't stay there anymore, you see. These days you just pick me up, drive me there, and then they give me a pile of pills to take and hustle me back out onto the streets again." His voice was muffled, almost echoing in the confines of the plastic oxygen mask.

"Do you have a home, Mr. MacAvoy? A place to stay?"

"Told you, I live out on the streets, Miss," Elbert said. "Not as bad as the jungle, no ma'am."

"Mr. MacAvoy, it seems you fell down and hit your head. We need to take you in and evaluate you. Is that going to be OK?" She took his pulse again while she talked.

"Suppose it isn't?"

"Well, that would make things more complicated, sir, but I suppose we'd have to involuntary you. Are you aware of what that means?"

"I guess I am," he said. "I'll come along quietly and spare you the paperwork."

"That's mighty decent of you," Lisa said. She found herself liking the man. He smiled at her through the mask, then closed his eyes. "Are you feeling well enough? Tired?" she asked him.

"Sleep when you can, that's what they taught me," he said. By the time they arrived at the county hospital, Elbert was snoring.

***

Elbert sat down in the plastic chair. It was bolted to the floor so he had trouble getting comfortable between it and the blue vinyl-topped table. His feet sounded strange, flip-flops on tile. "Used to be a water treatment room, didn't it?" The blue tiles on the floor and ceiling gave it away.

Lisa sat opposite. She wore a white cotton turtleneck, gray skirt, and her white lab coat. No jewelry, not in this place. Her hair was down, blonde going to gray. "Were you here back then?"

"No," he said. "How long you plan on keeping me?"

"You have some pressing engagements?" Lisa said, smiling.

"Suppose not, and the food hasn't gotten any worse. I could put my feet up awhile. But pretty soon you're going to try to make me take your pills, and then we aren't going to get along anymore."

"Suppose we start at the beginning, Mr. MacAvoy."

"Call me Elbert."

"Fair enough, Elbert. Help me understand how you ended up on that street corner, unconscious."

"Well, for that, you have to go all the way back. You want the beginning? The beginning is in 1954. I was thirteen years old in 1954, if you can credit that."

Two

"May I be excused, Mama?" Elbert still had food on his plate, some withered greens and a slice of toast, but his mother was busy with his little sisters. Twins, and each more than she could handle.

"Yes, go on now," she said, trying to brush one girl's hair and get food into the other one. The table was strewn with junk, old magazines and college books. "Is your homework done?"

"You know I'm no good at that math, not like you, Mama."

"I'm not so good at it either," she said. "I just work hard at it."

"Yes, Mama."

"And brush your teeth. When your Papa gets home, make sure he finds you safe in bed. No reading under the covers tonight, Elbert, I mean it. School comes early."

That it did, with a long walk to start off the day. Elbert put his plate in the kitchen with the others. It never occurred to him that he might wash it, being thirteen. His mind was mostly on whether Kathy-May might have read the note he'd slipped into her locker yet, and on the copy of Amazing Stories stuffed under his mattress. He got upstairs distracted. His math book waited in his room, pencils and paper laid out. Elbert didn't want to start on that yet.

So he took his transistor radio in the bathroom and set the volume as low as it would go while still being on. There was an advertisement for the local newspaper, and a thing about Bernie Cohen running for mayor – as though they'd ever elect a black mayor in this town – and then Jo Stafford came on. "*Make Love To Me*." If mama heard that song, she'd have a blue fit.

His toothbrush was on the edge of the sink, the toothpaste in a little tin jar on the other side. He swirled some toothpaste onto the brush, not liking the feel of the dry wood on his skin. A little water from the faucet spotted with rust – seemed like everything rusted fast in Arkansas – and then he set to cleaning his teeth. The sound was loud enough to drown out half the music, so he turned it up just a fraction.

Next up was "*Answer Me, My Love.*" Nat King Cole. Not as racy but twice as smooth. Elbert was really done with his teeth by then but algebra made him miserable, so he just stood where he was and listened for a minute. With nothing else to do, his eyes found the mirror over the sink.

It was old. A Coca-Cola promo product his ma had gotten by sending in proofs of purchase. It claimed Coke would relieve fatigue. The lettering was faded and flaking and there were rust spots behind the glass. It barely worked as a mirror. His dad shaved in it every morning, sometimes in the evening too if he was home in time for late service. He never missed a service if he could make it. Elbert couldn't imagine using this old thing to shave with.

But somewhere in there, behind the letters and words and in front of the rust spots, there was his own face.

He was thirteen, with just the vaguest hint of mustache growing over his upper lip. Broad nose, clear, dark skin. Thin brows that would thicken like his father's and then take over his face like his grandfather's one day, becoming great bushy caterpillars. And there were his eyes: clear, bright, brown like the Hershey's syrup Mr. Redman would put in his malted milk on days when Elbert could scare up a nickel.

He made eye contact with himself and held it. Nat King Cole faded away into the background, forgotten. Elbert's face slowly went slack, still. In those eyes, he saw something intelligent and real, and it held his gaze just as he held its gaze. That it was just light bouncing through glass and off metal didn't figure, not then, not to thirteen-year-old Elbert. He held the eye contact, and held it, and grew more and more certain that there was an intelligence in it.

And, slowly, he came to know that it meant him no good.

It was a creepy feeling, a certainty based on no facts. In that mirror, that rusty old Coke mirror bought with bottle tops in better times, was a mind. And that mind could make itself felt only through eye contact.

Elbert reached up and touched his own throat, not knowing at all what he was doing.

Thump-thump-thump.

Elbert's heart jumped like it was bursting. He knocked the radio off the sink. It smacked onto the floor, the battery door breaking off the back. Two Duracells rolled onto the tiles.

"What are you doing in there, boy? Is that music I hear?"

"Oh, Daddy, it's you," Elbert said. The door wasn't locked. He pulled it open. "I guess I just lost track of time."

His dad was a big man, a little over six feet and wide like an ox. Grew up pushing plows, share-cropping, getting beat up by the sun and the wind. Now he was a professional man, a book-keeper, but he still had the big, wide hands and weathered face of farmer. "Son, you look like you've been holding your breath past a graveyard. What's in you?"

But Elbert didn't know what was in him. Not then. "Guess I just didn't want to do my algebra, Daddy. I'm sorry." And he stepped into his father's arms. He was getting too old for such things and his father let him know it – after a minute.

"Come on," he said. "I'll help you. But only so you're done quickly. It's past your bedtime."

***

"That was your first break?" Lisa asked him. "Seems pretty mild. What else happened?"

"Break? Don't know what you mean. And nothing else happened. I did my homework and went to sleep. Except, it took forever to get there. To sleep, that is. That night, it was like reality was a canted table and I slid right off it. Where I found myself, I don't rightly know, couldn't say for sure." Elbert folded his hands on the table, leaned back as best he could in a chair that wouldn't move. "I never could quite shake that feeling. The feeling that something had gone wrong, that life had tilted sideways."

"Sounds prodromal," Lisa said, making a note in the file in front of her. There was a big black three-ring binder in the office with ELBERT MACAVOY along the spine, waiting for pages to fill it up. The manila file in front of her would furnish the first few sheets. "Prodromal means the period before the first break. People often experience strange sensations, mild psychoses, even personality changes."

"I know what it means," Elbert said.

"Yes, well I imagine you would. When was your first break, then, Mr... Elbert."

"Don't know what you mean," he repeated. "Never had a break."

"Fair enough. What were you doing outside the McDonalds?"

"Free country, isn't it? I can be outside McDonalds if I want to, or even inside it."

"Yes, Elbert," Lisa said. "But the question is, what were you doing? We have some conflicting reports and I'd just like to clarify."

"For the record?"

"For the record." She nodded.

"Well, in that case, what I was doing was faking a seizure so as you would have to bring me in here."

"And why is that, Elbert?" She thought she already knew, though. Eventually men like Elbert got tired of the streets, especially the older guys. The harassment, abuse, theft, even rape got to be too much and they needed a break, a couple weeks inside to put some weight back on and get some clean things.

"Why, Doctor Lisa, because you have one of them on you."

Lisa looked down at her notes. Wrote, "Fixed delusions very likely if not confabulation. Caution recommended." Then she looked back up at Elbert. "What makes you say that? And how could you know, given that we've never met?"

"Of course we've met," he said. "The grumlet distorts time, makes things very strange. What year were you born?"

"You'll forgive me if I decline to answer personal questions," she said.

"Always the same with you. I understand, though. You get some real crazies through here. Trust me on that one, I know it. But I'm willing to bet you were born in the last few weeks of nineteen sixty-eight, making you forty-seven."

"You're guessing," she said, trying to keep her expression bland.

"Basically, yes," Elbert said. "But I think I knew you before, and I've been trying to find you. I owe you one."

Here we go, Lisa thought. *I'm already part of his delusional system. Classic pattern would be to start on his side and migrate over as our goals fail to align.* But she just kept quiet. It was no good to mess around in fixed delusions. They were like a tar-baby out of the Brer Rabbit tales. Once you touched them, you could only get more deeply entangled.

"I owe you one," Elbert repeated. "You saved my life. Back in 'Nam."

"Well," Lisa said, "Looks like we're basically done, here, Elbert. I think you should stay with us for at least a few days. Get your three hots and a cot, see the barber. While you're here I'll see if there isn't something we haven't tried, some sort of treatment you could tolerate. Sally is our social worker. She'll be in pretty soon to see about your eligibility for some housing programs. Things have changed a little since Ronald Reagan was in office."

Elbert just smiled.

***

"He's quiet," Lisa said. She was inside the nursing station. The glass was soundproof and bullet-proof; speakers let in noise from the common room visible outside.

"The guys don't like him," Dylan said. He was twenty-four, brown and tall and wide and eager. "He's got kind of this vibe around them, like he's the only sane one in a house full of crazies. Like he's better. Hard not to notice."

"Yeah." Lisa watched Elbert. He occupied the armchair with the best view of the television. Shows had to be educational or informative and the news was too violent for this crowd so it was a cooking show. Elbert watched the wall behind the television. Other guys milled around, some reading, Barry just walking the halls as he did every day. Exercise. They talked to one another sometimes, sat together sometimes. Never with Elbert, though.

Dylan had Elbert's chart out in front of him on the table, laid open flat. The three binder-rings stood up, mostly empty in a place where the charts got thick fast. He read Lisa's summaries quickly. "Hey," he said. "What's all this?"

Lisa looked over his shoulder, saw her own notes on Elbert's story. "That's what he told me."

"But this is prose."

"Sure."

"We don't do prose here."

"I decided to write prose," Lisa said. "He's been in and out of here, Manhattan General, a half-dozen other places and nobody knows squat about him. They just throw a fistful of pills at him and let the guy go. I thought we should try to get his story down."

"For posterity?" Dylan said.

"For the record. How can you treat a guy if you don't understand his story?"

Dylan flipped to the med records, saw they were blank. "No prescriptions? Doc Killroy's going to go crazy."

"Not his case," Lisa said. "And like I said, we don't understand him yet."

"What's to understand, really?" Dylan said, opening the next book. "He's schizophrenic, right? Fixed delusions, like you said, so probably paranoid. We have meds for that."

"Meds that work at best a third of the time, and a diagnosis inherited from an in-the-breech assessment at Sinai in nineteen eighty-one. Let's be a little more thorough this time."

"You're the doctor," Dylan said, and concentrated on transcribing Killroy's semi-legible prescriptions onto the med sheets in front of him. "You want to let me in maybe on your thinking as you get to know him?"

Dylan wanted to be a psychologist. Not quite the same as a psychiatrist but they'd use the same manual for diagnostic codes. "Sure. School's treating you OK?"

"Too much reading. Hospital wants me to do overtime. Thinking of asking for nights. Could read some on nights."

"Forget it," Lisa said. "They've got night-shift doing half the janitors' jobs, auditing the med cabinet twice a night, auditing the records three nights a week. Those guys are busier than we are."

Dylan just grunted.

In the common room, Davy came over to stand in front of Elbert.

***

"That's my seat," Davy said. He was a short man, heavyset because of the Seroquel they gave him. He had fists like giant marshmallows and a face to match, doughy and strewn with craters left over from adolescent acne. Red hair and bloodshot eyes.

"I don't think it is," Elbert said. "I've been in these places before and for some reason they never let you bring in your own furniture." He smiled, showing brownish teeth. One needed a crown badly. He had on the thin pajamas and thinner bathrobe that passed for wardrobe in here.

Davy had on jeans and a T-Shirt. It proclaimed his fanhood of Pink Floyd. "That's where I sit," he said, changing tactics.

"I'm sitting here now, son," Elbert said. He didn't notice Lisa watching intensely from the nursing station. He did notice none of the orderlies – they called them Mental Health Clinicians here but they were orderlies – he noticed none of them were around right now. Room check time, probably. "You can sit here later. Or right here next to me if you like."

"Move."

"This is a power-play, right? Son, this isn't prison. You don't have to be the baddest, toughest young psychopath on the block. There ain't a block. It's just us crazies in here. Take a seat. Won't nobody try to hurt you."

Davy thought about it. Thinking was not his longest suit. His fists tightened up, not marshmallows now but big blocks of cheese, or maybe the peanut-butter that squirts out the side of an overloaded sandwich.

Then Elbert looked him in the eye.

Held his gaze.

Davy stood still as a mouse that's seen a cat watching it. His posture slowly relaxed. His mouth hung open a little, pink tongue like an oyster exposed to sunlight. His left hand shook just the tiniest bit. Then he sat down next to Elbert.

"OK," he said. "What's on?"

Elbert said nothing, just resumed staring out past the television, through the wall, into infinity.

"Oh, I like Rachael Ray," Davy said. "I wonder if she's married."

Three

Lisa waited in the interview room, pages laid out in front of her like a jigsaw puzzle awaiting assembly. Fixed delusions into which she'd been rapidly integrated; interpersonal charm (nobody talked Davy out of fighting); not much else to go on. Time-travel delusions might indicate guilt about a past event.

She butted the papers together, squared them off, slipped them into the manila file. Then she set a blank lined sheet on top.

Dylan knocked on the door. It echoed, boomed really, through the room's weird acoustics. Really a strange interview room, with marks on the floor under the table where the hydrotherapy tubs had once sat and burns on the table itself from when patients had used this space as the smoking room, before the ban.

"It's open," Lisa said, but it didn't have a lock.

Elbert entered, Dylan like a shadow behind him. When Elbert was settled in his seat across from Lisa, Dylan left them alone. The door boomed shut, the sound rocking back and forth through the room for a second.

"Hi, Elbert," Lisa said.

"Hello, Doctor Lisa."

"What would you like to talk about today?"

"Oh, I'm not really here for talking," he said.

"I know, it has to be hard with us poking and prodding on you. You didn't ask to come here and I practically coerced you into signing the papers. I see you've met the barber."

Elbert's hair was shaved down to scalp, just some gray stubble left in a circle from his ears around to the back of his head. "You did coerce me," Elbert said. "But I forgive you. It's hard to remain a free agent in this world. Anyways, *you're* the one that brought *me* here. Maybe we should start with what you would like to talk about. The sooner we're done with the preliminaries, the sooner I can be about my business."

"What business is that, Elbert?" Lisa said. But he didn't bite. So, after a few minutes, she said, "We were talking about the first time reality went sideways on you. I thought you might want to continue on with that story some."

"All right," he said, shifting around in his chair until he was comfortable. "Between the age of thirteen and going to Vietnam, I suppose you could say not too much of any real importance happened. Back home, the rest of the world discovered rock and roll, Jimi Hendrix and so forth. And drugs. Drugs, drugs, drugs. If not for the sixties, why, you wouldn't have a job, Doctor Lisa."

She smiled at him, waited for him to go on.

"I didn't do any of that, though. Well, that's for later. I suppose the next main event happens late in nineteen sixty-eight."

Lisa wrote, "Sixty-eight again," on her blank page.

"I was in prison, on the front lines in the jungle. Well, not really a prison, just a bamboo hut, really. But I wasn't allowed to leave. I was under arrest."

"What for?" Lisa said.

"You want me to tell it," he said, "then let me tell it." But he softened it with a grin, impish and impertinent.

"All right," Lisa said, and sat back to listen.

***

He got that feeling again when she came into the room, into his life.

Elbert had his feet up on a steel desk. His boots weren't shined. There was mud in the half-assed treads, which were really not much more than evenly-spaced thumb-prints in the thick soles. His uniform was dirty but it was camouflage so only his nose made that very plain. The walls were bare corrugated tin over bamboo poles.

She pushed through the door, dismissed the sergeant who had custody of him. The sergeant scrambled away like she was fire and he was made of rice paper. Elbert looked her over, the way a man looks at a woman, but she met none of those kinds of expectations. He looked again. And what he was thinking of was that time with the mirror when he was thirteen, that feeling of sliding right of the edge of reality.

She wasn't tall, maybe five eight. But she was big. "You're a black one, aren't you?" she said.

Out here nobody skirted the racism issue so Elbert wasn't too surprised, but the willies started. Gooseflesh held itself a parade on his forearms. "No blacker than half the boys out here," he said. "I think you got off the wrong stop, lady. MASH is back up the road a piece. This here is temporary jail until they figure out something more permanent."

She pointed at her collar. A subdued blue eagle rested among the random green and brown and black shapes of her camo. Name on her tape said WILCOX. "You forgotten your military bearing, soldier?"

Elbert's eyes widened a little more. He'd never seen a woman colonel before. Even the boss of the nurses didn't usually get farther than major. "I guess I just ain't met a colonel like you before." And he hadn't.

She had ripped the sleeves off her shirt, probably because she'd had to. Her biceps were like rugby balls in size, shape, color and texture. She had a linebacker's shoulders, all straining against the remains of her shirt, against the black tee she wore under it. She had pecs like a bodybuilder. And her face...

"You're in some trouble, MacAvoy," she said.

"My legal counsel advised I stay quiet on that particular topic until I get someplace civilized," Elbert said. The feeling of dislocation increased and he tried to talk steady, with confidence, but he was sure she could see the gooseflesh on his arms.

"You haven't seen a lawyer out here. But you're probably right: shooting an officer is a pretty serious offense."

Elbert crossed his arms, leaned back farther, looked at one of those blank walls like there was a window to see through.

"Black enlisted man shoots a white infantry captain with a shiny service record and a bunch of medals... Well, let's just say your aim was off."

Elbert looked back at her, into her eyes. They were set too far apart, brown like mud. Some folks might have said they were like a doe or a cow, but Elbert figured she was too ugly to be a cow. More like a bull. "I hit what I was aiming at," he said.

"Then you made a serious mistake. You know, your whole unit is mostly likely going down? Rest of the men, they covered for you. I guess they figured Daniels had it coming. Not every day an officer get fragged but it does happen. What doesn't figure is he doesn't fit the profile. He isn't a gung-ho young officer looking for glory and toeing the line. He's on his third tour. Doesn't take unnecessary chances, tried to stay out of the shit."

Elbert looked away again.

"Anyway, you'd have gotten through clean except for one thing. One mistake."

"What's that?"

"You didn't kill him," she said.

"Like I said, I hit what I was aiming at."

Wilcox was quiet a beat, then said, "I need you."

Elbert laughed, a sound more like a nervous cough than any expression of humor. "Lady, you ain't my type." And she wasn't. He didn't dig scars and she had some doozies: a nose that had been busted at least three times, a livid red mark that ran from over her left eye, across the bridge of that busted nose to under her right eye, a lacework of older white lines across her bare shoulders, healed-up bullet wounds on one arm. Plus she could probably bench-press him like some of the boys liked to do with the little Vietnamese women who congregated around bases.

"But you're exactly my type, MacAvoy. That's why I bought you out of here. Orders."

She reached in her shirt, came out with an envelope. It landed on the steel desk with a sound like a faraway gunshot. Elbert put his feet on the ground, sat forward. Poked the envelope with one finger. Finally, he lifted the flap. It wasn't sealed. The paper was thin, the cheap stuff orders were printed on. This was maybe the second or third carbon back from the original. He scanned over it, squinting to see the feint print.

"Detachment?" he said.

"Name of the game."

"Everything forgiven?"

"What's to forgive?" Wilcox said. "Nothing ever happened."

"I was looking forward to going home," Elbert said. "Maybe pick up where the good Doctor King left off, fight for something real."

"Can't do that from jail, Elbert. Not from Fort Leavenworth. The sit-ins at Leavenworth never end. Besides, what I got for you is bigger than all of that."

"Bigger than freedom for a whole race of people? You got my attention. There's only one wrinkle. Like you said, I left a witness."

"First order of business, corporal: do you believe in second chances?"

Elbert nodded slowly.

"Then saddle up. We're going to go and make amends for your mistake."

"Like, I toe the line, apologize, let him tell me off, and *then* all is forgiven?"

"Something like that." She turned and walked out like she expected him to follow. Elbert got up and looked around the room. "I was getting sick of bamboo anyway," he said to nobody, and did what she seemed to expect. He paused at the door, looking in every direction for an armed guard waiting to shoot him in the middle of an escape attempt. There was nobody.

Wilcox waited in a Jeep sitting in a muddy puddle that reflected a slightly overcast sky. Jungle encroached all around, practically screaming that this forward position was strictly a temporary inconvenience in the grand scheme of things, that vines and leaves and bugs would soon own all this land once more. And Elbert got that feeling one more time, that shivering, skin-crawling feeling like reality had just taken a big step to the left. He stopped dead halfway to the Jeep.

Elbert listened, and heard nothing. Nothing human, anyway. Birds, insects, the rasping of wind through the jungle. But no engines, no muttered conversation, no footsteps. No hammers or typewriters.

He looked around slow, in a circle. And saw nobody. The whole place, half a dozen Quonset huts, a couple of crew tents, a makeshift landing pad – all abandoned.

"Get in the Jeep, MacAvoy," Wilcox said.

He didn't see how he had any other choice. Go with the big crazy lady or spend the next couple decades making big rocks into little rocks. But he knew even then nothing good was going to come of this. Not one thing.

The Jeep coughed to life. Wilcox drove it hard, thumping through gears and slamming through obstacles. There was barely a track out of here and branches slapped at the front grill every few yards. There was green crud, plant blood, all over the window already. Wilcox acted like she could see. Elbert wished he couldn't. The jeep bounced over a fallen branch, bottomed out in a gully.

Elbert said, "Wherever we're going, is it important we get there alive?"

Wilcox just laughed and let her foot get heavier. Elbert groaned, threw an arm across his eyes, and waited for it to be over.

The outpost had been forward enough there was really only one way to go, and that was back towards the American lines. And that was through dense jungle, thick, hanging carpets of greenery. It was impossible to tell what time of day it might be until night took all the light from the sky. Elbert swatted at bugs, sleep a futile dream while the Jeep hammered at his ass and back. "Hey," he said, "you going to turn on the headlights?"

Wilcox was still driving at the limit, at the edge of what the Jeep could do. "Why?" she said. "Can't see anything though this crapped out windshield anyway. Plus, lights are targets in the dark."

"What's the difference if we die by gunshot wounds or in a crash? That how you got all those scars, driving in the dark?"

She smiled, a quirky, ironic gesture that didn't fit on her face anywhere. He wondered if she might once have been pretty, could be pretty still under all the scars and dirt and whatever feeling had made her make herself over into what she was now.

Another hour went by. Elbert watched the fuel gauge. Didn't seem to be any margin in telling Wilcox that it had been pointing at empty the last five miles. He couldn't tell for sure through the ruined glass, now crazed with cracks as well as bug-juice and plant smears, but he thought there might be lights in the distance.

"Right," Wilcox said, though he hadn't said anything. "Field hospital."

"I ain't sick," Elbert said. "Are you?"

"No, but this is where you make amends."

The Jeep held out another mile. When it came to a stop in front of a long, low building, headlights dimming as the engine quit, Elbert didn't know if it was because she shut it off or because it was finally out of gas or because it was dead, a mule flogged one time too many.

He climbed out. Wilcox led him through the front door of the place. It had been a while since he'd seen a place not cobbled together out of local materials combined with whatever would fit on one jeep. This place had steps, concrete ones. The jungle still loomed on every side, loud enough he couldn't hear the Jeep's engine ticking behind them, loud enough he could still hear it inside. *Even concrete is impermanent,* it seemed to say.

There was a hallway with subdued lighting. An empty desk. One desk lamp illuminated a medical text book. Someone had been sitting there, studying. Elbert could feel it. But now they were gone. Through another door, a swinging door that could open either way, there were two rows of cots. Men rested under thin army blankets, uniformly sweating. They all had white bandages someplace visible.

There was Daniels, down at the end on the left. His right shoulder was wrapped up in sterile gauze. It looked smaller than his left and that's because it was: a revolver pressed up against skin does a hell of a lot of damage. This soldier wouldn't be seeing any more action. That was good enough for Elbert.

Daniels' eyes opened as Wilcox and Elbert came close. Their feet practically boomed against the plank flooring.

"You," Daniels said – and he wasn't looking at Elbert.

But Wilcox was. "So," she said. "Go on, set it to rights."

Elbert didn't know what the game was. "I'm sorry I shot you," he said. "It was a mistake."

"Wrong answer," Wilcox said. "You were right to shoot the son-of-a-bitch. You know what your mistake was."

"Not killing him?"

Daniels looked from one to the other, his eyes gradually widening. He sputtered something half-coherent, tried to sit up. He had on a hospital gown, just a paper bathrobe really. His head shone where he was going bald around his widow's peak. Wilcox reached up and grabbed the drip bag connected to Daniels' arm, squeezed. He slowed back down, sagged, but didn't shut his eyes.

"Do it," she said.

"Do what?"

"Fix your mistake." There was a pistol in her hands, a sleek, square automatic. New. Deadly-looking. She had hold of the barrel, the grip right there for Elbert to take.

He took it.

"What is this?" he said.

"Summary justice. You know what he is. And you know what he'll do stateside. Did those little Viet girls deserve what he did to them? Did they? Will the little girls at home deserve it? You know he won't stop when he gets home. You know he's practicing out here."

Daniels muttered again, wooly, half-there. Elbert considered the gun. "I could kill you both and disappear," he said.

"You could. You've got a full clip. Do what you have to do."

"In cold blood?" Elbert said. Wilcox just looked at him, stared, like that mirror when he was a kid. Like the night sky if you thought too hard about it. He pointed the gun at Daniels. Center-mass. "He deserves it," he said.

"That's right," Wilcox said. "Rapist. Murderer. Torturer. Sadist. Worse. You don't even know the smallest fraction of what he's done, what he's setting up to do."

Daniels had seemed big out there in the jungle. Potent, competent, portrait of an Army officer. Here he seemed old, frail. Weak. Nothing.

Elbert pulled the trigger. Daniels jerked, a sudden, whole-body spasm, and then he was still. The smell of cordite mingled in the air with antiseptics and old blood and unchanged colostomy bags. The Captain's chest had a big hole in it: a concavity, a broken place that slurped and sucked at the weak light of the sick-room at night. Elbert shot him again, blew out his solar plexus. He resisted the urge to bite his knuckles in horror, to panic and jibber and run. Daniels would never finish going bald.

He turned the gun around, offered it back to Wilcox. She said, "Keep it. You're going to need it." She stripped the holster off her belt. Elbert put the gun in its leather holder and stuffed it in his pants. They'd taken his belt when they arrested him, should have taken his bootlaces too only they'd been so hot to lock him up it had escaped their attention. "Turns out I was right. You're exactly the man I need."

***

Elbert stopped. Lisa glanced up at the clock behind him. "We're out of time," she said.

He nodded.

"Did you really shoot that man, Elbert? Do you know if that was real or delusion?" It was a dumb question, she knew that, but it came out of her anyway.

"Of course I did. Not the first time, but the second. And I did worse. I did a lot worse, back then. Yes, we all did. But that's for another day. As you say, we are out of time. You have other duties to attend to. I think I shall go and lay down for a piece."

Lisa nodded, and Elbert stood up from the unmoving chair. He plodded out of the room, pushed through the door, and was lost to sight.

Lisa finished scrawling down what he had told her, writing fast. *Going to have to rewrite this later*, she thought. *Maybe need to record these sessions. Got an old voice recorder someplace.*

Four

"He's a strange one," Sally said. She was a tall, heavy woman a bit past fifty. She wore a pink cardigan the way Lisa wore her lab coat: as part of the uniform. Nobody would mistake her as anything but the social worker.

"Why do you say that?" Lisa said. The chair under her creaked as she shifted her weight, planted elbows on the big brown table between her and Sally. "I mean, I agree, even stranger than usual, for us. But what makes *you* think so?"

"Well, he was polite, well-informed, and didn't want one bit of help. He wouldn't let me talk him into a single piece of paperwork, any kind of benefits or subsidies or anything. He said our hospitality here was enough and in a few days he'd be back about his work."

"Anything out of line?"

"Nope," Sally said. "You warned me about his fixed delusions but those ideations didn't come up at all, whatever they are. His reasons were all strictly pragmatic. In short, he prefers to be homeless."

Lisa nodded, got up to pour coffee. Her hand ached from rewriting her notes from the last interview. As she turned to sit back down, she saw Elbert coming down the hall towards the common room, apparently refreshed from his nap. The other guys stayed out of his way. Davy, in the big chair in front of the TV, saw him coming. He got up and moved one chair away. Lisa could only see the back of his head, so she glanced at the black and white screen that captured the common room from a different angle, and saw that Davy had a smile on his face.

Fascinating.

"He strike you as charming?" Lisa said.

"Not especially," Sally said. "Maybe he's so charming we didn't notice."

That was possible. Years of dealing with sociopaths and antisocials equipped Lisa with a creep-detector, a way of recognizing false charm. It would take actual sincerity to get past her bullshit detector these days. "Wish I'd had one in college," she muttered to herself.

"What?"

"Bullshit detector."

"Yeah," Sally said. "Me too. I can think of a couple of boyfriends from back then who wouldn't pass muster today."

In the common room, Elbert had taken to staring at the wall behind the television again. Davy had joined him. On the screen, some guys with sleeveless shirts and dew rags were looking over an old car.

"What are they looking at?" Lisa said.

Sally followed her gaze, looked at the two men. "Not the TV," she said. Their heads suggested they looked up and to the right of there. That was just blank wall.

Except for the camera mounted there.

Lisa raised her head, slowly, sure what she was going to see. Her eyes passed over the four cameras giving views of the interview room, the library, two shots of the hallway. And they came to rest again on the view of the common room.

"The camera," she said, and Sally did as she had done, locked eyes with Davy and Elbert through the blurry, monochrome picture on the screen.

Sally's hand came up to her throat. "OK, that's a new one," she said.

"I'll say. What the hell does it mean?"

"Damned if I know, Lisa. You're the doctor."

"Right." She went back to her paperwork. Later, after reading her own notes twice, she looked up and found herself all alone in the nursing station. Two orderlies sat in the common room at the staff table. The clock said everyone else had most likely gone home.

"I wonder..."

Lisa went to the forward window, to the bookshelves under a counter there. Right under the screen, which showed Davy and Elbert and now Mike, too, staring up at the screen. Lisa shuddered but stayed on-task. Telephone directories were stacked in the tight space, maybe the last place other than public libraries to really keep them around. The guys weren't allowed to sign onto the internet.

The pages Lisa wanted had blue edges. She found a number quickly, sat in a wheeled chair and picked up the telephone. Dialed. Waited.

Of course it was after hours. A patient but mechanical voice came on, feminine and impersonal. "If this is an emergency, please hang up and dial 911. You have reached the department of veterans' affairs. Normal office hours are..."

"Shit." Just a hunch, though, and one that could wait until morning.

The back door to the station opened and closed. It was on the other side of a bathroom the size of a small closet, so Lisa couldn't see immediately who was there. When she rolled around to look, she saw James Killroy.

Oh, great. The Killjoy.

He was a white man of between seventy and eighty indeterminate years. He wore a blue button-down and a bowtie, the latter as clear an announcement of pedantry as you could ask for. Lab coat, navy slacks, brown shoes. His joyless face was slack, rubbery, shaven smooth except for steel gray eyebrows like Brillo pads.

"Still here?" he asked.

Lisa bit back her smart remarks – they never had any impact on The Killjoy – and just waited him out.

"Your clinical notes on MacAvoy are... very creative," he said. Drawled, really, in a Harvard kind of way. "I trust you've settled in here nicely, then, if you're already bored with the usual way of doing things. Keeping, for example, objective notes."

"I've been here ten years, Jim," she said.

"More than enough time, I'm sure," he replied.

"Is that what brings you to Unit Six, Jim? My time in service? Don't you get to make enough veiled threats up in Bean Counting?"

"I'm wounded," he said, not obviously wounded at all. "You know we run on grant money and donations, primarily, yes?"

"In addition to tax funding, Medicare and Medicaid, and private insurance in the rare cases that aren't snatched up by the not-for-profit-but-really-for-profit hospitals, yes. Are you here to nag me about putting MacAvoy on meds?"

"Wouldn't dream of it," Killroy said. "Unethical, that would be. Only, the sooner you're done writing his biography and he's on a state sanctioned treatment, the sooner those tax dollars can go to help the next person in line. There is a waiting list a mile long for court-ordered evaluations, you know. Men waiting in jail without trial until we have a bed and a specialist ready for them."

"Of course, you're right," she said, and relaxed into her seat. "I'm sorry."

"High stress occupation," Killroy said. "Easy to forget we're on the same team with the same objectives."

Like hell. "Look, Jim. This man is in and out. Classic revolving door stuff. Won't take help, won't transition into a home, won't transition into work, won't stay on the medications. I've got files in my office from nine different hospitals and he's never made any progress. Not one inch of it. I know it's bad for the numbers, and I know that affects our funding as well as our political support in the state assembly. I know all that. But..."

"The long-term good?"

"Yes," she said. "In the long run, if we take our time, slow down, really try to understand this man, maybe we can keep him from needing to come back."

"Don't write prose, Doctor," Killroy said.

"I'm going to write prose," Lisa replied. "I'm going to do it for one simple reason, really, just one: we've tried everything else. We've done everything by the book a dozen times in nine places, and none of it has helped one iota. "You know the definition of insanity."

"Yes," Killroy said. "Any condition the state will pay us to treat." He smiled – a grim expression, to be sure, but nevertheless an attempt at human connection. "Just one other thing."

Lisa waited.

"They didn't have black T-shirts in sixty-eight."

"What?" she said.

"Your notes indicate this person, this Wilcox, tore the sleeves off her shirt and had a black T underneath it. A colonel would have had her sleeves tailored, and only white was available in that year. I'm telling you this as a veteran. Just in case you were thinking about believing any of the story."

"Oh," Lisa said. "Thanks, Jim."

He smiled vaguely, glanced at the screens behind her, and left.

***

"Your phone call came in," Dylan said.

"What?" Lisa fiddled with her recorder, trying to remember how to make it record on a new track when she turned it on.

"You told me to expect a call from DVA."

"Oh, the veterans' office. What did they have to say?"

"They were very nice," Dylan said. "And they had a hundred seven records for Captains Daniels, eighteen for Daniels' killed or MIA, and none at all for friendly-fire incidents. She admitted they didn't keep great records on fraggings, that's what they called it back then. Because fraggings were not good PR. Bad press. The war had enough of that, she said."

"I can imagine." She'd just been a kid when they called that business off. "She say anything about a female colonel name of Wilcox?"

"No such person," Dylan said. "Almost no females of that rank in that year, in sixty-eight, and all of those nursing corps and accounted for. Plus, if there had been such a person, you'd need some kind of clearance or release to eyeball her records. She shouldn't even have said yes or no, really."

"Guess I kinda figured that."

"As for MacAvoy himself, he was in the years he said he was in, administrative discharge in seventy-one. Psych. Section-eighted out."

"After he did the time."

"Right. She said there was a medical file but we'd need a release to get it."

Lisa tapped her teeth with the business-end of a pen. "I'll ask him for it. Thanks, Daryl."

"No problem." He went back to inventorying all the pills with street value in the locking closet next to the toilet.

Lisa had the recorder about figured out, so she took it with her. Elbert stood outside the interview room. He still had on the thin pajamas and paper robe, meaning he had made no progress – no group attendance, no individual sessions other than these interviews, no points for making his bed or brushing his teeth. In short: no compliance at all.

"Hi, Elbert."

"Hello, Doctor."

She opened the door. Elbert could have done so but he let her go in first. As the door did not lock she was careful to check it for unauthorized occupants. Finding none, she took her usual place, and Elbert took his.

"Where were we?" she said.

"I was the man for the job after all."

She looked at her notes, but didn't really need to. They were engraved on the backs of her eyes right now. Lisa had read them twice more in the three days since their last meeting. "Good memory."

"I got that going for me. You aren't going to offer me any advice or interpretations?"

"You want any?"

"No," he said. "That never stopped any psychiatrist from trying."

She nodded, waited.

"I'll just go on then, shall I?" Elbert said after a beat.

Lisa nodded again, made sure the recorder was working.

***

Elbert looked around the room. The dozen or so patients were mostly staring at him, wakened by the shots. Only one guy was bad enough off he slept through in a drugged-out haze.

"I don't know we made the situation better," Elbert said.

"We'll be all right," Wilcox said. "These boys won't remember anything. Will you?"

A bunch of fellows shook their heads.

"Not what I mean, exactly. But let's get out of here," Elbert said. "If I wasn't a fugitive from justice before, I sure as hell am now. I'll be the most wanted man in Vietnam."

"Settle down," Wilcox said. "Like I said, nothing ever happened. I made it all disappear. The last link is gone. You're free and clear. Well, clear anyway."

They went out the way they had come in. Nobody came to check on the noise. Out front, rain had started to fall, tentative, like lovers kissing for the first time. Elbert had been in-country long enough to know that likely wouldn't last. The rain would soon fall in earnest. The Jeep sat in the edge of the storm, settling on its springs. It looked about a hundred years old, like it had been sitting there on the hardpan in the dark just about forever.

"That's not taking us anywhere," Elbert said.

"We'll walk from here," Wilcox said. She pointed off into the jungle, out back of the medical building. There were other buildings: a command structure, a mess, barracks, quarter-master. She ignored them. There were two packs in back of the Jeep. Rifles, machetes, a bandolier. There was a radio, too, but she left that. She tossed Elbert one of each of the other items.

"What are you made of?" Elbert asked as Wilcox took the first steps into the wild, plant-choked horror of the Vietnamese jungle.

"Same as you," she said. "We're all the same stuff, made of the same stuff. "

"I don't know about that," Elbert said, but he followed, gearing up as he went. The pistol hung on his bandolier and the rifle over one shoulder. Within about ten paces they needed the machetes to make any progress.

"We'll go about two miles," Wilcox said.

Elbert groaned. He was thinking about distance over speed and coming up with time. As in, lots of it. He ached from his captivity, the Jeep ride, being scared all the time. He just wanted to lay down and stop, right here at the start of the journey. But Wilcox set a brutal pace, hacking through jungle the way a starving man carves up a steak. "You aren't worried about leaving a clear trail?"

"Like I said, nobody will remember anything. They all knew what he was."

"What we did…"

"Was necessary," Wilcox said. "If you've got breath to argue, maybe we could push on a little faster."

Elbert laughed, because what else could he do? But sooner than he'd expected, Wilcox called a halt. There was the barest hint of a clearing, a space where they could string hammocks and a mosquito net and set up a camp stove.

"Is there dinner on this nature hike?" Elbert said.

"Packs. C-Rations. I brought tea, too."

"Tea?"

"Yeah. It will make you feel better. Here, boil one of these canteens while I fix up the hammocks. You want top or bottom?"

"Whatever I can get," Elbert said.

Soon he was swinging in a hammock, Wilcox somewhere below him, a tin cup of hot tea in his hands. He looked up at the night sky, what he could see of it through trees that spread out as if to use as much space as possible. The sound of rain picked its way through the jungle: so far, they had outrun the storm, but now it was going to overrun them. Rain pattered on leaves, filtered down from one leaf to the next and the next, mostly never finding its way to the ground. Thirsty vines sucked it up, and things with their roots up there in the branches. But some trickles of warm water found their way to where Elbert rested.

It felt good. Clean. He didn't mind one bit, and fell asleep listening to the pattering rain, searching for the invisible sky. His dreams were all nightmares.

***

"You still get them?" Lisa said.

"Nightmares? Not to speak of."

"That's a weird answer," Lisa said.

"I'm an old man from another time," Elbert said. "Sometimes the way we spoke back when don't cross over too good into the way you younger ones speak today."

"Been a while since someone called me young," Lisa said.

"Beats the alternative," Elbert said.

"What does?"

"Growing old. Looks like we still got some time. You want me to go on some?"

Lisa checked the clock, nodded once more.

***

Morning.

The storm had blown through in the night and the sun got ahold of the fresh water, turned it into steam. The jungle fogged up like wet eyeglasses in a warm car. Elbert rolled out of his hammock.

Wilcox was up already, doing some kind of weird calisthenics. She had on her camo pants and a black T-shirt. Elbert watched her while he made more tea. "You were right," he said. "It helps. What's in this stuff?"

"Just green tea," she said. She stood on one foot, her palms together over her head, the other foot flat against the standing knee. She sank down low, rose up again.

"What's that?"

"Green tea?"

"No, what you're doing."

"Yoga," she said. Which didn't help.

"Is that how you got so strong?"

"Partially. Yoga, tai-chi, isometrics, weights, discipline, contemplative prayer. Hypnosis. Pharmacology."

"I didn't get half of that," Elbert said.

"And you won't. There isn't time. Here, grab that bandage." She pointed to a long strip of gauzy material sitting on one of the packs. "Help me tie these down." Then she took off her T-shirt.

Elbert goggled. "What are you doing?"

"Tits get in the way in a firefight," she said. "You're going to help me strap them down, out of the way. All you have to do is hold up this end and I'll turn around until it's done. Look, man, stare if you have to, just get to work."

He stared, and he got to work. Wasn't much to stare at, really, but he'd been in country a long time.

"You never visited a whore?" Wilcox said.

"What?"

"I guess I should stop asking questions when I know the answers already. Your squad, they worried you might be gay."

"What?" he said again. The morning was starting out weird.

"Gay? Homosexual?"

"I know what it means," he said.

"Well, they noticed you never let any of the young ladies take your money. Like you didn't like them."

"Well, I like them just fine, never you worry," Elbert said. "It's just... I came from Alabama. You got any idea what it's like to be a black man in Alabama? I shouldn't think you would. It's like... I got my friends, the guys I went to school with, the guys who have farms around my folks' farm. Life ain't all bad. But if we should have to go into town, it's like we ain't people no more. Not human. We're second-class. Worse: we're things."

"And you don't want to treat a girl like an object. Something that exists to satisfy your needs."

"I guess you could say so," Elbert said.

"So why were you staring at my tits?"

"I apologize. I was surprised, is all, and I didn't know what was happening."

"Apology accepted. I know exactly what it means to be treated like an object, MacAvoy. I want you to remember that."

"Yes, Ma'am," he said.

"I'll start packing up. You'll want to take a few steps into the woods and cop a squat, no doubt. Watch where you put your... feet... This is hostile territory, and I don't mean the Vietnamese."

They were back on the move fifteen minutes later. Midges and mosquitoes whinged around them, zipping back and forth on their bloody errands. Wind rustled, and once Elbert saw monkeys watching them pass by from high in the trees. They sat side by side, still as cadavers, only turning their heads to follow his progress.

"You want to explain at all what we're doing?" Elbert said after a few hack-and-slash miles. "What's more important than the March?"

"What march?"

"*The* March. The freedom fight."

"Oh. How about the survival of mankind itself? How about understanding the very nature of existence, of what we are all made from?"

"Speak clearly," he said.

"OK. For now, we're going to recruit another team member. Then we're going north, into enemy territory, behind the lines. The Vietnamese found something up there and we need to find out what it is." She stopped, stuck her machete in the side of a tree and left it there a minute. "If we win, mankind continues to exist in all its racist glory. Maybe we'll have time to learn better."

Elbert thought for a time. Thunder rattled in the distance and the morning steam started to shred and tatter in a growing breeze above them that couldn't quite penetrate the undergrowth. "I need specifics," he said at last.

"You'll get them, in due time," Wilcox said. "First, we need a doctor."

"We just left a forward hospital."

"A particular doctor," she said. "Someone like you, the right kind of person."

"I don't like it."

"You don't have to like it," Wilcox said. "Read your orders again. You just have to do what I say."

Elbert followed along when she pulled the machete out of its resting place and started hacking again. *Back to feeling like a thing instead of a person,* he thought.

"I'll only use you as long as I need to," Wilcox said, and Elbert got that creeping feeling again. Like she was answering questions he'd thought but not asked. "And I promise, it's important. I understand what's being sacrificed here."

Five

"What was it?" Lisa said.

"I think you don't have time for that," Elbert replied. He glanced up at the clock behind his head, craning to look.

Lisa followed his gaze, saw they were a few minutes over. "Well, I suppose I'll find out in due time."

"Yes, reckon so," Elbert said.

"Are you going to do any of the program, Elbert? Keep up with some hygiene, maybe do a group or two?"

"Comply?"

"Not to put too fine a point on it, yes."

"No," Elbert said, "don't figure to. Don't see a percentage in it. Figure I'll be on my way in a few days in any event. Might as well rest as I can."

"Best chance of getting out is showing you can hack it," Lisa said.

Elbert just nodded. "There's something else you wanted," he said.

"Yes. How did you know?"

"Not hard to know what people are thinking, if you pay attention. I expect it's a paper you would like me to sign."

"Two for two," Lisa said, and slid the release form out of her folder. "This would let me find out what the VA knows about you. Might help us get you on your way quicker."

"You haven't been listening," he said.

"Hm?"

"I said, you haven't been listening. I'll be on my way in a few days regardless. Not much you or the VA or anyone else can do about that, either helpful or otherwise."

"Elbert, are you talking about suicide right now?"

"Oh no," Elbert said. "Only that my business here will be concluded, and then I have a job of work elsewhere to attend to. Slide me that paper and I'll sign it for you. Go ahead. The VA never helped me none, but they never hurt me, either. Go on and talk to them all you want." He signed, slid the paper back across the table with Lisa's pen on top of it.

"What is it?" Lisa said. "Your business here, what is it?"

"I already said. You have to listen. I believe I'll go and have some sleep now. Sleep when you can, that's what they taught us."

He left Lisa alone in the tiled room and it seemed she could hear her thoughts echoing back off the walls like voices.

***

The fax buzzed like a hornet caught behind metal blinds. Sheets rolled slowly out, one by one. Lisa had worried they wouldn't be very legible, and they weren't perfect, but it wasn't the fault of the fax. Fax machines had come a long way.

Just as obsolete as the phone books though, she thought.

Each page had Elbert's name and serial number on it. Some were copies of orders, photostatted from the original carbons and stored digitally and then reprinted and faxed. Here was a page detailing the reasons for a meritorious service ribbon. A Vietnam campaign ribbon. Technical training records, M-16 qualification, M-60 qualification, a rifle award. He was a good shot.

Then the medical records got started. A case of chlamydia in '67. Maybe he wasn't completely honest about his attitude towards prostitution – wouldn't be the first dishonest man in Lisa's experience. Broken finger in training, earlier in '67. Piles. After that, exhaustion and dehydration, the beginnings of malnourishment. That was the start of 1969. No cause given, just a list of treatments. A couple months in the hospital then returned to duty, stateside.

Orders said he pulled guard duty at Fort Knox.

Nothing else after that until 1971. Quiet duty in a place not much ever happened, a real change of pace from the jungles of Vietnam.

In 1971, Elbert's records said he made three back-to-back trips to Wilford Hall. The military psychiatric hospital.

Extreme exhaustion, combat fatigue, suicide ideation. Nightmares. There were pages and pages of psych notes, none of them more detailed than some sketchy differential diagnostics – no interview notes, nothing Elbert might have told a doctor.

Something was missing: if Elbert had been detached as he said, there should be a copy of the order in his file. Everything else was there, from his dental health in basic training to how well he kept his shoes shined in his Enlisted Progress Reports.

The last sheet of paper rolled through the fax machine onto the table. A DD214 – separation paperwork. Discharge type: administrative.

"Should be medical," Lisa said.

"What should be medical?"

She hadn't heard The Killjoy come in. She jumped as if caught with one hand in the med cabinet. "Oh, you scared me."

Killroy didn't say anything. No reassurances, no apologies.

Toad. "MacAvoy's discharge paperwork. Says administrative discharge, but he was on the psych ward at the time. Service-related psychiatric condition should get him a medical discharge."

"Happened all the time," Killroy said. "Especially to the black ones. Admin discharge means no benefits. No medical, no retirements, no GI bill."

"Oh." Lisa's face dropped a little. "Well, I'm sure we could get this corrected."

"A whole forest of paperwork," Killroy said. "Not worth the effort. But I can see you're going to try just because I said don't bother. Well, good luck with that."

"What did you want, Jim?"

"You didn't call in your census."

"Head nurse does that," Lisa said.

"I meant the plural you, as in this unit. Where's Juliette?"

"I'm in the can," came a voice from the toilet.

Lisa used that distraction to slip away, to her office off the unit. The hallways on this floor were dark, kept down to emergency lighting to save on the power bill. Her door had her name on it, a metal plate that offered a sense of permanence. Newer hires got cardboard rectangles instead, blue, with their name printed on them.

Lisa pulled out her ring of keys. Weighty, loud. They were attached to one of her belt-loops by an extendable nylon cord whose spring was not strong enough to retract the heavy load. She popped her door open, slipped the keys into her pocket, flipped on the light.

A figure stood up from her chair.

Lisa jumped back, clutching her chest, a scream buried in her throat ready to burst out like the gust-buster on Alien.

But there was nothing there, nothing to scream about. Her chair, a blue swivel with five radiating legs, was just where she had left it. The couch over against the north wall was cold to the touch, the blinds down, the computer humming away to itself quietly, two photos resting to the right of the monitor in their bamboo frames. Nothing out of place or disordered. No shadowy, dark figure anywhere to be found.

Lisa sat in her swivel chair, put her feet out in front of her, and waited for her heart to quit pounding against her chest. Her eyes strayed to the window seen in narrow slices behind the blinds: an autumn sky nearing dark.

"I'm jumping at shadows now," she told herself, but there wasn't enough light in the hallway to cast one into the office. Not when the lights were on in here. And no matter how many times she told herself she was remembering it all wrong, the gooseflesh stayed on her forearms and the nape of her neck continued to bristle.

***

"How long have they been like that?" Carl said. He had on a black and white uniform, police patches on the shoulders. Just his belt made him for a cop, though. It had everything but a gun and a TASER. Those weren't allowed on the premises.

He stared up at the monitor. Half a dozen patients stared back at him via the camera. In his peripheral vision he could see them again, all with their backs to him in their T-shirts and paper gowns and pajamas.

"Elbert and Davy were the first two," Dylan said. He stood on Carl's right, Lisa to his left. "The others started drifting in, one at a time, day by day. Now that's all they do. Tomorrow there'll be seven or eight of them. Pretty soon, they're going to have to start standing behind Elbert. No place left to sit."

"You don't think that's creepy?" Carl said.

"What's not creepy up here?" Dylan replied.

"I think it is," Lisa said. "It scares the hell out of me. Any one of these guys could be a major threat to society on their own. Wallace there raped three women. Barry sewed a man's lips shut and then tortured him until the guy tore through his stitches screaming. Steve raped eighty-six children. Eighty-six. They caught him after the first forty and rehabbed him, and after that what he learned was to quit leaving witnesses alive. Then he went straight back to raping kids, only then he killed them after."

Carl turned his eyes slowly away from the screen, looked at Lisa. "Guess you got a point."

"So maybe I get worried when they get organized, you know? We haven't had a riot up here since, I don't know, the eighties. Right?"

"Right," Dylan said. He hadn't been born yet in the eighties.

Carl's eyes drifted back up to the screen. "What do you think we should do about it?"

"Nothing yet," Lisa said. "I just wanted you to see it."

Carl grunted.

"Hey – was there anyone but me up on the office level last night?" Lisa said.

"Not that I know of," Carl said.

"You couldn't check, could you? The security log?" She held out her badge, a little white rectangle with her face on the front and a magnetic strip on the back. Theoretically all access to the office level was recorded by the computers.

"Something else up?"

"No," Lisa said. "Yes. Maybe. I don't know. I just didn't feel like I was alone up there last night."

Carl shook his head and Lisa couldn't tell if it was at her or at the guys all staring at the video camera. "I'll check it out later. After lunch."

"Thanks."

"No problem."

Behind them, the room was empty.

Six

The office computers were slow. Or the internet was, Lisa couldn't have said. But the page she was on took half a minute to load. She glanced around her office again, just a five by ten space with her desk, the chair under her, the couch against one wall. Nothing to inspire dread or terror.

Stars and Stripes back-issues. August, 1969. Her word search for "MacAvoy, Elbert, 1969" had brought up an article. "POW's released from Hanoi without explanation, negotiators overjoyed."

> Sunday, August sixteenth.
>
> Four service members crossed the border today into India following a long trek through Laos and Cambodia. William Ridley, Abraham Duncan, Elbert MacAvoy and Frederic Haynes were all released from a prison camp near Hanoi two months ago. Vietnamese officials reportedly gave no reason for this release and made no demands of negotiators. While prisoner exchanges are usual, lead negotiator General Peter Burns stated nothing of the sort occurred in this instance.
>
> "It's a gift horse, and we're not too eager to examine its teeth. These men are coming home. A lot of other men aren't going to. If our counterparts in Hanoi want to come over reasonable, I'm inclined to go along."
>
> When asked why the long trip rather than a standard beach or border pick-up, Gen. Burns declined to comment.

There were some grainy black-and-white photographs. Three white men who looked starved but happy, and a young man who might have been Elbert. His eyes peered out from the screen, tiny and distorted and haunted. Not much more than a couple of pixels, really.

A brief tour of Vietnamese hospitality explained Elbert's records. Dehydration and malnutrition. Said hospitality might have included torture and almost certainly included abuse: deprivation, mistreatment, humiliation.

Two pictures sat next to her monitor. One was a photo of her with her daughter and husband, about eight years ago. Behind them water reflected summer sunshine. The lake. A favorite spot, a favorite memory. He was gone now, and her with him, but he couldn't take away that day.

Next to that shot was one of her father. Edward Jayne. He was young in that shot, wearing a bomber jacket and Air Force blues. He'd survived the war and she had other photos but she liked to remember him like that, like from when she was just a girl.

"You never talked about it," she told the photo. "I guess you'd have said they were never great respecters of the Geneva Convention."

Lisa glanced at the time display in the bottom right corner of her screen. Almost time to meet with Elbert again. She took her recorder out of a desk drawer, selected a free channel, and talked into it. "Time travel fantasy possibly related to survivor's remorse. Records of detachment not in VA files. Detachment... meaning a small military unit detached from a larger one, or possibly a coping mechanism for trauma. Maybe it's a metaphor."

She turned off the recorder and left the office, checking twice that it was locked behind her.

***

They camped again, walked again, camped once more. And on that day they broke through the jungle into a wide cleared area, a real base.

There was an airstrip, with F4 Phantoms and F111s roaring in and out. Elbert gawked like a country kid in the big city for the first time but Wilcox could not be distracted. There was an eight foot fence topped with barbed wire and soldiers every thirty feet. She looked like she wanted to just cut through it but, instead, led Elbert around the perimeter to a guard house. There was a real road up there, a few Jeeps and bigger trucks rolling in and out.

Four soldiers waited at the gate. They looked jumpy. People didn't stroll in out of the jungle, not here, back from the lines.

"Help you?" one of the men said when Wilcox and Elbert were within shouting range. "You look like you been in the field a while."

"Just point us at the visiting officers' quarters," Wilcox said.

The soldiers got weird looks. "Uh, ma'am?" said the helpful guy. They all looked about nineteen. "Sorry, I didn't realize..."

"Realize what?"

"That you were a ma'am? Don't usually see women hauling all that killing apparatus," he said. "There been a policy change?"

"Has there? Isn't policy you salute officers and follow their orders?" Wilcox said. "It that policy has changed, I guess I need to know about it."

"No ma'am," he said. "I mean, yes... I mean... Take this street right here. Go about four blocks. VOQ is about five hundred yards down on the right. It's right under the flightline, I'm afraid, but you know, when it's jets, everything kinda is."

Wilcox didn't say anything, just turned and strode through the gate, Elbert in her wake. None of the soldiers even looked twice at him. "I can't stay at no officers' quarters," he said. "I'm lucky they don't got special barracks just for the black boys on enlisted side."

"We aren't staying," Wilcox said.

"What?"

"You say that a lot."

"You don't make sense a lot," he said. "Can't you slow down for one minute?"

"No. Survival of the human race? That ring any bells? Keep up. It's only for a little while, and it'll get easier as you start to get in shape."

"In shape? What was Basic for?"

"The basics," she said. "Consider yourself temporarily attached to an elite unit. And keep up."

He didn't have the breath left to argue.

It was a ten minute walk to the building they wanted, along a paved street with a green divider between lanes. It could have been any street in the U.S., except all the buildings were corrugated tin or concrete. VOQ wasn't much to look at, just a pile of cement with a sidewalk and a strip of grass. Looked like any VOQ anywhere, which was the point.

Wilcox pushed into the office, strode up to the counter. It looked like a motel room except it was done up in gray and army green. A young man stood behind the counter, again about nineteen. A lieutenant. Green uniform, soft hands, pimples. "Help you, ma'am?" he said, his voice professional but his eyes all over her.

"You like scars?" she said.

He paused a beat. "Uh, no ma'am?"

"There something wrong with my scars?"

"Uh, no, ma'am?"

"Eyes front, soldier," she said, and the kid made eye contact. "You see this rifle? Yes? You see this sidearm? Machete? I earned these scars, son. I earned these scars killing the enemy in his own territory. Now unless you want to earn some scars of your own, maybe you'll look me in the eye, salute smart, and ask me how you may be of service."

He did his best. Shakily, the kid said, "Ma'am, whatever you need, I am at your disposal. I just need your orders..."

"I'm not staying," she said. "Tell me which room is occupied by Captain Dana Smith."

"Uh..."

"Lieutenant? Now."

"Yes, Ma'am," he said, and flipped through his roster of occupants. "Smith, two-sixteen. Checks out tonight. Anything else?"

But Wilcox was already on her way out, Elbert right behind her. He faked a cough to keep his smile a secret.

Two sixteen was top floor, away from the street. Wilcox trotted up the aluminum frame steps, walked around to the right door. She pounded on it with her fist: *thump-thump-thump*. The door had been painted red and the diffuse reflected light made her fist look bloody.

A minute later, the door opened. A slender little woman peeked out. "Yes?"

"You're Dana Smith?" Wilcox said. Then she did the same trick she'd done with Elbert: pulled an envelope out of her shirt, slapped it in the lady's hands. "Orders."

"Detachment?" Smith said. She was just a little blonde thing, maybe a hundred and twenty pounds, with soft hair and soft eyes and soft hands. She smelled of lavender. Elbert made a point of not looking at her body although he wanted to.

But he said, "Guess you ain't never been drafted before, have you?"

"Not as such," Smith said. "Amounts to the same thing, though. These orders say I'm to come with you, detached into your care?"

"Care might be a stretch," Wilcox said. "But that's essentially the score. Grab whatever kit you can fit into one pack."

"I don't have a pack," she said. "I'm a scientist."

"Not a medic?" Elbert said.

"No. A parapsychologist."

"A what?"

"She studies extra-sensory perception, precognition, psychokinetics – unexplained and non-mainstream phenomena related to mental powers." Wilcox stared at Smith. "That's correct, isn't it?"

"If you want to sum it up crudely."

"Crude is my business," said Wilcox. "Get a change of clothes. Leave your valuables here. Better yet, seal them in an envelope and tell the lieutenant downstairs to mail them to you Stateside. We won't be coming back here."

"I need to make some calls," Smith said.

"Officers' club. Twenty minutes. You're one minute late, I come looking for you. We don't have time for games, Doctor Smith. MacAvoy, you're with me," she said, and marched off towards her best guess of where the O-Club might be. It was a small base.

Four hundred miles away, a band of priests prodded a mewling and kicking thing towards a fire. It was hard to see although the light was good. The priests were all old men, had been old men when the French had abandoned Vietnam to her own interests. They wore orange robes with yellow sashes and what little wisps of hair they might have had were shaved off.

The thing stopped struggling for a second, marched in the middle of the loose U formation the men created with their walking staves. Then it lurched to the right, tried to force its way through.

The men on that side made signs with their hands, called on the names of old powers, forced it back into its middle place.

It arrived at the bonfire, made one more charge to break through the line. But the men stuffed it in, encircled it. It got away twice, just a few feet out of the bonfire, a great roaring blaze. They pushed it back with their staves, pushed it in and held it down and watched it die.

One of the men said something that amounted to, "Damned French, stuck us with this problem."

"No," said another, "you know blame is unworthy, and the French unworthy of blame. This thing was always here."

A third: "Before there were men, before there was Buddha, it was here."

The first: "I feel anger. Burning this thing sullies my everlasting soul."

The third: "The soul is not sullied that accepts stains for the greater good. How many souls go unstained by your sacrifice?"

The first man sighed. "So we will burn it again when it comes back. And again and again."

***

"What's that, Elroy?" Lisa asked.

"What? What's what?"

"That bit of the story. That sounds like something you weren't there to see."

"Oh," he said. "That's some stuff I picked up later. Talked to people, found out what was behind some of the scenery, you see."

"You went back there, after the war?"

"I suppose you could say so. But let me finish this part of the story."

"OK, Elbert," Lisa said. She wrote "Dana Smith" on the legal pad in front of her, circled it twice. "Go ahead."

***

They walked into the officers' club. It was dark and hot. A couple of lamps shed orange light over tables and chairs that would have looked OK in a restaurant back home. White tablecloths with place settings, napkins, water glasses. There was a bar, too, and that's where Wilcox headed. She took a stool, Elbert taking the one next to her and awaiting the inevitable confrontation.

A barman came over, a White guy with a white shirt and black pants, short hair. He wore an apron. "What can I get you?" he said.

"Whiskey, double. Same for the soldier."

The barman seemed to notice Elbert for the first time, looked him over carefully. "You know we can't serve... enlisted men in here," he said.

Wilcox made eye contact and kept it. The barman looked at her as if expecting her to speak but she didn't, not right away, just kept staring. And the longer their eyes touched, the more the guy started to sweat. His mouth opened, a little at first, then more, until it was hanging open wide. The flesh around his face sagged, went sallow.

Then Wilcox said, "Same for the soldier."

The barman straightened up like a spell had been broken, snapped his mouth shut, seemed to shake off a daze. "Right away," he said.

"What was that?" Elbert said when the barman went away.

"People are easily influenced."

"Some kind of magic trick?"

"No, no magic. Just understanding people. You could have done the same thing. Just a matter of summoning up your will and endurance and making sure the person sees it."

"Ah," Elbert said. But he didn't think he could understand those instructions, never mind reproduce the results. He could get some things done in that case.

Behind them, Dana entered through the narrow wooden door. Took the stool on Wilcox' other side. "Base commander says you're legitimate," she said. "Possibly psychotic, but legitimate. I don't come cheap, though."

"Yes you do," Wilcox said. "You're under orders."

"There's following orders and there's doing everything in your power to succeed. You want my cooperation, well, you could have asked first, but I respect power plays. You want my enthusiastic support, there are conditions." She waited until Wilcox nodded, then went on. "One, this needs to be worth my time. In other words, this isn't just some ghost story from a grunt who feels guilty or lonely or wants an out. Two, whatever we find, my name goes on it somewhere. Three, if there's a buck in it, I need a cut."

"Fine," Wilcox said.

"Fine? No arguments or negotiations?"

"Would it do me any good?"

"No," Dana said. "But that never stopped anyone from trying. So, what have we got?"

"You ever hear of the wendigo?" said Wilcox.

"You mean, like the camper?" said Elbert.

"No," said Dana. "No, you're referring to the Indian legend, aren't you? Everywhere people have been for more than ten thousand years or so, we hear stories of half-men, man-like creatures that creep around the edges of villages or camps. At night. They leave big footprints sometimes."

"Oh," said Elbert. "I get it. You mean Bigfoot."

"Like Bigfoot," said Dana. "Yes, like that. Bigfoot shows up with the same frequency, except there's never any malice on the part of Bigfoot. Wendigo is said to be not just manlike and mysterious, but also evil. He can change his skin – go in disguise – and in some stories he likes to eat people. Is that what we have?"

Wilcox said, "The Vietnamese have something. It's important and it's beyond their capacity to deal with. They have local priests trying to contain it. They say it predates us, the French, maybe even them. We've been promised safe passage to go up and take a look at it."

Elbert didn't like it but he kept his opinions to himself. It had been a hairy couple of days and his immediate future looked about as predictable and sane as an acid trip, so he stuck to the now: and the now was officers' whiskey. A nice scotch blend, he thought, letting it sit on his tongue.

He signaled the bartender for another, pointed out Dana going thirsty two stools down.

"What's our imperative?" Dana said. "Get a look-see, or more than that?"

"Oh, much more than look," Wilcox said. "Depending on what we can get away with, study, capture or destroy. Maybe all three. Make no mistake: whatever they've got up there, it's more dangerous than Vietnamese communists with Soviet rifles."

The bar man set a whiskey in front of Dana, and she stared into it like it was a crystal ball, all the secrets of the future told in its amber hues. "Why bring me along?" she said. "Why not capture it or kill it and then send it home to dissect?"

"Can't handle it," Wilcox said. "The Vietnamese are very cagey people, don't let much slip, never ask for help. Certainly not from the enemy. Listen. We aren't the first team they've invited to come check into this, OK? You know who they asked first? The Soviets. They went in with a science team. Didn't get within five miles. Along the way all their equipment was smashed or lost, their trucks broke down. Men killed in friendly fire accidents, got lost and drove into a minefield. Last couple of men tried to walk in, complete the mission, only the Vietnamese say they went crazy and shot each other."

"Shot each other?" Dana repeated. "At the same time?"

"In the head, mutually assisted suicide."

"Now I see why I'm along," Dana said. "You'll heed my advice?"

"To the letter."

Elbert continued to keep his opinions quiet. He hadn't understood half of that and least of all his purpose in this operation. He was just considering finding out if he could get away with a third drink when Wilcox got to her feet.

"Bull session's over," she said. "Time to get back out on the road. Chopper should be loaded by now."

"Chopper?" Elbert said, following the women out into the hazy and uncertain sunlight. Inside had been hot; going back out was like a slap in the face when your face was already raw from shaving. *Now when in Hell did she have time to organize a chopper? She hasn't never been out of my sight since we got here...*

Seven

I guess the student loan people aren't getting paid this month.

It was maybe weird to go to a private detective in person. Lisa figured most people did their business over the phone. But here she was.

The guy was sixty-ish, huge and dour. He looked like he'd been a bodybuilder in his forties and all that mass was still there under a layer of comfortable, late-middle-aged fat. He'd shaved his head, probably because his hair was mostly gone anyway, and a roll of fat made a line from one ear, around the back of his skull to the other ear.

The office was just a room. Plain walls, white with dirty smudges. A steel desk that might have been army surplus. A desk chair somewhere underneath Hanrahan, and the computer. There were two doors: one to the hallway outside, one leading most likely to a toilet.

"Most of detective work is knowing where to look for people," Hanrahan said, his voice nothing that a glance at his body would suggest. It was high, melodic, with a trace of California to it. "I don't go out much, except when someone needs a husband caught cheating or something. Take the camera then. Mostly just sit here and call people and go through databases."

"Eight hundred dollars seems like a lot for a database search," Lisa said.

Hanrahan nodded. "I know it does, ma'am. But you have to know which, how to ask them, and you have to pay your dues. And then there's the rent on this luxurious palace. Plus it's going to be more than punching a few keys and shooting you off an email. Might take two days or a week, but if these are real people, I'll find them. Check them out for you."

"I don't need them checked out," Lisa said. "Just I need to know if they're real."

I'm as crazy as MacAvoy, she told herself. But his stories were so vivid, consistent. Nothing like any psychosis she'd heard before, despite their crazier elements.

"Whatever you say, miss... Jayne, was it?"

"Doctor."

"Sorry, ma'am. Doctor Jayne. Where do you want me to call you when I have something?"

She blushed just a little bit, fidgeted fractionally with her purse. "I don't exactly carry a phone."

"Work, then? What's the number?"

"And I don't want you to call there. They'd think I was losing it. Actually, *I* think I might be losing it. Never mind. I'll stop back in in three days. Fair?"

"Your show," Hanrahan said.

"In stories the PI always wants an advance. Half up front, that kind of thing."

"Yeah," the big man said. "Two hundred now, six on delivery."

Lisa dug around in her purse for a check. When she came out with the checkbook, Hanrahan's eyebrows sketched up towards where his hairline had once been. "I can take a Visa, you know. Got a card reader, goes right on my phone here."

"Oh," Lisa said. "I guess you get out more than I do."

"Are you gay or something?"

"What?" The room suddenly seemed too small and Hanrahan much too large.

"I guess you're supposed to ask now. If people are gay or straight. Before you ask."

"Ask?"

"If they'd let you take them out for dinner or something. Never mind. I'm sorry. It's just that you said you don't get out, and that made me a little sad, and I thought... But we got a business relationship now, so..."

Lisa let go a breath she hadn't realized she was holding. Leaned across the desk a little, touched Hanrahan on the forearm. "You're sweet," she said. Then she stood up. "And you're right: doesn't pay to mix relationships. Another time, I'm sure that would have been an irresistible opener."

"Really?" he said, a blush creeping up his face from under his shirt collar.

"Really. I am a psychiatrist, after all."

In the hallway, with the door closing behind her through the noise of traffic, a hundred air conditioners, and a baby crying someplace in the building, she thought she heard Hanrahan laughing.

His office was probably illegal. It was in an apartment building. An interior hallway stretched off towards a stairwell, the lighted exit sign the only illumination. The carpet was old and dirty and the air smelled of dust and cabbage. Ahead of her a doorway opened. A young woman came out with no shirt on, a baby latched on one breast. She looked both ways, saw Lisa, and stepped back inside. The door clicked gently as she shut it, again as she locked it.

The stairwell was worse. At least there was natural light through leaded glass windows, Art Deco things shaped like churches. The stairs were bare concrete, decades old. Cigarette butts had been swept into the corners by passing traffic, never actually cleaned up so that the edges of the stairs and landings had black, fuzzy nests of mold and rot. They stank of winter rain.

Lisa held her breath through that, barged through the door at the bottom of the stairwell and out into an alley. She almost hit a man in the face with the door.

"Oh, sorry," she said.

The guy looked at her, frowned, didn't say anything. But he let her hold the door for him. As Lisa turned to watch him through the door, she thought she saw someone else behind her.

Jumping at shadows again.

She wiped her hands on her pants. Let go of the door and watched it swing shut. Nothing wrong with the spring or the latch: the door boomed closed.

Back here was worse than the stairwell. Dirt, dog turds, a used condom. Fifty paces away, though, a main street was filling with artificial light in anticipation of the coming night. A bus trundled past, the one Lisa needed, but there was also a subway station nearby and her card was paid up.

She came out onto the main road, hiked down three blocks towards the station. Ahead of her, across another main road, a big glass building sat square in front of her. In its side she could clearly see the night lighting up behind her, where she had come from. Other people, dozens of them, milling around on their errands just as she was on her own.

But who was that behind her? Right behind her?

She spun, expecting to be confronted by a tall man in Air Force blue. The glass had shown him wearing the bus-driver cap and dress coat. But there was nobody. No thin man with white teeth and blank eyes, no hands that were just shadows stretched into grasping hooks.

She looked into the glass again, hand at her throat, eyes wide.

But she was alone. Just her, on a crowded street in one of the world's busiest cities, alone.

The rest of the way to the train, she alternated between looking into whatever glass was nearby and being too scared to keep looking. She walked at those times with her head down, watching her feet – and pretending she wasn't watching for an extra shadow on the ground before her.

The train ride was the worst. She sat opposite an empty space. The train was brightly lit, the night sky not so much, so that the windows in front of her became a mirror. Lisa tried hard not to stare at it but stare she did, and that was fine so long as she didn't look away. Nothing could creep up on her if she just kept staring. It was looking away and looking back that wracked her nerves.

The train pushed farther into the city. People got on, filled the seats around and across from Lisa. A lady with a winter coat and a suitcase sat next to her for a few stops, got off into the warm night. Across town, and more people got off the train than got on. Nearly home.

The train ground into a surface station. Lisa was alone in the car for a few seconds, then a skinny white man got on. He had on torn jeans, a T-shirt featuring a band she'd never heard of (Icicle Works), black boots with too many fasteners. He looked around, and she pretended not to notice him. In the glass, she was alone in her seat, and then she wasn't.

The young guy strayed into her reflected view. "You mind if I sit by you?" he said.

"There's a whole empty car," Lisa said. Unlike the suitcase lady, she was dressed for the weather, which was summer. Slacks, blouse, jacket. The jacket had a miniature can of pepper spray in the pocket. Her hand strayed there, slowly.

"But I want to sit here. You don't mind, do you?"

He did what he wanted. Now she was shoulder to shoulder with him. He watched her in the glass, and she watched him.

I wish I could just stare at him, like Elbert's Wilcox, and make him do what I want.

He touched her leg. His fingers found her knee, stretched around it, caressed her. Lisa's eyes dropped to the point of contact even as she tried to scramble back in a seat that did not move. She forgot about the pepper spray, just got up and walked away, backwards, towards the rear of the car. The man frowned at her.

"I'm sorry," he said.

Then he lifted up his shirt. There was a knife duct-taped to his stomach. He started picking at the tape, and that's when Lisa remembered the pepper spray.

The guy was obviously crazy, obviously someone who could wind up at her hospital. *What kind of lunatic uses duct-tape on their murder weapon?* That's why she worked across town from her place, to help avoid meeting any of her patients on the street. She was going to feel bad about using the Mace on him.

He was still fooling around with the tape, trying to work out how to get his knife free. *Maybe I don't have to Mace him.* Lisa backed to the door, thinking to go through to the next car, maybe find a security agent or just more witnesses. She bumped against the steel and glass, fumbled around for the latch, couldn't find it. She turned around to look, eyes sweeping across the glass window.

He was behind her again. The uniformed man. The window made everything gray, washed out the color, but she knew it was blue.

"Daddy?"

In the reflection, the man behind her strode towards the seat where the guy still fussed with the duct-tape around his belly. He looked up, saw... what? The man in front of him? Just a grayish cloud? Nothing? But his mouth fell open and his face went slack, and he sagged into the seat.

Lisa spun around, to confirm the reflection showed something real.

There was no uniformed figure behind her. The young man with the Icicle Works shirt was still in his seat. But now his knife was free from the duct tape, and protruded instead from his chest.

"No. No!"

Lisa ran back to him, slipped in blood and went down, skidding through a growing red pool. She got up, grabbed one slack arm, felt for a pulse. There was none. But she was panicked, terrified, and a calm part of her mind that had seen everything, done everything knew you couldn't take a pulse reliably when you were scared shitless.

She touched his neck, same result. Touched the knife.

Shit, don't touch the knife, you idiot...

Too late.

It was in deep, a four-inch blade with maybe only a half-inch still visible. Enough to touch the heart, to stop it. She couldn't pull it out. Like a thorn in a bicycle tire, removing it now would just make things worse. It was the only thing plugging the hole. She ripped off her jacket, stuffed it around the wound.

What is that noise?

There was a whining sound, rising towards a screech, scratching at her ears and consciousness. The train squealed and crunched and knocked into another station and, as a couple boarded, Lisa realized she was screaming.

***

The night was hot, humid, and sour.

Lisa sat on the rear bumper of an ambulance, breathing deeply from an air canister. Three paramedics, two in black and white uniforms, one in FDNY gear, hauled a stretcher up the subway steps about a hundred meters in front of her. When they arrived at the ambulance, her oxygen treatment would be over.

Some bloody towels rested in an evidence bag to her right. Across the busy road, an officer had all her clothes in another such bag. Lisa had on a hospital gown from the back of the ambulance and a blanket that was good for modesty but not so good for hot city nights.

Ahead, the paramedics cleared the top step and dropped the wheels on the stretcher, converting it into a wheeled gurney.

Lisa put up the mask, turned the oxygen off. As she stood up, a woman of about twenty-eight stepped around from the side of the ambulance as though she'd been keeping tabs – which in fact seemed pretty likely. Her police badge was prominent on her black uniform shirt. The shirt bulged over a bulletproof vest.

"Am I free to go?" Lisa said.

"Have you thought of anything else it might help us to know?" Reynolds, her name tape said.

"No."

"We still have some questions for you, Miss..."

"Doctor. Doctor Jayne. Lisa."

"All right, Jane Lisa. Try and stay calm. You've been in a serious incident. It would be best if you came down to the station. Give a more complete statement. Is there anyone you want to call?

"Like a lawyer?" Lisa said, and instantly wanted to snatch it back.

"Do you need a lawyer, Miss Lisa?"

"It's Doctor Jayne. Doctor Lisa Jayne."

"Just stay calm, ma'am." Reynolds had one hand on each hip: one by her service pistol, the other by her handcuffs.

"I'd say I was pretty calm under the circumstances, wouldn't you?" Lisa said, looking around for a break in traffic.

"Yes I would, ma'am," Reynolds replied, and Lisa knew she'd screwed up again.

"Actually, I think I would like to contact a lawyer. I think I shouldn't say anything else to you until I've taken care of that."

"That's your right, ma'am," Reynolds said, taking Lisa's arm and walking her through suddenly still traffic to the waiting squad car. "You have the right to remain silent. You should know that if you fail to remain silent, anything you say can and will be used against you in a court of law. You have the right to adequate representation by an attorney. If you cannot afford an attorney..."

The door was open, and Lisa found herself being pushed inside the car by Reynolds' body, with Reynolds' hand on top of her head. "Wait – am I being arrested right now? I tried to save him."

"Yes, ma'am," Reynolds said. "If you cannot afford an attorney, one will be provided to you by the state of New York at no charge to you. Do you understand these rights as I've explained them to you?"

Lisa discovered her mouth was hanging open. She shut it with a snap, turned to face the front of the car – a metal grille separated her from the front seats – and slid over a few inches so the door would not hit her when it slammed shut.

Reynolds pushed the door closed gently, secured it by pushing with her hip. She slid into the driving seat and her partner into the passengers' side. "The suspect has denied to communicate understanding of her rights," she said.

"Understood," said her partner.

The radio offered unintelligible chatter. Reynolds responded periodically, never more than a curt "roger that." Otherwise, the ride passed in silence.

***

"I've never been in a jail cell before," Lisa said. "It's nicer than I expected."

Killroy looked around at the used '90's furnishings: college couch, plastic chairs, dull gray rug. "You still haven't."

"Haven't what?"

"Been in a jail cell. This is just pre-booking."

"Oh. Well, that explains it, probably."

"I don't expect they wanted to mingle you with the general population," James said. "Some of the inmates have axes to grind against psychiatry. Others use us to learn how to game the system. In all cases, it's bad to let you mingle. Anyway, this is not a social call."

"I'm disappointed," Lisa said. "You sure you can't stay and chat for a while? After all, they did give me two chairs." All the furniture was turned away from the door, away specifically from the glass that surrounded it.

"I understand you're nervous, and you get sarcastic and antagonistic when you're nervous," Killroy said, leaning against the doorframe. "Why did you call me, of all people?"

Lisa had her head turned all the way to the right so she could make eye contact. Now she looked at the opening behind him, knowing just because the door was wide didn't mean she could leave. "Of all people? That's fair, I guess. Truthfully, you're the last person on Earth I'd expect to help me, Jim. At the same time, the only number I could remember was the hospital pager."

"They took your phone? What is it, evidence?"

"No, I don't carry one." She felt like she'd just confessed to peeing on the rug – and the look James gave her reinforced the feeling. "Look, I wasn't planning on getting arrested. Or for that goon to stab himself in my train car, alone, with no witnesses. Or for him to sexually assault me."

"I'm sorry," James said, and straightened up. "What?"

Lisa had tensed when he spoke. Now she tried to relax again. "Nothing. Not your fault. It's just, that's what he said. He said he was sorry, then he lifted his shirt, and I saw the knife."

"Oh. Sorry. Oh, damn. Well, anyway, I've been insensitive. Not used to breaks in the routine. It isn't easy..."

"Yes?"

"Never mind. I went by your place, as you asked. The police are searching through the bag I brought you. Underwear, jeans, sweater. You understand they're unlikely to let you have your own clothes unless they're letting you go. Toothbrush, hair brush, same problem. Those things tend to turn into weapons in here."

"That's right," Lisa said, putting her feet on the table. "You used to do community corrections."

"Long ago and far away," Killroy said. "The hospital cannot be involved in this matter, you understand. We and the government will not be able to provide counsel, legal or otherwise. I won't be able to visit you here again. And I'm sorry, but you're suspended pending this investigation."

"Ouch. Jim, that really-"

"Sucks, I know. It isn't personal. I don't hate you, contrary to your opinion on that subject. I imagined they would only let you make one call, although that's an outmoded rule usually only enforced in movies. So I took the liberty of calling my lawyer's lawyer."

"You have a lawyer?" Lisa said.

"More surprising is that you don't, given our line of work. Particularly if you are going to do the roundups with John. Anyway, her lawyer agreed to come in pro-bono, thinks this will be not much work."

"Thanks, Jim. I mean it. I mean, I know I'm a pain, really, but..."

"Goodnight, Lisa," James said. He stepped back out of the doorframe then turned to his right, walked out of her field of view. Lisa watched the doorframe for a moment, wondering with half a heart how long it would take for an officer to come and close it.

Turned out to be about six seconds. The door slammed shut, locked, and she could only have seen who did it through the six inch wire-embedded panes of glass to either side of the door. Since she was pointedly avoiding reflective surfaces with her eyes, the door-locker would have to remain mysterious.

Eight

A dream.

She knew it was a dream and still had no choice but to go along with it, be immersed in it, experience it as real.

"Dreams are the royal road to the subconscious."

A man with a pointed beard and round spectacles, a cigar in one hand. German accent.

"Austrian, thank you," he said. He was also Killroy. He didn't have Jim's face or body or voice but it was him.

"Are you gay?" she asked.

"What leads you to think so?"

"It's the cigar," she said. "Besides, I heard you should always ask. Before you ask."

"Ask what?"

"I don't remember," she said. Or did she just think it? But then they were someplace else. Someplace familiar.

"This is just a holding cell," Freud said, and puffed on his cigar. But there was no cell. Open spaces, wild green fields, chirping insects and birds. There was a line of trees on the horizon, green and lovely and absurd. "They don't want you to mix with the inmates."

Lisa turned to tell Freud to stuff it, but he was gone. Instead, there was a house behind her. A tumble-down place. The roof had wooden shingles. It was sway-backed, hopeless. There was a wooden door, dark, painted red so long ago that there was almost nothing left of color on it. Shuttered windows with cracked glass. Logs for walls.

A little boy came across the meadow at a run, shouting, joyful. He had a bunch of wildflowers in each hand, yellow and red and purple, bright like the bathroom light in the midst of a hangover.

He raced up, opened the door without putting any of the flowers down, dashed inside. "Stacey! Look what I brung you, Stacey!"

"Goddamn it Elbert, you go on back and shut that damned door. How many times I got to tell you..."

"I'm sorry, Stacey." Little Elbert sounded undisturbed, joyous. The door slammed shut again, and then Lisa was inside the house. It smelled of pine resin, of bacon, bread. A little bit of rain and countryside. It was dark, what with the windows being shuttered. Lisa looked up, saw that there were no fittings for electric lights.

Elbert and Stacey were down a hallway, through another closed door. Light coming underneath suggested it was better lit, maybe with a big window. The smell of roasting meat said it was a kitchen. She heard glass touching wood, metal touching metal.

"Oh, Elbert – they're beautiful. You're such a good boy. It's been years since anyone thought I was pretty enough to bring me flowers."

"You're the prettiest lady in the world, Aunt Stacey. Well, except for maybe my Mama."

She wanted to slip under the door, see these people, these strangers. But there was a voice behind her. A voice, but a voice with no characteristics. Not deep, not halting, not loud. Words only without inflection or tone, made by no throat.

"No, that's not what you're here to see," it said.

"What, then?"

"On the stairs."

There was a stairwell, the other way down the hall, in the dark. Wood almost black made up the steps and paneled the walls. And there in the dark was a little black and white cat. She stared at the door.

"That's why we couldn't leave the door open, no matter how hot we got. If we left the door open, the cat would get out. Old Stacey, she loved that cat. Well, for a time. Love don't never last, does it?"

"What happened to the cat? Elbert, what happened to her?"

But the dream was over, because Lisa was waking up.

***

She'd fallen asleep with her head on the table. Her back hurt and there was drool on her cheek. Someone was in the room with her. A man in a suit, looking impeccable and thin and handsome at... "What the hell time is it, anyway?" She scrubbed at her wet cheek with the back of one hand, because there was nothing else to clean herself with.

"Good morning," the man said. "I'm Dave. David J. Hammond, attorney at law. The time is..." he pulled up one sleeve an inch and looked at an expensive watch. "Four fifteen in the morning."

"I'd offer to shake your hand, but..."

Dave pulled a handkerchief out of an inside pocket, clean and fresh and white. It smelled of starch. "May I sit?"

"Of course," Lisa said. "I'm sorry, I'm just a little..."

"Yes, I understand. Lisa, I've asked the sergeant to let you have your clothes. She says they haven't had time to inventory them yet, which is of course bullshit, but they agreed in principle."

Lisa tried to think past a picture of a cat sitting in a dark stairwell. "That means they don't mean to keep me here?"

"I don't think they do. You have some support at the county morgue."

"Really?" She thought of zombies, of dead men, of her father.

"Yes. The victim, the dead man, has a number of prior arrests. The subway really is quite pestilential with inappropriate touching. Sex assault, as it were. And he was one of the pests. Anyway, it took me so long to come here because my first stop was there. The morgue. I... encouraged? the mortician to accelerate his preliminary investigations.

"The knife, Doctor Jayne. It was lodged in his sternum. Very deeply. Do you remember your basic pathology?"

"Yeah," she said, finally starting to feel with it just a little bit. "Takes sheers to get through it. Whoever stabbed that guy in the chest wasn't a middle-aged woman with no discernable musculature. Not me, in other words."

"Correct. They'll be in after shift change. Say, in another two or three hours. They'll want another statement. Be sure to tell them all you can, but be sure not to say anything new or different."

"You aren't staying?" Lisa said. There was a queer feeling in her stomach, like fear.

"I don't think you need me. Listen, I'll be back around six-thirty. Bring you a donut and a cup of coffee. All right?"

"All right," Lisa said. Her voice quavered a little. "Thank you."

Dave stood up again, headed for the door. One step shy, he turned around. "People aren't routinely very kind to you, are they?"

"What? Kind? No, I suppose not. I seem to attract a different kind of energy."

"There's someone I want you to talk to. The hospital is going to want you to be in counseling before they let you go back to work. Not through it, but in it. Don't worry, your benefits will cover it." He reached into that inside jacket pocket where the hankie had come from, produced a little gray business card. "My sister," he said.

Lisa looked at the card:

Hildebrand Dallas
Psychic readings, personology
Spiritual counseling, life coaching

There was a phone number, an address in a way nicer building than the private detective occupied. When she looked back up, it was to see the door closing behind Dave. She felt a cold draft before the door slid all the way shut, and that said something about what it was like to be alone again.

***

"You can go, Miss Jayne."

"It's doctor," she told the man. He was a balding, fifty-ish man of middle height and more than middle weight. He looked like the black uniform was the only structure to his body, like he'd been poured into it from a giant flask, over-filling it.

"Whatever," he said. When he left, nobody locked the door behind her.

And he left a paper bag on the table.

The bag was dirty, wrinkled and torn. No special care had been taken with it. It overflowed with clothes that Killjoy had probably packed very neatly because he did everything very neatly. Parsimoniously, anal-retentively, with great precision, and neatly.

Lisa experienced a sudden vision of The Killjoy standing in her bedroom in front of her chest of drawers, a pair of her white cotton panties in his hands. He held them up to his face and breathed deeply. Then he folded them on top of the chest, using a ruler to make sure they were perfectly square.

She laughed. Then she laughed because she was laughing. An officer looked in on the disturbance and found her pulling on her underwear while holding her stomach, tears coursing down her face.

"You all right, ma'am?" he said, and she was grateful it wasn't the boneless man. This chap was young and tall and handsome.

She just waved him away, continued dressing.

Outside, at the counter, another new person gave her back her purse, keys, wallet, shoes. "What about what I was wearing?"

"Sorry," she said. "Evidence. You can fill out a-"

"Never mind. Listen. All I've had in about twenty hours is a cup of coffee and a donut. What's the nearest place to get some food around here? And where the hell am I, anyway?"

"Deli on the corner, ma'am. And you're about a thousand feet from the subway."

In New York, there were two ways of understanding your geographic position, and distance from a subway entrance was usually the most helpful from Lisa's perspective. In the light of recent events, however, she thought she might just hail a cab.

"Thanks," she said, and she wasn't sure why. Outside, down some concrete steps, she blinked her way into the light of nearly-noon. There was the deli, as promised, and she could just about smell the sauerkraut and corned beef.

Nine

"What'd I miss?" The staff meeting was about ready to start. Around the big dark table were: the two social workers, Sally and Mark; the shifts three mental health clinicians, Dylan, Chad and Bryan; and the shift's two nurses, Ellen and Alan. And Lisa, dressed in a long wool skirt and turtleneck sweater, both in navy blue.

"You were only gone two days," Dylan said.

"I know. That's an eternity in here."

"Still not enough time for anything to really change," Sally said. There was a coffee stain on her jacket. "The boys stopped staring at the camera. I guess there's that."

Alan said, "I hope you're feeling better."

"Better than what?" Lisa replied.

"Killroy said you were sick. We didn't hear anything else. Assumed it must be pretty bad – you never missed a day before." Alan squared his papers.

"Oh. No, I wasn't sick," Lisa said. "Some guy tried to stab me on the subway and ended up stabbing himself instead. Aren't any cameras or anything – can you believe that? In twenty-fifteen, no cameras on the trains? Anyway. Took a couple days to get squared away. Why are you guys all looking at me like I'm an alien?"

Dylan said, "Because it's been all over the news. They said you stabbed him. Prominent local doctor offs homeless man. Like that."

Lisa felt almost like snorting or laughing. She knew she should, show derision for the idea. But she couldn't – she still wasn't certain what had happened. "Damnit..." her hand shook, spilled her coffee.

Four people stood up to get paper towels as the coffee spread across the table. Everyone had paperwork in front of them.

"You going to be OK?" Ellen said. "Your hands are shaking like crazy."

"Just tired," Lisa said. "Nightmares."

Everyone commiserated. Then they got to business.

"First patient," Ellen said. "Elbert. He's not on anything yet. No florid psychosis, but I don't like the way he's gained control of the milieu. When he pops it's going to be big, and all those guys are going with him."

"I don't think he's as dangerous as all that," Lisa said. "Nothing in his records indicates violence, and he's been in and out a bunch of times."

Ellen pointed to the ceiling. "Them upstairs are saying get him on something or get him out of here."

"Well, that's fine, but let's not get into justifying their policies with our observations. Let's give him a few more days."

"You're responsible," Ellen said.

"Yes," Lisa said. "I suppose I am."

When the meeting was over, when everyone had offered her to help with whatever she needed in a way that made it clear the offer was only valid for help that didn't involve money or food or legal help or anything actually useful, then it was finally time to go and meet with Elbert.

I've missed this, Lisa thought. She sat down, adjusted the recorder to just where she wanted it. *I shouldn't have, but I missed this*.

Elbert came in a few minutes later. "Welcome back, Doc," he said.

"Hello, Elbert. You feel like talking today?"

"Yes I do. Shall we get straight into it, then?"

***

Jungle skudded by below like it was clouds and Elbert was lying on his back on a windy day. He watched for tell-tale signs of enemy movements, but that was the problem: there weren't any tell-tale signs. From up here, the ground might as well have been the bottom of the ocean.

He glanced up at Wilcox. She was sitting on her helmet in the open doorway, unaffected by the height – they were low enough to call it height rather than altitude, a word that made things seem too abstract to Elbert. She was playing with the .50 caliber machine gun mounted in the doorway, maybe figuring to take it with her. The weapons she had all looked like toys next to her; the fifty-cal seemed to fit.

They were going too fast. Elbert was having trouble keeping up with events.

There were three other men on board. Two white guys and a man of uncertain heritage, small and tough-looking like the meat Elbert's grandma used to jerk in the fall.

The white guys had their heads together, talking. With the noise of the chopper their words were lost, but one of them looked up at Elbert, who looked away.

Dana was on one of the bench seats, hands wrapped around her restraints. Elbert yelled, "First time on a chopper?" but the noise of the rotors and the air rushing through the cabin snatched his words away, tossed them out into the air. He thought she looked silly with that helmet on, those green fatigues. She looked like what she was: an academic playing soldier. She couldn't know how dark it got out here.

Elbert stood, stepped over carefully, touched her chinstrap and mimed taking off the helmet. She raised her eyebrows: a question. Elbert pointed to Wilcox, sitting on her helmet, his own helmet stuffed under the bench seat where his ass had been a second ago, the row of goons that had come with the chopper all sitting with their helmets under their butts.

Dana understood, at least enough to comply.

Elbert went back to watching the scenery. They were low, sometimes running between the tops of the tallest trees. That put them at about a hundred feet. A troupe of monkeys watched, unfazed perhaps because choppers racing by seemed routine to them. The war was hardly nascent. They had red faces framed in golden hair.

Wilcox had the .50 off its mount and now she had the goons stripping it down, scrounging all the ammo boxes they could. Two big white men with grease-paint on their faces and arms, sleeves ripped off their shirts just like her only no T-shirt for modesty underneath. The one who had been watching him while his buddy talked watched him again while boxing up ammo. One smaller brown guy, maybe Mexican, maybe Cuban. He clasped a cigar between his teeth while he worked. It wasn't the first time Elbert had ever seen a war trophy, but still the guy's necklace of severed ears disgusted him.

I got to get level, he thought, but he didn't really know what that meant. Only that nothing had seemed real for days. He looked at the necklace again and thought about shooting Daniels. Two shots, each lethal on its own, a horde of witnesses. Had Daniels deserved it?

He'd been doing worse than taking ears off dead men. Much worse.

The little brown guy looked up, caught Elbert looking. Saw his eyes were on the trophies. Elbert wanted to look away but his eyes slid up to meet the other guy's eyes, betraying him. The guy touched one of the ears, caressed it gently. He smiled with his mouth but his eyes were dead.

Now Elbert did look away.

What the fuck am I into?

They didn't set down. The sun set behind rampant jungle and the chopper changed its attitude: rather than leaning into forward motion, it settled even, hovered. Wilcox tossed out cables, attached to a winch inside. She helped Dana onto one of the lines with a harness and some fancy climbing gear painted Army green. One of the goons went down with her and there was never any question she was going no matter how scared she looked.

Elbert got his gear together. Wilcox saddled him with an extra ammo box for the .50 and Dana's pack and he slid down a cable into the treetops. The line didn't reach all the way to the ground, so he took hold of a tree like he was home at last and it was his Mama. The tree shook and rattled all around him in the chopper's downwash. He didn't bother trying to move until it was out of his space, thumping away back the way he had come.

"Will you quit screwing around up there, Elbert?" Wilcox called from below. She lit a flare and then he could see her down there, about sixty feet under him. She had that absurd machine gun in one hand with the ammo belt draped over her shoulder. How she'd climbed down in the downwash carrying that thing, all her other gear, and apparently a shaken Dana Smith, Elbert didn't want to think about.

He climbed down, branch to branch, getting more confident as the branches grew heavier and steadier nearer the ground. Until he put his hand right on a snake, completely oblivious.

It was like the branch itself turned to attack him. It whipped around, bullet-fast. If he'd gone bare-armed like Wilcox and her squad, he'd have been done for, but its teeth snagged in the loose fabric of his shirt. He fell out of the tree before he had any idea what was happening. The snake stayed where it was.

The three guys laughed at him as he met the soft, black earth under the tree. "You OK man?" said the guy with the necklace. He had an unplaceable accent, not quite Spanish or Mexican. He put out a hand to help Elbert up.

Elbert took it, got to his feet. "It was only a few feet," he said. "Was thinking of jumping it anyway. I'll have a bruise or three, but mostly just my pride."

One of the white guys, his name tape said DENNIS, reached in one pocket and came up with a blunt. "Cure for what ails you," he said, and he also had an unplaceable accent. Different but equally foreign to Elbert's ears. Not Russian, not quite, but too guttural for German or the like. Sinister, almost.

Can an accent be sinister? Or is it just the way he watches me? "I don't smoke dope," Elbert said, and all the guys laughed again.

"Not what I heard," said the third one, the White guy whose tape said "FLOYD." "Heard if a guy wanted to move some product around..."

"Enough," Wilcox said. "Dust him off, slap her until she stops shaking, and let's get on with it. Front moves every day, every hour, but we should have about twenty miles before we're out of nominally friendly territory. Let's make the most of it."

"You don't want to camp?" Elbert said.

"Why? We've been sitting on our asses the last six hours. Let's move, ladies."

There wasn't much to sort out. They started marching, in a formation kind of like geese flying: Wilcox in front, Dennis and Floyd to her left and right and slightly behind, Elbert and Dana behind and to the right of Floyd, the trophy taker smoking along behind and to the right of them. The undergrowth was forgiving here and Wilcox set a hard pace, her eyes everywhere.

What she could see was beyond Elbert. All he could see was dark and whatever came within a couple feet of his nose. She'd tossed the flare before they started. No other light presented itself.

Dana got a little closer, panted, "Hey, what was that with the helmet?"

It was on her head again, and her pack on her own back. She marched like she was wearing high heels and a pencil skirt. "Got to cover your ass," Elbert said. "Sometimes the Cong, they like to snipe at passing birds. And choppers are light. Can't carry too much armor. Bullets come up through the floor, they can get you right in the..."

"I get the picture," Dana said. "Thanks."

"She for real?" Elbert asked, quiet-like.

"Oh yes, she's for real. In psy-ops circles, we try to avoid her. A little too aggressive for our minds. You know, we prefer to do propaganda broadcasts and leaflet drops, get into their heads, but she likes to get behind their lines and carve some of them up. Make it look like spirits, or better yet like they did for each other."

Elbert thought a little. He tripped over a branch, got going again, found he'd lost the train of his thought. Later: "You don't just do psychology and head-shrinking, though. That's what you said."

"I was on post for a briefing on remote-viewing. Had a promising candidate."

"You gonna make me ask?" he said.

"I guess you just did. It means being able to leave your body, astrally project to someplace else. Get a good look at what's around you, report back."

"Sounds like bullshit to me."

"The world is a weird place," she replied. "A lot of things you'd take as false, well, they keep turning up real and matter-of-fact. Remote viewing hasn't yet shown practical application. But a thing like this, this war, you've got to look at all the angles. What if you're wrong, and a person could see the situation far away, and we could save a few lives?"

"I don't know," Elbert said.

"That's just it. I don't know either. That's a good attitude to have."

Elbert's nose got ahold of a smell just then, the burning-rubber, distant skunk smell of marijuana. He hated that stink. If only he hadn't gotten into it with Daniels, none of this weird shit would've happened.

But he'd still be in the jungle someplace, trying not to get his ass shot off, so on balance he'd say he was about even. Wilcox was terrifying but the whole jungle was terrifying. One night he'd seen a leopard snatch away a full-grown man who just went out to piss, carried him screaming into the jungle.

"At least this is interesting," he said, and felt a little better for a second.

Then Dennis said, "You sure you don't want a taste, MacAvoy?" He tittered, and his buddies giggled like they were high, too. Floyd had a knife out and was fondling the blade, testing the edge.

And Elbert felt like he was naked, vulnerable. That they knew everything and he had nothing on them.

Maybe interesting isn't what it's cracked up to be...
***

Elbert stopped talking. He steepled his fingers, leaned back, waited.

"What were their ranks?" Lisa said.

"Who?"

"Floyd. And..." She looked through her notes, cursing her own handwriting. "Dennis. Floyd and Dennis."

"Didn't have none."

"You said they had on uniforms."

"Yes ma'am. And they were subdued. Undercover, even. Those weren't their real names and they didn't have on no ranks. If they had, they'd have been lies."

Was it time to push? To see how much Elbert could take of reality? Or would that just shut down the story?

"Can I ask you something, Elbert?" she said.

"Go right ahead."

"Do you think that's likely? I mean, after all this time, might you not be remembering it just right?"

He smiled, and that was not a great sign but far from the worst sign. At least he wasn't probably about to get violent.

"I remember it just right," he said. "It wasn't back in sixty-eight. The first time it was, but I dream about it every night. About her, Wilcox. About Dana. Poor sweet, doomed Dana. And about those two scary cats with their weird ways of speaking. And Osho. You forgot to ask after him. But us bush pigs, we didn't wear the uniforms right. We modified them as we needed to, you know? Tore off ranks so the Cong wouldn't know who to shoot. Tore off the sleeves. Cut them up for bandages or headbands or whatnot."

Plausible, Lisa thought. *I wonder if I know anyone who was there. Verify. Not Killjoy, though. He's... not right.* "All right, Elbert. I'd say that's good enough for today."

"Fair enough," he said. "But we should start to hurry this along. Running out of time, you know? Maybe I should talk for longer next time."

"All right. I'll see what I can do."

He nodded, stood up, plodded away.

Lisa scratched on her legal pad: *heretofore Mr. MacAvoy has been relaxed, unhurried. Laconic, even. Today is his first sign of urgency. Meaning...?*

Ten

Lisa put her grocery bag in her left arm where it fought her purse for space. Her right hand held a ring of keys.

Too many keys. Each one an obligation.

Her hand was shaking. The key skittered and danced over the lock plate. Then she dropped the ring completely.

"God *damn* it!" She looked around like there was someone around to hear her. All the other doors on her floor stayed closed, so Lisa set down her bags, picked up the keys, used both hands to open the lock. Then she held the door with one foot and moved everything inside one item at a time.

You're losing it. Overreacting.

Dinner didn't help settle her stomach. French bread with cheese melted over the top was the height of her culinary effort these days. She ate over the kitchen sink in her underwear, clothes strewn across the floor. There wasn't anyone to see or care unless one counted the roaches. The building manager had just fumigated last month, anyway.

Lisa washed her hands and face. Two doors left the kitchen: one into a hallway with a bathroom and a bedroom, one into a small sitting room. Eight hundred square feet, palatial for the city. There was always TV to numb the mind, but she had a new flat-screen that was all black and shiny. Might as well be a mirror when it was off.

Glass shattered by her bare feet, and that made her realize she'd abruptly jerked her arms, knocking a water glass to the floor. She swore again, bent to pick up the big pieces she could see. She stacked them on the counter then got to work on the smaller pieces, doing her best to not move her feet at all.

Her shoes were in the entryway, cast aside by the apartment door. Socks, too.

Finally she had enough picked up to feel like she could walk over by the fridge, pull out the broom from between the fridge and the wall. There was a dustpan back there too, and she brought it.

I can't go on like this.

It was a weird thought, heavy with despair, and it pissed her off. Lisa was never one to surrender to hopelessness.

But it wasn't her thought, not really. That's what her father had said. The last thing he had said. "Daddy? Are you sure this is what you want? Completely sure? Because when you push down on that plunger, there's no going back."

"I can't go on like this."

She'd left him there, knowing what he was going to do. Sure, back then, that it was the right thing – the merciful thing. He had just enough strength left in his right hand, just enough control to push down on the plunger and overdose on morphine. He had no strength left to do anything else. To enact any decision but that one. Kinder to let him have it, that last bit of decision and dignity.

I can't go on like this.

No, Daddy, and neither can I. But she'd make a different decision. There was still strength in her arms and legs. Her eyes still worked as well as they ever did.

The bathroom held a big make-up mirror, a hold-over from the twenties. It had little light bulbs all around it and was made of amazing glass, clear like a still pond in autumn. *Time to go settle this*, she thought, and strode across the kitchen.

The thing about broken glass is no matter how careful you are, you can't ever see it all and therefore can't ever clean it all up. A little shard just a bit bigger than a grain of sand poked into the bottom of her bare foot, the left one. Lisa shouted in outrage and pain, then slipped in her own sudden blood. Her head contacted the murky linoleum and then all thoughts about mirrors were done. All thoughts were done.

Until the nightmares began.

***

Four men sat with their backs to a burned-out bonfire. Their orange robes were all black in the darkness, with only a little starlight to light them. Three of them were asleep, semi-upright, arms thrown around their bent knees. The fourth was in almost the same posture except his eyes were on the sky, watching black clouds that could be known only by the way they obscured the stars they passed.

In the ashes of the fire, something moved.

A weak, burned thing crawled out. It was only darkness, no real form or substance, blacker than the ashes that clung to its smoky skin. It stank of char but, so close to the fire, everything stank so.

It clawed its way onto the dirty track, resisted a mewl of pain. Looked around. It thought of creeping away from the four men, disappearing into the jungle after more interesting prey. Something new was coming, it knew that, something... delicious. Worth waiting for.

But it was hungry. Just so hungry.

The thing slipped soundlessly over the dirt track, between ruts formed by centuries of hand-carts and barrows. Flowed over one of the sleeping men, towards the wakeful one. Tasted his despair.

Ripe.

He felt it touch the back of his neck, started, began to stand. But it dragged him back down by the neck and stuffed itself into his mouth, nose, eyes, ears, aborting the scream that his human reflexes demanded.

Like the smoke from the bonfire, the burned, mewling thing was gone.

Came the small hours, the glow over the trees in the east of a sun not yet risen, one of the monks woke up. He stretched, rubbed his eyes. Pissed into the shrubs that lined the track. He saw the watcher had gone to sleep. If he had spoken English, his words would have been, "Damn Hein, sleeping instead of watching." But there was no malice or any real anger in it: it was part of the game, part of the story they and the monster were telling each other. Over and over. It came, they burned it, they went to sleep, it slinked away into the jungle only to return a few days later.

Only this time, Hein wasn't really sleeping. "Not this time," he said. "This time, it needs flesh."

"What needs flesh?" Nguyen said.

"The thing that has taken me, that which I am." Then Hein picked up his staff.

"What are you doing?"

Hein didn't answer, only swung the heavy stick. It caught Nguyen on the temple, sending him sprawling. He grabbed Nguyen by what remained of his hair, dragged him towards the burned-out embers a few paces past the camp. The others woke up, struggled to comprehend what was happening with sleep-addled minds, lurched to intervene just as Hein put Nguyen's face into the ashes.

They were stone cold. For a second. And then the burned-out thing, the wispy, shadowy creature, let loose all the flames and heat it had absorbed in its various deaths. The bonfire leapt high, twenty feet, thirty. Nguyen died. Hein's body was ruined beyond redemption. The other two men were knocked back, eyebrows singed off and robes set alight. They rolled around in the dirt.

When they were ready to think about something beyond surviving the moment, they looked up, looked around for Hein.

Hein sat on Nguyen's back. Bits of ropy muscle hung from his mouth, the ends charred black. "He despaired," Hein said. "Nguyen was right: to torture the thing to death stained your souls. But he was willing to pay it. Hein, poor weak fool, tried to bargain it away. As if despair could be bought and sold."

"This, too?" said one of the remaining humans. "Must we do this, too?"

"We have done so much already," said the last. "What difference one more murder? Or let him continue this way?"

"No, you are right."

They took up their staves and forced the body of their friend into the ashes, into the flames it called up, and held him there until his body was still.

"Is this mercy?"

"No, I hope not."

***

"Alice?"

"What? My name is Lisa."

"Alice, is that you?" There was a man in her apartment. Maybe a man. He smelled of grass and gun oil. "Alice, I have to find you."

"Not Alice. Lisa."

He didn't seem to hear, and Lisa didn't want him to. When he came into the light and she saw who he was, she was glad this was only a bad dream, that she was invisible.

***

The clock on the microwave said **3:38**. Then the eight changed into a nine.

I can see clearly. The back of the head, which Lisa had smacked on the lino, held the visual cortex as well as the major center for balance and coordination. Seeing the time was a good first sign. Standing up without being ill would be a second.

She rolled over from her back onto all fours, peeling her hair out of a pool of tacky blood. Up on her knees now, she felt at the back of her head. There was a small abrasion and a pretty good bruise. Head wounds generally bled a lot even if they weren't serious, so she wasn't that worried yet.

She used the countertop to lever herself upright.

So far, so good.

She leaned there for a minute, thinking about running the sink. She was thirsty, dried out. But the priority was to rule out a concussion, and that meant letting go of the sink and walking around the apartment.

So that's what she did. Her injured foot protested. Just a tiny glass cut could hurt like hell down there. She left a little red spot in every footstep, then stepped through the blood from her head wound and turned each step into a bloody print. Off the lino and onto the carpeted hallway, marking up the cheap builders'-grade beige with her mortality. Into the bathroom and back onto linoleum.

In the drawer under the sink was a hand-mirror, a magnifying one for doing things like tweezing eyebrows. She took it out, hit the lights around the dressing-room mirror, held the hand-mirror behind her head. With her other hand she tried to spread her hair to get a look at the injury.

It was hard to see clearly, to keep a good angle on it, but it didn't look bad. If it were someone else she'd suggest maybe a stitch or two. Given that she couldn't stitch herself, though, it was probably not worth a trip to the emergency room.

Lisa lowered the hand mirror and thought about a shower. She could wash the blood out of her hair and see from the color of the water whether the bleeding had stopped on its own.

But her eyes brushed across their selves in the mirror.

There was something behind her. In her peripheral vision it looked like a shadow except there were lights overhead and lights around the mirror. There should have been no shadow. She remember the smell of crisped flesh, the sound of Vietnamese language she had somehow been able to understand.

But her eyes were locked to the reflection. To the eyes of the woman staring out at her.

She watched her own face fall slack. She looked old, tired. Dark, puffy bags hung below her eyes and her lips were white, bloodless. Her eyes, brown and dark and liquid, were full of red veins.

Is this mercy? No, I hope not.

The room seemed to turn around her. Slowly, like the night sky turned overhead, like the world turned under that sky. But her eyes stayed latched onto that mirror.

Who was in there, behind those eyes?

Is it me? Am I in there somewhere?

No, not her. Something else. Something...

The telephone started to ring. In the kitchen, on the wall with a short cord. *Ring-ring, ring-ring.*

Lisa turned away from that mirror, walked back to the kitchen. Halfway there she realized she was cold, and her skin was covered in gooseflesh. But she went straight to the phone, telling herself along the way that she'd been about to look away, that the mirror had no hold on her, that she was just creeped out from nightmares.

"Hello?" The phone smelled of old plastic, old rubber. Feint, persistent odors.

The line was open. She could hear that, the not-hiss of a connection made. She thought she heard someone there, maybe breathing very softly. And then the line went dead. No click, just a switch from open to shut, from signal to no-signal. A second later, the deadness of the line was replaced with a dial tone.

Lisa put the phone up on its cradle. "Maybe I'll take that shower now." But she left the mirror lights off.

Eleven

The building still stank. Outside, like urine and decomposing cardboard. Inside like death and old cigars. The ones with the black band her daddy used to smoke.

She climbed the stairs with one hand on the wall, careful to step over the black, spiky growths. Her other hand held a hankie over her mouth and nose. The one Dave had given her. She didn't know what those black things were but they were probably fungal, and you could inhale spores and die in old places like this.

All the doors stayed shut this time as Lisa all but crept down the hallway. Behind the papery walls she could hear early-morning life going on: kids talking, parents yelling, a spoon touching a bowl. Farther down, someone breathing with a ventilator. A telephone ringing and ringing and ringing, nobody answering.

Here was Hanrahan's office. She tried the handle, found it unlocked, stepped inside. The big man was at his desk, little windows behind him making him just a shadow, a silhouette.

He didn't move, or greet her.

He's dead. He died in the night, calling you, and his killer hung up the phone.

Don't be stupid. "Hanrahan?"

"What?" he said, starting. "Oh, it's you. Crap. I think I fell asleep. Man, I've been in this chair all night. Come in, sit down. I'm sorry." He bustled around the desk, pulled out a chair for Lisa that she could have taken with no help at all. "Just need to hit the head. Be right with you." He disappeared through the little door she had supposed was a toilet on her last visit.

A minute later, he came back out, wiping wet hands on his slacks. "You're early. I thought you said Thursday?"

"It is Thursday," Lisa said. And then noticed Hanrahan had stopped walking, was standing behind her.

"What did you do to your head?" he said. "Looks pretty gnarly."

"I hit it. Bumped it. Not worth any stitches, I don't think."

"Stay there." He went back into the toilet, came back with a small white case with a red cross on the front. "It's bleeding slowly. Not gushing like a fresh head wound. But I've got just the ticket. Band-Aid won't work, too much hair and I doubt you want a bald spot. Can't do a stitch..."

"Really, don't worry about it."

"Never take advice from a patient," Hanrahan said. "I was a combat medic. Gulf War, the first round. Desert Shield, Desert Storm. Here it is."

Lisa looked around at him. At his hands. They were big, like bunches of baby bananas. One held a tube of superglue. "That's in your first aid kit?"

"Always keep one. Now sit still. This is going to hurt like a bitch. Sorry, it's really going to sting. Solvents."

She sat still. "I'm not made of glass, you know."

"Still, it'll hurt."

"I know that. I mean, the language. I'm not a delicate flower. Say what you want."

"Really?" He paused waited for her to go on.

"Really."

Then the sting. It was about as bad as the worst shot she'd ever gotten, Novocain right in the roof of her mouth. But the pain faded after about fifteen seconds.

"You can shower, and you can rinse out the blood if you're careful. Try not to use any shampoo for a couple of days." He put his glue away, extra careful with the cap. The white case snapped shut.

"Thanks," Lisa said.

"So. Thursday, you were saying."

"All day."

"Huh. Well, I don't have much for you. Not yet. Lots of Wilcoxes and Smiths. Smiths like you wouldn't believe. But I think Dana Smith was a real person." As he talked, he rummaged through the drawer in front of him, making a hollow, booming sound against its metal floor. Came up with a sheet of white paper. A printout of a newspaper article.

Parapsychologist busts Johnny James

Johnny James, local psychic, palm-reader and mentalist, met his match yesterday at the Homburg Auditorium. Dana Smith, professor of psychology at the University of Madison, proposed a series of tests. Cont. on page 7.

Lisa scanned the page for more clues. There was a story about a dog-food plant going bankrupt and a ribbon-cutting at a mall. "Where's the rest of it?"

"All I could get was the front page," Hanrahan said. "They didn't keep these things back then, you know? And most of what they bothered to archive isn't on the net yet. This was a small-town paper."

"Back then?"

He pointed to the date at the top of the page: July 3rd, 1964.

"Huh. How many parapsychologists could there be named Dana Smith? Smith is pretty common, but parapsychologists aren't, and Dana isn't. Are they?"

Hanrahan made some notes on a memo pad with Grace Memorial Hotel printed across the top. "Guess I could try and find out. Not likely, though, I think. I think that's your girl. One of them."

"Any luck on Wilcox?"

"VA is no help. Nothing in the marriage, divorce or death rolls. No property transfers. Or, I should say, too many. So many Wilcox' that it's impossible to narrow the search down sufficiently. A first name would really help."

"Try Alice."

***

"Got any tape?"

The med closet was closed but the half-door was open, allowing Lisa to lean in. Ellen was on duty. Sixty-ish, lean and dour-faced. She was on a step-stool, pulling pills from a drawer up near the ceiling. "Counter," she said. "Bring it back."

"Thanks." Lisa took a second longer than she needed to find the tape. Back at the staff table, she taped Hanrahan's article into the log notes. Dylan watched over her shoulder, reading the last few words about the Vietnamese monks burning their friend.

"The Killjoy's not going to like that," he said.

"What?"

"Any of it. That's a dream you had? Not something he said? And newspaper clippings? I can hear him now: *this is a testimony, a sworn testimony of our treatment and interactions, not a scrap-book.* Why keep pushing him?"

"You ever hear of a folie a deux, Dylan?"

"Must be a higher-level class. Wasn't in abnormal psych."

Lisa closed up the book, set it on its shelf between Lannington and Miller. "A shared delusion. Two or more people experience the same psychosis."

"You're as crazy as he is?" Dylan sat down at the table, put his feet on the chair in front of him.

"Not exactly. You do have to be a little nutty to work here. But psychoses are transmissible, like strong emotions. That's the theory. If it's happening – if my dream is verifiably part of Elbert's story, then we'll have a concrete record of something we've never been able to study before. Well, there's religion, but faithful people will never admit their faiths are mad. And there's the Heaven's Gate cult, but they're all dead."

"Heaven's Gate?" Dylan leaned forward now. "Sounds familiar."

"Hale Bopp comet? Before your time, really. Nineties. They all believed if they killed themselves in the right way at the same time, they'd go to a kind of heaven on a spaceship in the tail of the comet. Castrated themselves then drank the proverbial Kool-Ade."

"They did what?"

"You heard right. Anyway, I'm obviously not that crazy and I'm keeping one foot firmly in the realm of doubt. But it's my duty to document everything. Like The Killjoy would say, it's a legal document, an attestation. We can't just attest to the things that we do right, we have to also include the weirdnesses and inconsistencies and material evidence. That's science."

"Speaking of which, there he goes," Dylan said, pointing to Elbert walking by the side door towards the interview room.

"Guess I'm a minute or two behind. See you on the other side." She gathered up her legal pad, recorder, a pen. Touched something in her pocket. Walked out through the side door. "Hello, Elbert."

"Doc."

She opened the door and they both went in, took their accustomed places. Lisa turned on the voice recorder and waited.

Elbert began talking.

***

Dennis puffed on his toke. Watched water starting to boil over the fire, bubbles growing against the bottom of the pot, waiting to break loose and roil around. "It's getting worse," he said, and then he giggled. "Real spook parade, boss. We aren't alone out here."

Elbert had a feeling like someone was staring at him. Figured maybe Dennis wasn't really watching the pot at all, but was watching Elbert out of the corner of his eye. Elbert sat up, giving up on getting any more rest, wiped morning dew off his face. A hammock would have been nice but camp was no camp at all, just a couple of hours resting as they could in the mud and dead leaves, among the millipedes and beetles and worse. "That tea you're making?"

"Yeah," said Dennis. "Colonel hook you on it?"

"Makes a man feel human," Elbert admitted. "For a piece. Until she tries to march him to death."

Dennis giggled again, scrubbed a hand over beard stubble. Some of it was gold, some red. He sprinkled the now-boiling water with leaves from a pouch; they were curled up into tight balls like roly-poly bugs, but the water would entice them open. Elbert went into the trees and came back a few minutes later. Dennis handed him a cup, steaming only marginally more than the jungle itself steamed.

Wilcox sat up, sudden, like a machine that had been off and now was on. She went to her own ablutions off in the jungle. When she came back, rather than indulge in the tea now steeping away from the fire, she said, "Exercise. Now and every morning at this time."

Elbert complained. "Marching all day is exercise, isn't it?"

"These exercises will make the loads lighter and purify your mind, open your chakras."

"What's a chakra?"

Dana was awake now, too. "Body's energy centers," she said, "for want of a better word. That giant machine gun is just for show, Elbert. We're going into spiritual warfare here, where bullets won't avail you and a hard heart is no armor."

"You all got to learn to speak English," he said.

Dana just said, "Trust her."

He didn't trust Wilcox, not even a little bit. She was the one with the leash on the hounds, was all, and he didn't want to be around when she let them slip. There was Dennis, setting his toke half on and half off a flat rock so it would keep. Never turned his back on Elbert and always looked away when Elbert caught him looking. Floyd, doing his exercises with a knife in each hand, face fat and sagging as he concentrated. Osho, moving like he was born to these alien movements, but with fingers that kept seeking out the dead flesh on his necklace as if for reassurance.

They did poses. Warrior stance, down dog, backwards cat, standing kring. Elbert thought it hurt like hell and couldn't see how this was going to lighten any loads. Half an hour later, Wilcox said, "Enough. Pack up, drink up, saddle up."

Dennis giggled.

"What do you see?" she said.

"We're not alone out here," he said. "Not by no long shot, Chief."

"Bad?"

"Not the worst. Old ones. Spirits so long in the trees they were *in* the trees, you know? But whatever the Gooks found, whatever they woke up... Even the ghosts are running from it."

"You know how I feel about that word," Wilcox said.

"Sorry, Chief. I mean, the Vietnamese."

Elbert looked a question at her as he shouldered his kit. "To dehumanize the enemy is to render them beneath us," she said. "And to fight things that are beneath you sullies your spirit. A warrior does not kill children, or animals, or weaklings; a warrior looks for enemies worthy of respect, gives that respect, and rises the higher."

"Never heard it put that way," he said.

"You never called them Gooks though, did you?" Wilcox said.

"No, no I didn't. Too much like what some other people get called. Back home, I mean."

"I know what you mean." There was nothing of threat or accusation in the words but all the same Elbert felt like that was some kind of challenge, a provocation from which he was intended to back down.

So what am I supposed to do? Do her the way I did Daniels? With no other viable options, he looked away, grabbed his field pack. He saw Dennis look away from him, pretend he'd been contemplating his joint the whole time.

They moved. Wilcox took point again and they fell into roughly the same formation as before. A couple of fighters thundered overhead, seen just as white streaks in the sky and then heard seconds later. They shook the trees. The jungle was quiet a long time after that.

Elbert waited until Dana looked like she was ready to talk. She had dirt and sticks in her hair and ashes on her face, but for all her mincing steps she looked fresher than Elbert within a couple miles. "What was he talking about, about ghosts?" he asked her.

"I don't see them," she said. "Must be the hash. But they're everywhere. Not really ghosts, not literal spirits left behind after the body dies. More like... impressions on the environment from strong wills. The Earth remembers. And a place like this, an old place, it will have known many strong wills."

"And something even stronger is chasing them out."

"Like deer run before a forest fire."

"What can I do?" Elbert said. He didn't know if he was ready to believe in ghosts or spirits.

"Be who you are. She called you for a reason, dragged you out here for a reason. Trust yourself. Be who you are."

"Could I see them?"

"No," said Wilcox. She hadn't seemed close enough to hear. They'd been talking quiet, unsure the territory was friendly any more. Up ahead, distant, a pair of fireballs rose over the treeline. Black smoke followed, overtopped, started to spread with the wind. "The reefer does it for Dennis. You don't have any sight at all, that I can see. That's why I want you. Someone who knows the difference between right and wrong, and who's mind is closed to emanations."

"Why aren't we moving?" Elbert said, realizing everyone had stopped dead. He'd caught up to Floyd, almost walked past him. There was no formality to their formation, but it felt like a boundary about to be crossed.

"Because," said the little brown guy. Osho, his name was. "Another two steps and you set off that Claymore mine."

Now Elbert took his mind off spirits and hash and whether any of these people were sane. His eyes crawled along through the dirt, the dead leaves, the few spikes of grass trying to weed through. "I don't see..." But then he did. The faintest glimmer of a wire. "You guys are good. Trippy, but good. Why didn't you tell me?"

"Didn't have to," said Floyd. He bent down, got a better perspective. "Better just step over it," he said. "Don't want to trigger it, don't really want to take it down, neither."

"Why not?" said Elbert, stepping carefully over the wire as Dennis did the same.

"Because it's one of ours," Floyd said. "Means we're getting closer to contested territory. Weapons ready from here." His knives were all put away now. He had an M-60 with a grenade launcher attachment. It looked too big for him.

"No," said Wilcox. "We have safe passage."

"I don't like it," Elbert said. "How they gonna know not to shoot us, out of all the Americans creeping around the woods playing soldier?"

"They'll know," she said.

Twelve

Lisa wrote while Elbert talked:

Patient speaks now in a more pressured manner. He stated before that time is increasingly a factor. This is demonstrated in sometimes hurried or rushed speech. At the same time the subject matter is decreasingly of ambiguity and increasingly of personal danger; of traps, tripwires, unseen threats more concrete than paranormal activity. He relates a world at the last where we don't know not to shoot one another, where one requires safe passage and signs to not be killed just in the ordinary course of events.

She looked up, realized Elbert had stopped talking.

"I should go on," he said. "If you're listening."

"I'm listening," she said. "And I'll listen again to the recording."

"Don't trust them," Elbert said.

"Who?"

"Recordings. Anyway, I can see the world out there is a lot safer than the world in Vietnam. It isn't ordinary to be murdered. Then... I still sweat when I think on it. Maybe I'm as crazy as you think I am. That's the only solution to the problems we were presented. Staying sane in the midst of such carnage, tragedy, such horror – that would be truly mad."

Lisa stared at him as though he had started to speak in tongues.

"Time is shorter and shorter," Elbert said at last. "I'll go on, then."

And he did.

***

A bunch of soldiers stood around a dead body. There was a sniper rifle near one of its hands, Soviet-style. The Vietnamese boy was dead, no doubt about that. Half his face was missing and most of his torso was bullet wounds.

Wilcox approached with her weapon high over her head in both hands. The others followed her lead, hanging back just a little until peaceful contact was established. "What you got there?" she said.

One of the men turned around. He was maybe twenty-five, clean-shaven. The other guys were painted up but he hadn't bothered. Subdued rank badges made him a lieutenant, and his tape read "RODGERS." "What are you?" he said after a moment, looking Wilcox up and down just as she did him. "Reporter?"

"Colonel Wilcox, Special Investigations," she said.

"JAG?"

"No, intelligence."

Nobody saluted anybody. Elbert thought that was sensible, made everyone here veterans. There was always a sniper watching, and if they could take out an officer, they'd take the shot.

"Sniper," Rodgers said, echoing Elbert's thoughts. "He dropped a matchbook while we were walking under him, or we'd never have known he was here."

"Good work," said Wilcox. "You have any more recent contact with the enemy?"

"There's Gooks all up and down this alley," he said, meaning the dense forest between two rising hillsides. "You coming or going?"

"Going," Wilcox said. "You look like you're coming in."

"Yeah. We laid a pretty hefty perimeter so I advise watching where you place your feet. We're pulling back on rumors of a major assault getting prepped on the other side. Whatever you're doing over there, best get it done fast, Colonel."

"Teach your grandma to suck eggs, Lieutenant," she said. "I look like I mean to go over there and fuck around? Maybe ask gentle questions?"

"Uh... No, I guess not. And you look to have brought some hard boys."

"They're just the back-up band, son. I'm the rock star here. And this' my instrument. You hear people dying up ahead, you can be sure I had a part in it."

"Yes ma'am," the young man said.

"One more thing: don't call them Gooks. They're people, same as you."

The lieutenant and his men looked sideways at one another at that. One of the other guys said, "Willie, grab one of this guy's legs. Let's get him posed up like the Captain taught us. Might slow 'em down a pace."

Couple of the guys set to with quiet "Yes, sergeant." Didn't do to sir, ma'am and sergeant one another too loud out here for the same reason as saluting was a bad idea. The Vietnamese hadn't figured out yet that NCO's were worth more than officers, but they would. They were no dummies.

"You want some help with that?" Wilcox said.

"What do you know about it?" said the sergeant.

"The captain who taught you. Was it Daniels?" The sergeant nodded. "Well," she said, "who do you think taught him?" She pulled out her belt knife, a fat, wicked thing with a saw-blade on its back side and a runnel for blood. "Going to be messy. Floyd, get these recruits out of here. Dana never had the stomach for this. MacAvoy, stick to her like her life depends on it."

Elbert shifted his pack, not sure he understood what was happening.

"Let's go," Dana said. "She's right. I never had the stomach for the wet stuff." They passed among and then through the other soldiers, emerged on the hostile side, closer to enemy territory. "The science doesn't really support mutilations making them scared, either. Seems to just piss them off. Us, too. Our boys find one of our soldiers strung up with his dick cut off and stuffed in his own mouth, their mind doesn't go to, 'that could happen to me.' It can't. Humans have a hard time thinking about their own death or vulnerability, especially in the jungle with guys trying to kill you. It goes to, look what they did to him. That could be my buddies."

Floyd said, "Scared, angry, who gives a shit so long as it makes them stupid? You get emotional, you stop thinking about what you're doing."

"Because angry, vengeful men will fight on with wounds that would take out a regular person," Dana countered, stepping over a twisted root. She braced one hand against the trunk of a tree. It was smooth and white, seemed to live without bark.

Nobody had an answer for any of that. They marched on, stumbling, half-climbing in places. "Up ahead is the end of the alley," Floyd said. "Another mile, maybe two. Bottleneck. We want to get there fresh, full daylight. It's gonna be a chokepoint, full to shit with snares, traps, all kinds of bullshit from both sides."

"Camp?" said Dennis.

The little brown guy pointed at a stand of those weird white trees, about a hundred yards further into the bush.

"Yeah," said Floyd. "There looks good."

Elbert helped tie up hammocks. "Looks like were not sleeping in the mud tonight."

"Don't get used to it," said Floyd. He spat to one side.

Dana set her stuff down and wandered off a little north. Elbert made to follow. "You mind?" she said.

"What? Oh..." But then he remembered what Wilcox had said. "I should stick close," he said. "I'll turn my back if you want but boss-lady said you get full coverage."

"Fine. But I think you misheard."

"Huh?"

"It's not my life that depends on it, soldier. It's yours."

Elbert shrugged to conceal a shudder. "In that case I'm staying twice as close. You got a nice skin, but I'm a little more attached to mine."

Dana laughed, a throaty sound better suited to a room full of low conversation and the clinking of glasses. She wandered a little further, found a likely-looking stand of shrubs. She picked up a white stick that looked like a snake, poked at the bushes to make sure nothing with big teeth was concealed in the foliage. Then she disappeared back there. After a moment, Elbert heard the inimitable sound of urine landing in dead leaves and a sigh of relief. Made him kind of need to pee, too.

"All right, let's head back," Dana said, fixing her belt.

Gunshots. Tap-tap-tap. Tap-tap.

"Shit." Elbert unslung his rifle, checked the safety and the auto-fire toggle as he ran, set the selector to triple. The rough camp came into view seconds later.

Nothing seemed amiss. Osho and Dennis laughed. Dennis slapped Floyd on the back. Floyd turned to see Elbert charging in with his rifle ready.

"Shit man, relax," he said. "It ain't the end of the world, it's just dinner." He strode off under a stand of some weird tree that looked half-banyan, with big, grasping roots. He reached down and came up with a monkey about the size of a housecat. "Dinner," he said.

Dana said, "Gross. But no worse than K-rations. She going to let us have a fire?"

Elbert built one. Dennis lit it with a match from a book with a red cover and Asian lettering all over it. "Hey, where'd you get that?" Floyd said.

"That pussy lieutenant had it in his pocket."

"You picked his pockets?"

"I was bored. Probably came off the sniper. Guy said he dropped a matchbook."

"Yeah," Floyd said.

Osho butchered the monkey. Floyd made a rough spit and Dennis impaled the carcass. Within the hour the whole jungle smelled of roasting flesh. That and reefer smoke, clouds of which clung to Dennis and everything around him now that they weren't marching.

Elbert thought the monkey tasted like crap. But Dana was right: it was still better than whatever shit the government packed into those tinned rations.

The jungle darkened and Elbert tried to rest while he could. He claimed a hammock and lay in it, eyes shut against the night. Floyd and Dennis muttered to one another, too low to understand, the sound becoming a drone like bees congregating around a fire.

Later, half in and half out of sleep, he heard footsteps coming from south of the camp. Heavy ones, someone not trying to be quiet. His eyes flicked open and the men fell silent as he swung his legs out of the hammock, got to his feet. He snatched up his rifle, ran quiet as he could with short, mincing steps, scanned the trees around their little stand. Whoever was coming could be a distraction from an assault and that assault would be from a different direction.

"Settle down, MacAvoy," Wilcox said. Loud, from about fifty yards away. She seemed to know where every person was in the dark. "Just me. You other soldiers best check out his example though. There's a man who's almost scared enough to survive this adventure."

Dennis giggled. "You got it boss. Meantime, we saved you the ass cheek of this monkey."

Elbert came back, swung himself back into his hammock. It was strung up under Dana's and he could see the shape of her body up there in the flickering firelight. No good thinking about that too much, so he watched Wilcox tear apart the stringy bit of burned flesh they'd left her.

His eyes roved over her muscled shoulders, her scars, heavy brows. Her jaw, working delicately, like a steam shovel striking a match. Her hands.

Big, mannish hands. Wide, flat, with thick fingers and nails like nickels.

There was something all over them, up to the wrists. Dark in the darkness, black. Elbert could practically smell it over the wood smoke, the pot smoke, the burned meat.

***

It was late once again by the time Lisa had gotten all the notes in, dealt with test results for other patients, reviewed logs and prescriptions. Outside the hospital, rather than use the bus or train, she hailed a taxi.

The hospital was right downtown, and the address in her pocket was just a few blocks away. The cabbie didn't speak any English so Lisa just handed him the card. He turned on the dome light, looked at the card for a moment, handed it back. The light went off and the car eased into movement.

Minutes later, Lisa climbed from the back. She gave the driver a twenty because it was all she had. If he was grateful for the nine dollar tip, he didn't say so. The address was a brownstone, an old house carved up into several offices. There was a buzzer on the door. A bunch of names next to little lighted buttons.

She found the one that said "Dallas, H.," jabbed at it with a finger. The intercom came on and made the sound of a phone ringing. Nobody picked up but, after the sixth ring, the door buzzed and the lock retracted with a click.

She went through two doors, steel and glass, into a brightly lit atrium. The house was a hundred, hundred-twenty years old, but the interior was all modern. There was a black leather couch, a metal coffee table covered in books, modern art on the walls. Black and silver tile on the floors and a tin drop-ceiling that might be the room's only nod to antiquity.

Lisa looked for the staircase, found it behind a folding screen of a style that belonged in an old dressing room but painted in Anime themes. It seemed to tell the story of Kagemusha in Manga-style cartoons.

A door opened upstairs. There were footfalls along a creaky wooden floor, then a man came down the stairs. He was tall, taller than Hanrahan. Dressed in a gray suit, he had long gray hair, gray eyes behind little round spectacles, hands like spiders. He didn't look up or make eye contact, just walked across the room and out through the two sets of doors.

Then, from upstairs, a woman's voice: "Lisa?"

"Yes," she said, and started up the staircase. On the wall to her left were pictures of women and men, couples and families, seeming to stretch back to the dawn of photography. Previous owners of the home? Most were pretty old, and the newest looked to be from the sixties. A man in a turtleneck that awful brown-yellow color characteristic of that decade had his arm around a woman with a short beehive haircut and horn-rim spectacles.

"The Masons," came the voice from above. "They were the last people to live here."

Lisa looked up, saw a figure silhouetted against the light from the hallway up there. "Is that when this got turned into offices?"

"Oh no," said the woman. "Wasn't until oh-eight. Place was derelict until then."

"Shame. Why?" She was almost to the top of the stairs now.

"Haunted."

"You're kidding?"

"No. Mister Morris killed Missus Morris. In sixty-nine. Said the spirits made him do it. It was the eighth murder in this house. I'm Hilde. You're Doctor Jayne. Welcome. My office is down here on the right."

Lisa followed with a backwards glance at the photos on the wall below. How many of those faces were of murdered people?

Hilde sat in a plush-looking office chair, more of a captains' chair really. She sat directly under a fluorescent light as if volunteering to be looked over. She was average height, maybe five-six or five-seven. White heels, long black slacks, white silk blouse. She had on a ring of little blue flowers. Cornflowers? Her hair was black and steel though her face said thirty-five or so. She had on a silver bracelet set with all kinds of stones, semi- or non-precious. Onyx, jade, rhodochrosite, others.

There was one other seat, a loveseat with too many pillows. The room was too warm and even warmer down in that seat. Lisa looked around the office: Indian rug, pictures of stylized, idealized Native Americans on the walls, incense burner, laptop computer on a desk made of salvaged wood.

When it was obvious Lisa had looked around sufficiently, Hilde said, "Welcome. It isn't much, but this is my place. David said you needed my help."

"Yeah. Actually... I went through something pretty bad. I'm OK with it, but work needs to know I'm talking to somebody. I'm not sure this is all my speed..."

"I get it," Hilde said. "This looks like a crunchy kind of place. I've been at this a long time now and I know the look. But you don't need my help with an employee certification."

"I don't?"

"You could get that anywhere. You saw my business card. You could have tossed it in the garbage."

"David was good to me," Lisa said, leaning forward. Her palms were hot and she scrubbed them on her slacks.

"He'd never have known one way or another. He can't. You know how this works. You could have gone anywhere, but you came here. I suspect I fit your expectations."

"A little."

Hilde smiled. Her eyes agreed with her mouth, a real smile. "So, as long as you have to see someone, maybe you can decide to make the best of it."

"I've told patients the same." *Did I say something like that to Elbert?*

"Let's start with your hand."

"My hand?" Lisa's hands were pressed against the tops of her knees.

"The right one is best. Are you right-handed? Yes, I thought so." Hilde held out one of her own hands, waited for Lisa to comply.

"I don't believe in any of that stuff," Lisa said, but extended her right hand anyway.

"Me either," Hilde said. She touched, prodded, felt, then just held Lisa's hand between both of hers for a minute. It was warm, comforting. "You need that," she said.

"What?"

"Comfort. There's nothing in your life. It's empty. You live in an empty place, and it doesn't get fuller when you get there, does it?"

"You can tell that from my hand?"

"No, dear," Hilde said. "I can tell that because you're crying."

***

"And then he died. My brothers didn't help with anything. They never did, not once. Not when Daddy got sick and not as he declined and not as I had to take care of him. I think Roger sent a check once for a couple hundred bucks like that could get him off the hook. Like it could buy him out of the grief or the guilt for not grieving, all the grieving I did on all our behalf. And I can't believe I just told you all that."

"Lisa, you've done so well. You came in really guarded, I was worried for you." Hilde straightened up, moved a little closer. Their knees were almost touching. "You're so close to it now."

"Our time's up. Isn't it?"

"We don't do it that way here. By the hour like whores. Come on. Finish the job. It's what you came for."

Lisa leaned away. Her palms were sweating again. The back of her neck felt like there was a cold breeze on it. "I can't."

"I think you can. Anyone who did as you have done, who has borne up as you have... You can do anything. Come on, finish the job you came here to do."

"I have to go to the toilet," Lisa said, but she didn't stand up. "No, I don't. I do, but I want to run away. That would be a good reason to disappear for a minute and come back with the moment destroyed."

"Yes."

"So, here goes." She took a deep breath. Two. Then let it go, blurted it out like spoiled food that the stomach has rejected: "He's still with me. He's behind me, all the time. He's behind me right now. My father. I killed him, and now he's damned to be with me until I myself die. And he killed that man on the subway."

Hilde put her hands on Lisa's knees. "Good. Good, Lisa. Our dead cannot leave us, not until they've had their say. And they can never talk to us so long as we pretend they aren't there."

"I don't believe in ghosts," Lisa said.

"Neither do I, dear. You know better than to reify such concepts. You don't think Freud *really* meant we wish we had penises like our fathers."

"Of course not." She thought, and when Hilde sat back, took away her hands, Lisa wished she'd put them back. "But whatever stabbed that man on the train wasn't a metaphor. Whatever was behind me in the mirror. My eyes in the mirror. And Dana Smith, she was a real person. Elbert didn't invent her."

"Let's just stick to you for the time being, shall we? You know, I can see him back there. He's really angry."

"I thought you said he was a metaphor."

"No," said Hilde. "I said not to make your abstractions too real. You know why he's angry?"

"Yes. I murdered him. In hot blood or cold, what difference does it make? Now he's damned. Who wouldn't resent damnation?"

"He's not the one who's damned," Hilde said. "That's why he's angry, dear. Because he loves you, and he has to watch you damn yourself every day."

Thirteen

Another nightmare.

It started with Hilde touching her legs, only her legs were naked. Hilde leaned in and in, closer and closer. "You need this," she said. "You need the comfort." And Hilde tried to kiss her. Lisa tried to squirm away but she couldn't. Hildebrand's teeth smelled like rot and mustard and her face was just paint, her eyes hollow and blank. "You need this..."

Lisa pushed back. Hard. Right through the loveseat, into a different place and time.

Someplace hot, close. An office. A picture window looked out over... nothing. Just gray. The world outside did not exist. The world inside was composed solely of two men. Vietnamese men in uniforms with insignia she did not understand speaking a language she did not know.

"Containment has failed," one officer told his superior. A major and a colonel, essentially.

"The monks?"

"Dead, mostly dead. The ones that lived... Well, they aren't going to be of any further use."

"Unfortunate," said the colonel.

"If not unexpected. Did you really think those zealots could solve our problem? Maybe if the things were Buddhists. But the priests never had any luck converting them."

The colonel laughed, a sad sound. "Containment has never been an option, not a real option," he said. "At least, not for very long. Just hope they did well enough, long enough."

"A delaying tactic?"

"What kind of protégé are you? Of course a delaying tactic."

"To what end?" said the major. "Awaiting what? Lose the war and let the Americans handle it? Bring back the fucking French?"

"Calm yourself," the colonel said.

"Sorry, sir."

"It can't be contained or destroyed. It will have to be displaced. Transplanted."

"Transplanted?" the major said. "Pick it up and move it?"

"In a manner of speaking. I want you to clear out zone three. The people we talked about before, the American spook doctors, they're on their way. We expect visual confirmation in the next few hours. It is imperative they arrive untouched."

"Like the Soviets?"

The colonel steepled his fingers. "The Russians did not take our warnings seriously."

"The Americans did?"

"We'll see. Just keep any overly enthusiastic fighters away from the Minh Cong trail for the next few days."

But now there was someone at the door, and Lisa needed to wake up. They were banging, pounding, hammering...

***

She opened the door, neglecting the chain and the security bar. Her eyes were full of sleep-sand. Outside, a giant waited.

Am I still dreaming?

"Ms. Jayne? Doctor, I mean..."

"Hanrahan?"

"Yeah."

As her vision cleared she saw his face in the sketchy light of the hallway. "What are you doing here? I mean, come in. And then tell me what you're doing here. How did you find me?" She made room in the doorway, and only then realized she only had on jockey shorts and a sports bra.

"What kind of private detective couldn't track down one of his clients?" Hanrahan said. He came in, keeping his eyes firmly on the floor. There were tall stools in the kitchen and he took one, still looking away.

"Excuse me a second," Lisa said, and made for the bedroom, sure he would be looking at her behind. Her fault, really. She threw on sweats from the "clean" pile on the floor by the bed. Right side was clean, left side dirty. The clean side was getting low. *Laundry: Sisyphus' rock.*

In the kitchen, Hanrahan waited with the size of a boulder, if not the patience. "You're in danger," he said.

"I thought the palm-reader would say that. She said I was safe. Guess someone had to say it."

"What?"

"That's my question," Lisa said. "You want some coffee? I'm going to make some coffee."

"I'd appreciate it. Thanks, ma'am. Uh, danger. "Alice" turned up some hits. She's here. In New York City. At least she was in eighty-nine, and again in ninety-seven, and once more in oh-one."

"It's a big city, Hanrahan. You sure you didn't just want to see me in my underwear?" Lisa filled the coffee pot with water, started to pour the water into the machine.

He blushed. Looked away. "I couldn't have known..."

"Shit. I'm sorry. Of course you couldn't. I'm just..." She set the pot on the counter, empty.

"I know. Well, I know some. I'm not a woman, so I can't know everything, but some. I'm sorry. I guess I did have more than work on my mind. An excuse, you know? But a real one. Listen. She isn't just in the city. She's been to your hospital."

"What?"

"She was there in oh-eight. Her last records in the city. Arrested in Central Park over a very bloody murder. Guess where she was transported?"

"Shit. What happened to her after that?"

"Don't know," Hanrahan said. "No more hits on her after that. I've got the whole network lit up, you better believe that, though. All my friends in the industry, on the force. All their computers. We'll find her. If she's alive."

Lisa finished setting up the coffee pot, pushed the "start" button and the "strong" button. Two tiny ovoids, almost too small for her fingers. She watched the brew drip into the pot, sizzling and gurgling as it went.

"Did you get anything else, Mr. Hanrahan?"

"Pete."

"Who's Pete?"

"I am. I'm Pete. Peter J. Hanrahan. I guess you should call me Pete, on account of I've seen you almost naked."

Lisa laughed, a startled sound that surprised her. "You want some coffee, Pete?"

"Yeah," he said. "I hope it's no trouble. Lots of Daniels', like I said. A first name would really help. Most of them came home, not all of them did. I've got two killed in action. A Danny Daniels and a Mark F. Daniels. Danny seems to have been a black guy. You source give you demographics?"

"He was white. I'm almost certain he was white."

"That must make it Mark. Killed, September nineteen sixty-eight. No details on the death. Nothing in the news, no medical or pathology that I could find. Buried with honors at Arlington."

Lisa pulled the coffee pot out. It was half full and little drips spat their way through the cut-off valve to land on the hot-plate where they cooked and stank. She poured two mugs, grayish stonewear from her mother's house. "Thanks, Pete. Anything more you think you can do?"

"About Daniels? I can look for known associates, make a few calls. Get a story, maybe. About Wilcox? If she was here, we can find her. Someone knows about her. Thanks for the coffee."

She sipped at her own. It was bitter, dark tasting. The coffee was too old, stale. "I'll ask some questions too."

***

Pete was gone. It was just Lisa and her empty place. She sat by the counter with a cup of coffee forgotten in her hand. The other hand was in her pocket.

I shouldn't. I can get in so much trouble...

There's only one way to know, though.

But I shouldn't.

Her hand came out of the pocket holding a little twist of plastic wrap. In the center of the plastic was one white tablet. An antipsychotic.

I must be crazy.

That's the point.

She unwrapped the pill and looked at it. Such a small thing to have such large ramifications.

She took it. Put it in her mouth, washed it down with bitter coffee. Grimaced from the heat and the taste. The pill tasted like nothing at all, but the coffee was like chewing aspirin.

What happens now?

A pointless exercise, probably. Antipsychotics took weeks to build up in the blood. At least that long to have a noticeable effect beyond sedation.

She waited. Drank coffee. Soon she fell asleep.

Fourteen

Morning. The light battered through dirty glass, the tiny window her kitchen had to satisfy legal requirements. Lisa had a headache and her mouth felt like it had spent the night stuffed with dry newspapers and silica gel.

Is this what it's like for the patients? How can they stand it?

The coffee pot had turned itself off long ago. The coffee in the carafe was still warmish, warm as fresh blood. She poured a mug, gulped it, poured another. Her bladder asked for her attention.

Well, only one thing for it.

She got up, leaving the coffee behind, and marched to the toilet. When her business was done, she turned to face the mirror. Flipped the switch to turn on the lights.

Behind her, nothing. Just the empty room.

In a horror movie, she could open the bathroom cabinet and when the door swung closed again, bringing back the reflection, something would be behind her. But she didn't have a medicine cabinet. The mirror was fixed, unmoving. She looked away, looked back. Still nothing.

Lisa sighed in relief. Turned on the shower.

The water was too hot and she wanted it that way. Her skin felt dull, lifeless, and the heat brought her closer to aliveness. Steam filled up the room, filled up her sight. Later, when the water was just starting to run a little cold because the whole building was taking showers, she reached out for her towel and shut off the water. The towel was starting to smell of mildew: time to wash it.

But she patted dry, stepped out onto her fluffy pink rug. Her eyes dragged across the mirror.

Nothing but steam.

She went close, wiped away a patch of condensation. Made watery eye-contact with her reflection. Laughed at herself, went to the bedroom to dress. Back to the kitchen to see if there was anything decent to eat. In the hallway, she thought about what Hilde had said. Sweet, goofy, deranged Hilde. *You go home to an empty place and you don't fill it up.* Something like that. Maybe it was time to make some changes, to finish kicking Charlie out all the way. Put some real food in the fridge, do some cleaning, maybe paint a little.

In the kitchen, she stopped in her tracks. "Who's here?" Her coffee mug was just gray shards on the kitchen floor. Spilled coffee was everywhere, all over the counter, the floor.

"Who's here, goddamn it?"

Nobody. Nothing. The front door was locked. She'd locked it behind Pete and nobody had come through. The apartment only had the one stupid window. She was alone in here.

So what had knocked over the coffee cup? Earthquake?

She got a towel out of the hall closet, the last clean one. Put it back, got the dirty one off the bathroom floor. Threw it over the mess on the kitchen floor, remembering the cut she'd gotten there just the other night. Looked at the counter, really looked at it.

The coffee spill wasn't random. The splashes and eddies spelled a word.

LISA

She backed away, hands at her throat, creeping towards her mouth.

"Go away. Leave me alone. You're dead. Go lay in your grave."

Something touched her, the back of her neck. Light, fluttering. She started screaming.

***

The telephone was ringing.

Lisa was pressed up against the kitchen cabinet, one arm around her legs, one fist stuffed in her mouth. She didn't know how long she had screamed or when she had stopped.

She stood up, brushed herself down like her panic was dust, answered the phone. "Hello?" Her voice shook.

"Lisa? It's Hilde."

"Hilde?"

"You remember."

"Yes. But why are you calling? Now?"

"You don't sound well," Hilde said. "You should come in and see me again. Tonight."

"All right. I have to go to work."

"Of course you do, dear. And you should get out of that place for a little while. Come and see me. Don't go home tonight."

"Yeah," Lisa said. "How did you know you should call?"

"I don't know," Hilde said. "I had a dream you were screaming, and I thought I should call you. Check in on you."

"I'm glad you called," Lisa said. "I'll tell you about it tonight."

She hung up the phone. In her bedroom, she packed a bag. Some underwear, shirts, pants. Toothbrush. *I'm not coming back here.*

But it's not the apartment.

That was a thought she didn't want to examine to closely.

***

"Lisa, can I talk to you?"

She stopped in the doorway, the big conference table a pace away. "Ellen?"

"We were short a pill yesterday. We count twice a shift. Can't throw anything away without a signature and countersignature. Nothing on the floor."

"I'm sorry."

"Seems like you're into some trouble right now, Lisa. I just wanted to say, nothing in that medicine closet can help you." Ellen wore blue scrubs today. They made her look severe and too old for the work she was doing. The unit was a physical place sometimes.

"I didn't take your pill."

"I know you didn't, dear. We all come to a point though. When we wonder if there's some way out, a cheat, a fix. I don't know if there is. If so, it isn't in there."

"Thanks for the pep talk."

Ellen sighed, turned away, started pulling charts. Lisa grabbed Elbert's chart and retreated, too. Back to her office for her recorder, careful to leave the lights off and look only at the floor. Then to the interview room. She was early, but didn't want to deal with anybody. Least of all The Killjoy.

Maybe he wouldn't come today. Maybe he'd stay up in his office where he belonged. Maybe if he came he wouldn't want her. Wouldn't look in the interview room.

Lisa changed seats, took one too close to the door to be seen through the narrow window.

When Elbert knocked an hour later, she jumped like his gentle rapping was gunshots. Gasped. "Oh, god, Elbert. You frightened me."

He came in. "I'm sorry, Doctor Lisa. I'm afraid I'm not done yet."

"What?"

He took his regular place like everything was ordinary. "I have to keep telling you the story. You have to keep trying to understand it. Nothing is OK. Are you ready?"

The hair on Lisa's arms was erect, like monkey fur. Patients said weird shit all the time and this should be no different, so she grabbed the recorder, turned it on, shoved it in front of Elbert like her troubles were his fault. "Tell it, then," she said.

He did.

***

"It's hairy," Dennis said.

Elbert grimaced. "You eat so much spook-smoke I don't know what to make of you, man. What's hairy?"

"My ass," Dennis said. He chuckled at his own joke, then gestured with his rifle. "Like the lieutenant said. This place is bugged to hell and gone with wires and Claymores and shit. This side is all done in ordnance. That side is all out of their fucking asymmetric warfare manuals from fourteen-hundred."

"Their what?"

Floyd's head was straighter, so he picked up the narrative. "We ain't the first foreign army they bogged down out here, champ. They been doing people like this for centuries. Even got an ancient manual on guerilla warfare. Half the little traps they set, they come out this old folk-hero book."

"The ankle-grabbing spike trap, the shit-smeared spears down in holes, all that stuff?"

"Yeah," said Dennis. "And all that stuff is other side of these wires and shit. Glad we got a good night's sleep. Hate to come at this without a clear head." He coughed up bluish smoke, giggled, set down his gear. "Gonna be a minute working up a plan."

Wilcox got up by Elbert. He was taller than her but still felt little, like a kid next to a grown up. "See, we could cut all the trip wires, uncover all the pits and so on. But then we deny our boys a tactical advantage when the offensive rolls through here. We want to leave all this work intact. But going over, around or through it each carry their own risks. Maybe we have to de-activate a couple things and--"

"Got it," Dennis said. "Follow me."

"Or just follow him," Dana said.

"Put your feet right where I do. And watch out for that fucker right there." He pointed into the woods, into a dark patch. Some kind of thicket.

Elbert looked, just saw prickly bushes. He wondered if they had blackberries in Vietnam. Why wouldn't they? "What's in the bushes?" he said. "Mine? We're not going anywhere near there, are we?"

"Dead guy," Dennis said. He stepped over a wire. It caught on his boot so that he had to stop, wait on one foot while Floyd pulled the wire ever so fractionally, let it slide down the outer heel and free.

Elbert wondered if that were a threat or if he'd just misheard.

"How bad?" said Wilcox.

"Bad."

Elbert peered into that dark patch some more. "I don't see no flies or nothing. Birds, carrion eaters. Why be scared of a body?"

"Told you," Dennis said. "It ain't the bodies. Lots of dead out here and they're scared and pissed off. That one's watching you."

"Me?" Elbert froze in place. Behind him, Dana did the same, one hand on his shoulder for balance. He didn't believe it, not with the front of his brain where the human lived. *Ghosts? Don't be stupid.* But he was still unsettled, and that meant he was lying to himself about what he believed. "Why me?" he said, and the lie was revealed completely.

"Fuck should I know?" said Dennis. Then he giggled. Moaned, "It's coming closer."

"Don't fuck around with me, man," said Elbert.

Dennis took a mighty drag off his toke and held it. Ten seconds, twenty. He started to sputter, little wisps of smoke escaping his mouth and nose. Then he blew it out, all at once, about three feet ahead of Elbert.

The smoke swirled around and dissipated. But for a second, half a second, a quarter, Elbert saw it.

The shape of a person.

It had mad, crazy eyes in a sad face, a raceless face. Skinny, small, hands like claws.

He started to panic. Dana had a hold of him, stilled him with her touch. "If you run you'll blow us all to hell. Close your eyes. Close them. And your nose. I'll plug your ears. Can't give it a way in."

"A way--"

"Just do it. And squeeze your cheeks tight. Not your face. Yes, like that."

"I can't breathe."

"Take one deep breath. Quick. And hold it."

He did.

He stood like a statue, not even breathing, clenching his ass shut. Seeing nothing and hearing only the roar of his own blood in his ears. No sense of presence, nothing touching him but Dana, but fear coursed through his veins like the blood in his ears. He shivered.

It got harder and harder not to breathe. *I'm going to suffocate before any spooks get me.* But he held it, held it. It became a force, his breath, trying to push up out of his lungs. And he could feel the thing, the ghost, the spirit. He could feel it crawling over him, touching his face with fingers made of cold. It touched his hands. His mouth. He pinched his mouth shut tighter, moaned in his throat against the dread, against the pain of held breath.

It touched his hips, his back. His crotch. Elbert pissed in his pants but still didn't move.

Dennis did the trick again with the pot smoke. Elbert smelled it all over him, a skunk's used jock strap. Then Dennis slapped him on the shoulder. Elbert hoped that meant all-clear because he couldn't hold it in any longer. He blew out his breath, sucked in a fresh one, gasped for air. "Gone?" he panted, opening his eyes. Dana let go of his ears.

"No," said Dennis. "Went back to its spot, though. Right over there. Watching."

"Bullshit," said Elbert. But also, "Hurry up, man. Let's get out of this minefield. If they catch us here they'll tear us apart. We ain't got noplace to run."

Wilcox said, "The Vietnamese you can run from. The unquiet dead, though, are everywhere. MacAvoy, you got to get right with what you believe and what you don't. You're getting their attention with your ambivalence. And that attention you don't want."

"Yes, Ma'am," he said. "I'll get on that just as soon as I clean the shit out my drawers. Dana, what the hell happened to not literal ghosts, just impressions on the environment?"

"You can bet if I get back in one piece I'm coming back here with instruments. A monograph, maybe a Pulitzer prize."

"God," Elbert said, "I wish you people would learn to speak English."

Dennis said, "What she means to say is, there wasn't never any proof of spirits or ghosts what look like the dead people what left them behind, but now she's done seen it, she done believes it."

And Elbert tried to tell himself the could touch had been no more than suggestibility and imagination, memory of the stories his folk told around the stove at night, but he couldn't quite make himself believe that.

***

"You aren't going to like this next part," Elbert said.

"I haven't liked much of this at all, to be honest," Lisa said. "It's fascinating as stories go, and if it were a novel

I'd read it twice. But, Elbert, there's a lot of pain in this story. You really can't trust anyone, can you?"

"You go on and take that advice to heart," Elbert said. "Don't trust anyone, Doctor Lisa. But that's not why you aren't going to like it."

"Why, then?"

"Because of the cat."

"What cat?"

"You'll see." And he got back into it.

***

"It feels weird to be out of the jungle," Dana said. "I was getting used to not being able to see more than a few dozen yards and picking bugs out of my ears."

Wilcox had that giant gun up on one shoulder and her head on a swivel. Increased visibility should have made everyone feel more secure: no places for snipers to hide or soldiers to set up ambushes. Elbert watched Wilcox, though, and Osho and Floyd, and just felt what they felt: exposed. But he'd felt that way since the ghost in the thicket. He'd watched everywhere at once knowing there would be nothing to see, just a cold touch. And then... what?

"My sister in law had a cat," he said. "The cat had kittens. She gave them all away, all but one. That one she kept inside. It wasn't never allowed out and wasn't never all too interested in trying to get there. It would come up on your lap and love on you, sure thing. Wrap round your ankles like cats do. But it didn't never go near the doors.

"And one day it pissed on her bed, and she said that's it, you'se an out-of-doors-cat from now on. And she grabbed it and tossed it clean out the front door.

"Now that cat was scared shitless, that's a fact. She stood by that door and cried for a week. Curled up close as she could to the doorstep and watched out, scared of every little thing."

"This story got a point?" said Floyd. Dennis giggled like that was a great joke, smoke snorting out his nose.

"Just that I know how that cat feels," Elbert said.

"What happened to it?" said Dana. "The cat, what happened to it?"

"Fuck difference does it make?" said Floyd.

Dana said, "I want to know. Elbert, what happened to the cat?"

"Fox got it. Coyote, maybe, I don't know. They just found little bits of her around the yard."

Floyd swore, snatched out a knife even though he really needed both hands for the big machine gun. Elbert felt like Floyd might come at him even though the guy was facing away.

"You're just as scared as me, aren't you?" Elbert said. "I pissed my pants yesterday but I got more balls than you. Because I know I'm scared. I ain't scared of being scared. You, you're making like you ain't scared at all, stroking that knife all the time like a kid with her favorite doll."

Floyd did turn around then, and there was madness in his eyes. He opened his mouth to say something, but Wilcox beat him to it.

"Fox isn't getting us," she said. "But look lively. See those men just below that ridgeline?"

She pointed, and ten sets of eyes focused on the hill in question. It was a dusty, sere kind of brown, darker than bleached-out bone but not by much. Elbert thought, *As much rain as I've seen, why isn't that sucker green?* All the grass was dead. And there, moving just along the horizon, were the tops of two heads.

"On the other side?" Elbert said.

"Looks like," said Wilcox. "Floyd, go find out who they are. Make sure you see them before they see you."

Floyd went, glaring at Elbert until he tripped over a root and decided he'd do better with eyes front. Dennis giggled, drew heavily from his joint, and limbered up his weapon. He saw Elbert watching. "You got to be prepared," he said. "Wasn't you all gung-ho last night?"

He had a point. Elbert checked his settings again, wiped dew off his scope, took a stance. He scanned that horizon with the scope, zeroing in on one of the heads. It moved, left, down, back up into view, right again. *What is he doing over there?* The hat appeared to be a beret. Some weird insignia on the front. The Vietnamese did not, in Elbert's experience, wear berets. "Not theirs," he said.

Wilcox grunted and he kept watching. That weird insignia flashed through his scope again as the man turned. "Got it," he said. "That's British special forces. I'd bet my combat pay on it. My nephew is into badges and ranks and so on, had him a book on it. Color photos and everything. When I got drafted—"

"Why the hell would they be out here?" Wilcox said. "Smith, you know anything about this?"

"Out of my purview," said Dana. "I have nothing."

There was a little excitement over there. The two visible heads were joined by two more, at a run. No gunshots, though. And then five men came over the ridge: four burly-looking British soldiers and Floyd, grinning and chewing a bit of dried-out grass.

The two parties approached one another. "Wilcox," said Wilcox. "Colonel. On detachment. What are you doing here?"

"Waiting for you," said one of the men, a square-jawed fellow with golden hair and beautiful teeth. "Her Majesty the Queen got wind of something up between you and the Communists. Our French allies were quite excited that you not pursue what they are offering you."

"How do you know what they are offering?" Wilcox said.

"Little birds. Some Soviet ones, some French ones. Maybe even a highly placed American or two. In any event, they were quite excited and, if they're not spouting complete rubbish – always a consideration with the French – then it seems they have a certain amount of cause."

"Get out of the way," Wilcox said. "I'll forget you were ever here."

"Well, that much is true," the fellow said. "Officially, we're well off the record, as it were. I never was here. As to getting out of the way, well, Her Majesty has requested the honor of your company, Ma'am."

Several people started to talk at once. Dana said, "A euphemism, no doubt, for a room with no doors or windows."

Floyd said, "Like to see you make that stick. We've been in the field long enough to know how to make problems like you go away." Elbert imagined that was true, only Floyd was looking at him when he said it.

Elbert said, "Always wanted to meet me a queen."

The British officer just smiled, and his mates stood quietly, fingers near the triggers of their rifles. Then Wilcox made eye contact with the blond guy. And held it.

His smile faded, slow, like the sun going away behind a slow-moving cloud. Then his face started to sag. Absent any motivating energy, his jaw slacked open. His gun came down from ready, hung loosely in his right hand, dropped to the dirt.

The three other Brits looked nervous of a sudden. "You well, Dover?" one said. "Dover? What's happened?"

Another: "I think he's had a hemorrhage. Remember Wallace? Too long in the lorry?"

They started to fuss over him, weapons forgotten, Americans forgotten. Wilcox strode passed. "Fall in," she said. Floyd and Dennis formed up on her, Elbert and Dana hurrying to catch up. Osho strolled along backwards, watching the show come to an end.

"Stop them," said one of the soldiers, and they remembered their job. Rifles came up to ready again.

"Hold," said the blond man, reanimated – the sun had emerged from the cloud once more. "Let them go."

"But Captain, our orders..."

"New orders," said Dover. "Much more important orders. Let's go."

"Has he gone barmy?" one of the soldiers complained.

"Perhaps," said another. "But do you plan on shooting a NATO ally in the back without some higher-up to cite?"

Their argument dwindled. Elbert was keen to make a lot more distance between him and them. "We can't move any quicker, can we?" he said.

"Told you you'd toughen up," said Wilcox.

***

"How did you know about the cat, Elbert?" Lisa said. Her frown wasn't one of puzzlement but of anger.

"I have the right to see my files."

"You most decidedly do not have the right to see your narrative notes."

"Doctor's discretion," Elbert said, leaning back in his chair.

"I'm your doctor."

"No, Doctor Killroy is. He took you off my case two nights ago, as primary. Prescribed a fistful of medications. Don't worry, I haven't taken any of them yet and I'm not going to. And it will take a week to get an order for emergency medications. I've been down this path before, I guess."

Lisa just sat in stunned silence for a minute. Eventually, she said, "So you know everything."

"Yes. First time anyone wrote themselves into my narratives. I must say I'm a little bit flattered. Thing is, this is not folie a deux, as you wrote. That's when two people have the same crazy, right? Only it's no crazy. Been trying to tell you. Wherever the stone is, time goes a little screwy..."

"Elbert."

"Yes ma'am."

"Shut your damned mouth for a minute."

"Yes ma'am." He smiled, showing gaps in his teeth.

"I think we're done here for the day. I have to go straighten a few things out."

"OK. But time is almost up. This will all be over real soon, Doctor Lisa." He was halfway out the door when he turned back, and said, "You ask him. Ask him about her. He won't want to tell you but you ask him anyway."

"You should leave."

He did.

Lisa looked at her watch. It was almost too small for her to see the time, barely more than a bangle. But the time was after office hours. Killjoy would be long gone, which was good, but records would be closed, too. Lisa took her gear out to her office, careful not to linger, and came straight back to the nursing station. Ellen was still there, putting pills into pill cups.

"Ellen. You remember a female patient, name of Wilcox? She was here about twelve years ago."

"Lots of women here twelve years ago," Ellen said, keeping her eyes down on her work.

"She'd have been pretty memorable. Five-eight or so. I guess ordinary face and hair and so on, but really built. Like one of the girls on American Gladiators, built up like Schwarzenegger."

"I've always been up here on the troubled unit. All males up here."

"Shit," Lisa said. "Well, thanks anyway."

"But I remember her," Ellen went on. "Because we got called down there twice a week to help control her. Get her into seclusion and restraints. She was a bully, a psychopath. Strong as any two of the guys up here. That's how Frank got hurt, got his medical retirement. She busted his chest with her fist."

"Frank..."

"Before your time, I suppose," Ellen said.

"OK. That sounds like her, though. A hundred percent mean from what Elbert says. So what happened to her?"

"Happened? What happened to her?"

"Yeah," Lisa said. "Where did she go after she discharged?"

"Cemetery," Ellen said. "She died in restraints in two thousand four. There was a whole investigation. A negligence thing. She didn't have no family or anything so nobody sued. Coroner put it down to misadventure. Nothing came of it. Except the usual orders to reduce reliance on seclusion and restraint. Her type, though, isn't nothing we can do but tie them down and shoot them up."

"She died. You're sure."

Ellen finally looked up, made eye contact. "No, Lisa. I'm not sure. Like I said, it was a dozen years ago and I don't remember the names. You know how many people come through here, and most of the hopeless cases. You forget. But I remember her. She'd look right through you..." Ellen shuddered, looked away, put her eyes back on her work. "Excuse me. I have to get back to work now."

Lisa thought she should say something. Thank you, sorry for the bad memories, something like that. There didn't seem to be a way to say it that wasn't weird, so she let it go. She had a sweater on a peg by the door. She grabbed it, threw her purse over one shoulder, and left.

Fifteen

"I told you this place was haunted," Hilde said. She was in her captains' chair, legs folded under her body. She looked gray and ephemeral. "That wasn't always true, though. I mean, we always believed it, but the evidence was pretty slim. Lately, though... Lately, when I'm here late at night, I can hear voices. In the walls, in the plumbing. Not clearly enough to understand their words, but they are voices. And I get cold chills in the back room. The file room.

"That was where he did it. Where the last tenant did the last murder."

"Why are you telling me this?" Lisa adjusted her own body to match Hilde's position, drawing her legs underneath herself. She was cold and all her hairs were dancing like there was a loose live wire in the room.

"None of it was always true," Hilde said. "I'd do the palmistry thing, but really I was watching your reactions and feeling where you had calluses and how long you'd been without your wedding band. That kind of thing. Read your auras, but really using what I already knew to try on some guesses and see how they fit."

"But that's started to change. Like the voices in the walls."

"Yes," Hilde said. "And that frightens me. Because if some of it is true, all of it might be true."

"All of it?"

"Yes. God and angels and demons and devils. And the Devil. Hell. Judgment."

Lisa shuddered, pulled her sweater tight. "I don't want it to be true. But I don't want to be crazy, either."

"Then say it was all a coincidence," Hilde said. "The phone call, my dream, your dream about Elbert's cat. None of it is real: just coincidences, chances, things mis-remembered. Altered perceptions and fatigue."

"I can't."

"Neither can I," Hilde said.

"But they can't hurt us. The spirits, ghosts, whatever. They can't hurt us, can they?"

"No," said Hilde. "They're just echoes, reverberations through time and space. Not things or entities, not as you'd understand the terms."

Lisa nodded. "My father's ghost came to me. He told me Wilcox' name. And he wrote my name in a coffee spill on the counter. Threw a mug to the floor."

"Ghosts can't do that," Hilde said. "They aren't really real."

"Like the voices in your wall, like the auras you're seeing now, I think they're getting realer by the minute."

"How?"

"Maybe Elbert is totally ill. And maybe he also knows something about something. I don't even want to think he might be right about anything but a scientist has to consider all the possibilities. So there's some object, I forget what he called it, that he says screws up time around itself. Maybe that's found its way into the neighborhood somehow."

Hilde thought. "I think you should be careful. I don't think it's your father disturbing your apartment."

"What do you think it is?"

"I think it might be you."

"I don't think so," Lisa said.

"Not consciously. Subconsciously exercising a power you've never had. Through a troubled subconscious. That's why the word in the spilled coffee. "Lisa." That's you, telling you who did it. Signing your name."

"Do that thing again," Lisa said, leaning forward. "That thing where you make me feel better. Provide comfort."

"We both know I can't do that now," Ellen said. "You have to go. I see you getting up to leave. Just... be careful. Please?"

Lisa nodded. She stayed where she was a minute more, then did as Ellen had seen.

***

Lisa walked the dark streets under sickly orange lights that made all colors black. She didn't avoid reflective surfaces. Here a store window, here a passing limousine. She looked and saw.

He was there, behind her.

Maybe he doesn't want to be gotten rid of.

Psychopathology class. Oh, fifteen years ago. Dr. Chaires in her horn-rim glasses like it was nineteen sixty-eight. A hairstyle that was more modern, shoes that spoke of a life walking hallways.

"Where do they go?" Lisa had asked. "The personalities in multiple personality disorder. Where do they go when the patient is cured?"

"Go?" Chaires had said. Claire was her name, Claire Chaires. "There's a lot of controversy over whether that's even a real diagnosis or if the patients are play-acting roles assigned them by their therapists. Iatrogenic illnesses. Is dissociation a real thing? If so, does it go as far as the creation of a real and fully discrete personality?"

Lisa stepped down a curb, looked both ways. Ahead and a little on the left was a motel sign. VACANCY in blue neon in the window. On a letter board outside: WEEKLY RATES ENQUIRE WITHIN.

Not quite correct, she thought, and that stirred up more of the memory of that long-ago lesson. "It's not quite correct to say those personalities are annihilated upon cure, even for those who fully believe in the phenomenon of multiple personalities. More correct to say that they are reabsorbed back into the whole person. Ideally, therapy reintegrates the split-off parts of the person."

"What if they don't want to be reintegrated?" Lisa said. Both out loud, here and now on the street, and in her memory.

"Well then we have a rough ride on our hands. But ultimately it doesn't really matter if they're real or not real. The cure is the same. Either the spilt-off personality fragments are reintegrated or the patient believes them to be and in either case we have the same result."

"Mental health?" Lisa had asked.

"Haven't you been listening?" Claire had said.

Lisa was at the motel now, stepping in the door. The rest of the thought would have to wait because there was a small man in a neat blue suit behind a piece of clear plastic. She imagined it might be bulletproof. She slipped an ID and a credit card through the little steel tunnel under the window.

"How many hours?" the clerk said, avoiding eye contact.

"Hours? I thought you had a weekly rate."

"The girls don't usually stay for a week."

"The girls? Oh, maybe I've come to the wrong place."

The clerk looked at her for the first time, really looked. Squinted, even. She had a gym bag, a purse, a sweater. Nothing to really distinguish her from any of the working girls just booking in. "So you're not a..."

"No," she said. "I'm a psychiatrist. I just need a place for the night. A clean place. With clean sheets."

He frowned. "Can you wait ten minutes? I'll have Hector make up twenty-two for you."

There was a couch, ratty and rough in beige and brown and what might once have been white. She sat on the arm, gingerly, and waited.

The clerk came back a few minutes later, through the front door. There was a big man with him, vaguely Latino, with a white T-shirt, a red and white bandana, jeans, leather vest. "That's Hector. He'll show you your room."

She looked up at Hector. Hector didn't look back, just gestured with one arm that she should go ahead of him. Rough place if he was afraid of having little old her behind him. But she obliged, watched the numbers on the doors. At Twenty-Two, Hector opened the door with a steel key on an orange plastic tag. Out here, it was the only thing with color, catching the orange street lamps and reflecting back the light.

Lisa went in, felt around a light switch. Behind her, the big man held out the room key in a surprisingly dainty hand. She took it and he closed the door having never said a word.

There was no coverlet on the bed, just a blanket and crisp white sheets. The blanket looked old but smelled all right. The carpet had oil stains, ground in dirt. An air conditioner sat dormant under the window with a street-level view of a less than wonderful neighborhood. Outside, she saw them for the first time: women. Here and there, scattered, alone or in pairs. They were dressed like eleven-year-olds' fantasies of adult sexuality. Men cruised around in cars with the headlights off, stopping, talking, sometimes picking up one of the women. Sometimes parking. A few of them came towards the motel.

Walking in, she'd been so in her own head that she'd missed all of them. Oblivious.

Is that how it is? Is there shit going on around us all the time to which we're oblivious until someone points it out?

She looked at the window now. Not through it but at the glass itself, the reflection it offered of the room behind her. He was there, standing partially in the double bed like it didn't exist. Because he didn't. He was clearer now, clearer all the time. Tall, thin, gaunt even. In his dress blues and a long trench coat – was that part of the uniform? The bus-driver cap, what they called the big round hat that went with dress blues.

His eyes were hungry. He looked at her back, not at her eyes in the mirror. Maybe ghosts couldn't see reflections.

She turned around and he wasn't there. She looked back in the glass and there he was, standing back, keeping his distance.

"You're scaring the shit out of me, Daddy," she said. "You don't have to stay stuck to me, you know. You can go on to whatever awaits."

He moved then, for the first time. He pointed to the window. She looked again, through the glass now rather than at it. Outside, there was darkness. And a few people out there doing what they could to get by, others exploiting them.

"I don't understand."

When she refocused on the reflection, he was gone. And that scared her more than anything.

***

The bed was damp.

The damp came from humidity in the room and gradually settled over Lisa, over the sheet, the blanket she'd kicked down to her feet. Her skin, arms and hands by her sides on top of the sheet.

The air.

It was cold and clammy but if she pulled the blanket up it would just be hot and clammy. And besides, there was no way in the world she was sleeping.

Her father was in the room with her, somewhere. Her dead father, who she had killed. She'd given him the means of suicide, of expressing his ultimate despair. She'd made it happen. And he was stalking her.

If she did sleep, she couldn't say she'd have none of Elbert's dreams – of cats trapped in houses, of Vietnamese officers discussing strategy.

Lisa took a deep breath, tried to relax.

Insanity is a defense. Who'd said that? *Insanity is the only rational manner of coping with the terrors of war.* Was that Laing? Close enough. *Sometimes you just have to go crazy.*

Her heart pounded. Blood buzzed in her ears. She couldn't slow her breathing. She just lay there, waiting for something to happen. For something to touch her, maybe, like in the apartment. For something to stab her, like the man on the train. *Does he hate me?*

Someone pounded on the door.

She jumped, part of her torso actually rising up off the bed. She'd drawn the curtains and she could see someone out there, a shadow thrown against the holed, worn curtain backing by the street lights.

Lisa sat up, edged back against the wall – there was no headboard, not in a place like this. Whoever was out there pounded on the door again. "Stacy? Open up, you bitch, I know you're in there. If you've OD'ed again I'm going to kill you."

Lisa put her hands over her ears, shut her eyes. *Look what you've done to me, Daddy. Look where I've come to run from you.*

Outside, a bigger shadow crossed the window. "You be quiet out here now, you hear?" a voice said. Hispanic, maybe, or not. Weird vowels, clipped endings. Sinister. "Stacy, she isn't here. This here's a respectable customer. You fuck off now, hear me? Go away."

"I ain't going without Stacy." But the voice was already farther away.

"She in that alley over there. Big black car." Fading. "You'll get your money."

Lisa gave up on sleeping. Packed her things in the gym bag, put on her clothes and shoes. It was three in the morning and she didn't at all want to go out there with the street-walkers and the pimps and the Johns. But she had a feeling a taxi wouldn't come near this place.

So she went out, dressed in jeans and a sweater and no make-up or jewelry. A working girl going off-shift. Nobody bothered her, she bothered nobody.

The milling and flesh-peddling went on for a range of about two blocks around the hotel. Soon that noise was behind her, and Lisa quickened her steps. There would be a bus station or a taxi rank somewhere near. There always was.

If I had a phone, I could call Hanrahan. But that was an empty thought, idle. She just wanted his size, to shelter in his gravity and feel safe. And no guarantee he'd come out to find her.

Lisa was alone now, walking down a street with boxy apartments on her side, to the right, and empty lots across a two-lane road to her left. Bits of masonry, girders, plumbing stood up from the ground in the dark like grave markers. Like the bones of the world.

Ahead of her, someone moved. Ran across the street, disappeared into the black rectangles of one of those lots.

Lisa stopped. Stood still in the dark between street lamps.

It can't have been. He's locked up right now.

But he was voluntary. That means he could maybe get out if he wanted to.

He's nearly eighty, she thought at last. Even if Elbert had talked his way off the unit, even if she chanced across him in this huge city, there was no way a man his age in his condition was sprinting across the road in the middle of the night.

Pure imagination.

She pushed on, finding what she wanted two blocks farther down. A taxi depot sat open to the night, refreshingly white light spilling out of its bays into the road. She walked up the path, through the cloudy glass door, into the office.

"You guys taking any fares?" she said.

A mature-looking woman sat behind a desk, feet up on the flat surface, a hero sandwich halfway to her mouth. "Sorry, honey," she said. "We ain't allowed to take walk-ins."

"I understand," Lisa said. "But maybe someone could meet me right there. On that corner."

The lady smiled, put her feet down, and picked up a cell phone from the table. "Gimme five minutes," she said. "Where you going?"

Lisa gave her the address of the hospital.

Sixteen

Lisa sat in a squarish chair made of wood and orange fabric. She thought it was the worst fabric in the world, with a color guaranteed to turn the stomach and a texture that whispered to the skin of fleas and nettles. No way to get comfortable. Nevertheless, she was dead asleep when the hallways lights came on.

It was the sound of clogs on tile that woke her up. She felt bleary and recognized that as a welcome change from terrified. Down the hall, heels clocking along, was Steph Granger.

"Morning, Steph," Lisa said, rubbing at her eyes. If she'd been smart, she'd have taken a minute to neaten up in the toilet.

"Hi. Is that..."

"It's Lisa. Lisa Jayne. Team Six."

"Well good morning, Lisa." Steph came ever closer, keys jangling against her purse in one hand, coffee in a cardboard cup in the other.

"Can I hold something for you?"

"I got it," Steph said, and managed to open the door while retaining a grip on all her things. "Come in if you want. I'll need a minute to turn all the machines on."

"Thanks."

Steph had the same chairs in her office, against the back wall. Behind her desk was a proper office chair, black leather, functional. Lisa couldn't see from this side of the desk but she imagined it would have wheels, and there would be a plastic cover on the carpet so the chair could roll.

Steph sat, pushed a button on the side of her computer screen. "Early," she said.

"I couldn't sleep," Lisa said.

"Looked like you were doing fine in the hallway."

Lisa grunted. "Maybe that's what I should do."

"What brings you up here before civilization has gotten started, hon?"

Lisa sat, dragged the chair up close to Steph's desk. "I need to see the files on Alice Wilcox."

"I can't show you those," Steph said, looking away.

At least she didn't deny knowledge, Lisa thought. "It's relevant to an ongoing case, Steph. And I already know she's dead. Dead patients don't have any rights. Plus I know she had no family, so even if she had some rights, which dead people don't, there's nobody to ask any questions."

"That's not why I can't show you that," Steph said, turning her back to fuss with a printer set against the far wall.

"Then why?" Lisa thought for just a second, looked at the shape of Steph's back as she heard the question. "Shit. The Killjoy, right?"

"You shouldn't call him that," Steph said.

It was as good as a confirmation. "He probably also said to phone him if I stopped by."

"I'm sorry," Steph said. "Maybe there's something else I can help you with." She turned back around, looked at Lisa's shoulder rather than her eyes.

"Maybe there is," Lisa said. And she didn't know why she did it, or what she thought would happen, but she put her left hand on Steph's chin. Guided the other woman's face to face her own. Steph kept her eyes down and away but Lisa said her name, soft and firm. "Steph."

Steph looked at her. "I could file an assault charge," she said.

"You won't." And Lisa stared into her eyes, just as she'd stared into her own in the mirror.

"He said you might try this." But Steph didn't look away. Only held Lisa's gaze.

It's not working. Stupid thing to think. But now she was stuck, kept on staring. And Steph didn't look away, maybe couldn't look away any more than Lisa could. Then her mouth went slowly slack, and her cheeks fell, and the muscles around her eyes let go. Her whole face went dead.

The door opened behind Lisa and someone took a step into the door. "Sorry, I'll come back," a man said, and went away again. Steph didn't look up, didn't break the gaze.

I'll take that file now, Lisa thought. *I need that file.*

Steph perked up, smiled. Took a sip of her coffee like it was an average morning in normal-town. "Doctor Killroy took the paper file with him yesterday. You could ask him for it if you want."

Lisa's own face fell. So easily defeated...

Then Steph said, "But if you hang on just a minute, I can print out most of it for you from here."

***

She approached the unit from the office side. There was noise coming from the other side of the security door, maybe a scuffle, so she knocked and waited rather than open the door.

A second later, it opened. Carl stood back, let her in. On the floor in the hallway, Elbert lay on his back. Dylan had one of his arms, Sally the other, and Paul, the other officer on duty, had hold of his legs. Ellen stood over him with a hypodermic needle. Empty.

Lisa stepped in, waited for the door to click shut behind her. "Problem?"

"Not really," Ellen said. "Elbert was out wandering last night. Don't know how he got out but he was outside the front door this morning."

"Elopement and returning requires sedation now?" Lisa said, sure what was in the syringe.

"Of course not. He was pretty excited, though. Couldn't get him to calm enough to say what was happening. When we tried to get him in seclusion as a precaution, he started swinging."

"Elbert, did you swing at them?" Lisa said.

Elbert just looked up at her like a scolded dog.

"Looks like it's all under control now?" Lisa said.

"Yes," said Sally from the floor. "Changeover meeting will be delayed a few minutes."

"Naturally." Lisa went into the office to look at her acquisition. Carl came in a minute later.

"You remember what you asked me to check?" he said.

"What?"

"About whether there was anyone in that hallway with you. Last week."

"Yeah. Oh, yeah. What did you find?"

"Key logs said empty. Except for you and him."

"Him?" Lisa said. "Who him?"

Carl pointed. At the front of the station, looking up at the monitor screen, stood James Killroy. As Carl pointed, Killroy turned around. "Good morning, Lisa."

***

Killroy's eyes were on her face, but Lisa knew what he was really interested in. She picked up the file, a plain manila cover with about twenty sheets of paper inside, and hugged it to her chest. "Good morning, Jim. Come for our change-over meeting?"

"I think you know why I'm here."

She shivered, tried to keep the expression from being too obvious. "You must mean Mr. MacAvoy," she said. "Pretty weird for someone to get out at night, even weirder for them to come back."

He just stood there, looking. Maybe he was wondering whether to call her bluff.

"I wasn't here," she went on. "I just got here, in fact. Ellen or Sally could help you."

"We should talk up in my office," Killroy said.

"Shift change. Got to sit through the meeting. You want to stay?"

He looked at her some more. She waited him out. Finally, he said, "One hour."

"OK, Jim. Have a good morning."

He looked some more like he was trying to communicate something, but she didn't want to know what. Finally, he turned and left.

"Weird," Carl said.

"Yeah," said Lisa.

"Never seen anyone beat him before."

"What? Beat who?"

"Beat The Killjoy at a staring contest. He always gets what he wants."

Lisa grunted, went to the table to look at her file.

There was no prose, just medical papers, medication administration sheets, a few pages of log notes. But it all took shape in her mind, a story of Alice Wilcox' last day on Earth.

The co-ed unit was usually for low-risk people. Depression, histrionic personalities, that kind of thing. Brian looked up and saw Alice coming out of her bedroom and wished for not the first time that day that she had male sexual anatomy to go with all those muscles. The only thing keeping her off the all-male unit was her sex.

Then he hoped she would go to the breakfast table and get some Wheaties or something. But she didn't. She came straight to him.

"I want to see the psychiatrist now," she said.

"Good morning, Alice."

"It's Colonel Wilcox, I told you that. Now go and get the psychiatrist. I don't have time for this."

She looked silly in the paper hospital gown and pajama pants they'd issued her. She'd come in coated in blood, like she'd been wallowing in it. A shower had erased all that evidence but she still looked bloody-minded. Sixtyish, tall for a woman, all bloated muscle.

"He'll be along in his own time, Alice," Brian said. The psychologist had told him never to call them what they demanded: Jesus, Mr. President, Napoleon, whatever it was. That would just give their delusions power over you.

She reached across the table, grabbed Brian by the shirt. Stared him in the face. "He'll come if I hurt you, isn't that right?" She dragged him close, across the spindly table staff used when they sat in the unit. Brought him nose-to-nose with herself. "He'll come right away if I hurt some people."

Brian's soft-self-defense training dribbled down his leg as he looked into her eyes. Some of the people down here were crazy, no doubt about that. Tommy thought President Clinton had killed him. That was crazy. But this lady, behind her eyes... In there was madness. Infinity, chaos, the universe whirling through space towards its own inevitable death. He grabbed her wrist with both his hands and tried to pull himself away but she was exactly as strong as she looked.

"Get the psychiatrist. Now." Alice tossed him against the wall behind him. The wall to the nursing station, mostly glass infused with steel wires. The noise brought out the other orderlies.

Steve, a big man of indeterminate race. Hong, a smaller guy who wore a white t-shirt too small in order to show his muscular chest.

"Problem?" Hong said.

"Bring that psychiatrist down here right now," Alice said. And she stared into Hong's face.

He stared back, life slowly ebbing out of his expression.

But Brian stood up behind him, holding one arm across his chest. "Bitch broke my ulna," he said.

Alice grabbed the table under the lip with both hands, tossed it into the air like confetti at a wedding. It came down with a crash, broke into pieces. Hong and Steve tackled her.

It was like tackling the wind. She used her fists and elbows, drove them down, into the tiles. Her feet slipped in their blood and she went to her hands and knees, red stain getting back under her fingernails.

That's how Carl found her. Bloody and grinning and savage, just like the night she'd come in. Blood on her teeth, between the wrinkles of her knuckles, on her cheeks.

"You done?" he said.

"Is this enough to get the psychiatrist down here?"

"Sure," Carl said. "He's going to want to talk to you, for sure. Through some bullet-proof glass, though. Come on, I'll walk you down to the seclusion room."

"I'm not going back in there," she said. And she turned at the sound of boots on tile. Coming down the other hallway were two more safety officers. And they'd brought cops with them, real cops with Tasers and handcuffs.

"Well, Colonel," Carl said, "You're most certainly going in that seclusion room. There are some other questions, though. Like, how much force is it going to take to get you in there? And, are you going to be able to talk to any psychiatrists once we've had to pump you full of Ativan? You remember Ativan? And here's the best question of all: is old Brian here going to press charges? Those cops can march you right on out of here right now. Frankly, that's how I prefer to handle it."

Alice looked at him, looked at the black and blue wall forming around her. "Guess I'll walk," she said, and she looked smaller. Deflated.

But no less dangerous.

She let them march her to the seclusion room. Brian watched from the hallway, writing with his good hand. Messy notes that would be the only real documentation of the incident, handwriting that looked for all the world like speech through clenched teeth.

Steve and Hong were in no shape to help. Carl got the restraints out of the closet, brought them into the little stone room with the metal bed like a table in the middle. "Gonna need you to lay down here, Alice."

"I don't think so."

"Look around, man. Colonel. You can't win."

"I already have. That's what you don't understand. What I found out there, in the jungle..."

"Alice," Carl said, patience running thin, "I need you to sit on the edge of the bed right now. I'm going to secure you for our protection. Otherwise these gentlemen are going to put voltage into you and cuff you."

"They aren't going to do anything," she said.

"I'm tired of this," said one of the cops. "That's enough to book her right now. You want we should take her off your hands?"

"Bring me the doctor." Alice seemed to grow as she talked, re-inflate. Her muscles swelled up like a cobra fixing to strike. "Bring him to me now."

"Take her," Carl said, and that's when all the officers, the cops and the safety officers, all fell to their knees holding their ears. Only Carl remained standing.

"You never killed a man," Alice said, "so I can't command your ghosts. But I can still rip off your balls and stuff them down your throat."

Carl did the only thing he could. He punched her in the mouth as hard as he could. Busted his finger, cut it up real bad on her teeth too. He used the other hand to punch her in the neck. Threw her against the wall, rattled her lights out.

The doctor arrived at that time. He oversaw her restraint. He advised taking her to the medical hospital but nobody was in much mind to hear that: they had their own wounded to care for, and ambulances *en route*.

She was strapped face-down onto the bare metal. Mattress would be a suffocation hazard. When she started to struggle, the doctor said, "This isn't safe."

"Then knock her out," Carl said. "Do it properly. She just bought a ticket on the Ativan train."

"Dangerous," the doctor said.

"So is she, doc."

One of her hands came loose from the canvas restraint. It seemed impossible, but there it was, clawing towards the other hand.

"Hold her down," said the doctor. He went into the office to unpack a syringe. A minute later, he came back with the pre-loaded dosage. He pulled the cap off the needle, stuck it into the meat of Alice's right buttock, depressed the plunger. She struggled like a bull for a few more minutes, then went quiet.

***

A drug overdose, or some combination of trauma and drugs, or an injury sustained in the fight. Whatever, that doctor had killed Alice by not sending her out. Killed her as sure as if he'd held a gun to her face and pulled the trigger.

The one thing Lisa could not find was his name. It was redacted from every report. But she knew his name.

Her hour was up. It was time to go to The Killjoy's office.

Seventeen

"Come in," he said. "Sit down."

Sunlight sliced in through window blinds set almost to blankness. The room was dim and full of motes of dust dancing in the light. His jowls hung loose, deep purple bags under his eyes.

Lisa sat down in the chair opposite his desk. He had a big black leather chair. She had one of the orange itch factories that were in all the offices. "How can I help you, Jim?"

"I'm old," he said.

"Only one cure for that," she said, "and I don't think you want it."

He nodded. "I'm old, I'm tired, and I've seen just about everything. I've seen psychiatrists lose it before, Lisa. I've seen them get into drink, into drugs, into the pills in the cabinet."

She held her breath just for a second, willing color to not appear in her ears, her throat. She looked around the place as if casually. The insipid painting on the wall, all muted color and no content. A picture of Jim in an army uniform someplace hot, younger and thinner. A piece of shiny metal on the window ledge. Lumpy and random like a meteorite but shiny, like chrome. Did silver come in nuggets like gold?

"You're losing it," Killroy said. "Or you've lost it already. That stuff you wrote about *folie a deux*... In my day, we had that kind of courage, you know. To experiment? Try things out, see if they worked. Jump the tracks when more formal, more traditional treatments weren't getting the job done. Take risks, by God."

"What happened, Jim? Not age, I think."

"No," he said. "I think you know what happened."

"Yes."

"Anyway. The modern age does not tolerate risk. The modern age requires proofs, evidence based practices, conformity to the code book."

Lisa leaned back. This was a dressing down she could handle. "You think I should remove myself from the case."

"I think we should let Mr. MacAvoy go. He's no crazier than you are. Nothing diagnosable, anyway. Some story-telling reminiscent of Korsakoff's-style confabulation, but nothing we can continue to hold him for. He won't take the medicine anyway, and he's too old for a lot of pills."

"Let him go." Lisa ran the phrase through her head once or twice more. "You don't think he's a potential danger?"

"No. What has he ever done? Pretty soon he'll age off the street, into an indigent-care nursing home."

"Or die."

"We can't save everyone," Killroy said. "Come on, let's take a walk."

"I thought you brought me up here to fire me."

"Not a chance. You're the best and the brightest. Come on."

"Where are we going?" said Lisa, standing.

"Team Seven," Killroy said.

"There is no Team Seven."

"Not anymore. That's why I want you to see it." He grabbed his jacket off the back of the door, levered it over his shoulder, fumbled the zipper. He led her out the door, along the tiled hallway to the elevator. Down to the ground floor, along another tiled hallway. Outside, across the parking lot, across the road, into a low, disused building.

Lisa had been in there before. Human Resources was over there, and the training rooms, and the gym. Plus four or five big, sealed doors like the ones to the operational units. Killroy led her to one of those. It was unlocked already, meaning he'd planned this excursion earlier.

"Just in here," he said.

The place was dark. Clean – nobody had been in here in two decades, meaning no dust had been generated to settle over the flat surfaces. They shone in weak light from around the edges of the window-blinds. Floors, counters. Door handles. The nursing station lacked glass, lacked a wall. There was no furniture, which made the common room look very large.

"Why are you showing me this?" Lisa said, leaning against one wall. "It's neat and all, I guess, but what's the point?"

"If you keep on how you're going," Killroy said, "this is what all the units will look like."

Lisa sighed. "Whatever, Jim. Let's get this over with. I assume you want me to look in each of the rooms and get all sad."

"Ideally."

"Fine."

The floor was laid out like all the others, like the active units. To the left was the big common room, straight ahead the ruined nursing station, to the right a short hallway with four doors along the right-hand wall and one at the end. That sole door would lead back off the unit. The four doors were seclusion and restraint rooms. She went that way first, past a six foot by eight cell. She paused, looked inside. There was no exterior window in this one, making it just a square of darkness with a little light coming around her shoulders. She moved down to the next one, peered inside. "Are the beds still in there?" she said, "or did they take them out?"

"I don't know," Killroy said.

She stepped closer. "I just can't see." Another step.

Then Killroy hit her in the back. Shoved her. He wasn't strong but she was unprepared, overbalanced. She fell into the room, knocked her head against the tubular steel rim of the bed. The door crashed closed with a noise like a timpani and the dark hit her as hard as the sound: total, complete, inexorable.

Lisa tried to stand but fell down, dizzy. Blood dripped onto the floor with a tiny noise. "What the fuck are you doing, Jim? They'll have your license for this."

No response. No footfalls, no laughter, nothing at all. He was already gone.

Lisa screamed. Angrily at first, rageful. She got up, dizziness notwithstanding, beat on the door with her fists and feet as she'd heard so many patients do before and screamed at it.

The door had been there eighty years. It was solid steel with no viewing window, not on this side. They'd put them in during the nineties, after this side was already closed. The lock was a deadbolt rather than the electronic locks up on the active teams, but it might as well have been a dump truck backed up against the door for all she could move it. It had been designed to stop big men at their maddest.

Her screams began to lose their anger, to retreat into panic.

Her words faded away into incoherence.

Lisa's hands grew sore and bloody, leaving invisible but sticky prints on the steel.

Part of her mind knew exactly how screwed she was. She'd seen so many men locked into these rooms, watched on the video screen as they struggled and then eventually gave up, calmed, rested in a fetal position on the steel bed.

But none of her mind could stop raging, panicking. Not yet.

On the active units, Safety supervised seclusions and restraints. Someone was always watching. When you calmed down, you got a mattress. Water. A toilet break. Someone would unlock the door, let you eat, let you out when you were not obviously dangerous anymore.

But this unit was disused. Nobody could hear her, nobody knew where she was. She and Jim had been the first people here in twenty years. It could be another twenty or fifty or forever before someone thought to look in these dark cells.

Eventually, Lisa grew tired. They always did, the patients. They didn't calm down because they forgave the voices in their heads or their hallucinations stopped, but because rage and terror are exhausting. With no clocks or even lights to tell time, she could not have said how long it took her but, eventually, she just leaned on the door with three contact points: each fist and her forehead.

She breathed in the smell of cold steel, of blood, of her own terrified sweat. Breathed deep and hard, like after a long run.

There was no way out.

And it could not possibly be any worse. Her future appeared to be solitude, loneliness, sharing space with her own eliminations for as long as they happened, eventual starvation.

And then he spoke from behind her. Her father, her long-dead father who she had killed with her medical knowledge.

"Lisa..."

He touched her shoulder with a hand that felt like cold made concrete. And from somewhere deep inside herself, Lisa found the energy to start screaming again.

***

It might have been night or day. Lisa had no cues, no clues. She was curled up against the back wall, farthest from the door, in the fetal position she had observed so many times in so many patients. Eschewing the bed was the only act of rebellion available and there was nobody to see it.

A door clanged open nearby. The next cell over, it seemed like. Feet tramped down the hallway, nobody talking. At least three people. Lisa's ears strained to hear, to capture everything, to log it away. Was that the sound of something being dragged? Bedding, maybe a mattress? She'd been good. They might bring her a mattress.

"Put him in here."

"Carl?" she said. She'd thought she would shout it, scream it, but the sound barely made it as far as the nearest wall, did not echo back at all. *My voice, I've screamed my voice away.* "It that you, Carl?"

Something thudded against the steel bed in the next cell over. A body, limp.

"Should we strap him down?"

Is that Dylan?

"No point. He can't get out of here." Carl again. "Nobody cares if he hurts himself. Records say we let him out an hour ago, dropped him off at the bus station with a ticket to Colorado and twenty bucks and drugs enough for two weeks."

"I don't want to do this."

"Then you shouldn't have killed that girl at that party. Then she couldn't control you."

Lisa filed all that away, even though it sounded like nonsense. Dylan, a killer? Gentle Dylan who balked at restraining patients for their own good?

"Just shut the door," Carl's voice said. She still wasn't sure it was Carl and Dylan. "It's the guilty feelings she wants, you know."

"Doesn't make it right."

The door slammed shut, the lock rattled in it fittings. The two men walked back down the hall, much more lightly than they had come in. And that third set of footsteps, lighter than the others, no voice attached to it.

Maybe a woman.

Or maybe Killroy.

Lisa went to the left-hand wall, shared with the room where they had dumped whoever they had dumped. Touched it with her hands, her face. No way to see in there, or to hear more than the sound of the blood rushing in her own ear.

"Dead. She's dead. They killed her."

"Shut up, Daddy." Her voice was too hoarse to waste on spirits, on imaginings, on psychoses. Her brain was too hoarse to waste energy on knowing the difference.

"She tried to be nice to you," he said, whining. Petulant. He was never petulant, not in life, not until the end. At the end, weakened by drugs, by sickness, by pain and starvation – the illness wouldn't let him eat or keep the energy from eating – at the end he was weak. Sad and useless, capable only of complaint.

"I said shut it, Daddy. I don't have time for you."

"You only have time for me. They've killed you, too. And he won't feel a thing about it. She won't. Maybe that's for the best. I can finally rest, and I'll know you aren't tied to her. You can go to whatever hell or oblivion waits for us after this."

That's my own voice talking to me. He never talked that way, sounded like that. That's my own voice in my head.

"What difference does it make?" he said.

"Just be quiet. Please."

"When you've chewed your fingers off for want of food and smashed your head against the wall to quiet the silence, then you'll wish you hadn't said that."

"Well, shut up until then." But those words cut. Did she hate herself so much as to say them? And that was just the future she feared the most, the inevitable end to this confinement. Starvation, bloody stumps, the madness inherent to solitary confinement. If she wasn't crazy yet, she would be soon enough.

I wonder if there's a way to commit suicide before all that happens.

The thought came not as a voice from outside, not as a haunt, but seemed just as alien. Intrusive, even, in a way that her father's voice was not. More solid than his hand on her neck, brushing the bones of her spine.

"Don't touch me."

"I can't help it."

She backed into the corner, against the rear wall again, and imagined that would stop his spectral touch. He couldn't be behind her if there was a wall. Then she put one fist in her mouth, bit her own knuckles, concentrated on not screaming. If she started to scream again she'd never stop, not this time.

***

She was dreaming.

Sleep must have come to her out of exhaustion as she lay in the corner, pretending not to feel her dead father's hands on her back, to not hear his voice in her ear.

In the dream, she climbed up the short flight of steps to the brownstone, Hilde's brownstone. Pulled the heavy front door open, noticing it was quarter-sawn oak, tiger oak. She stepped over the threshold, into the waiting room. There were foot prints on the rug, footprints in blood. Heading out, the way she came. She followed them up the stairs, past the paintings and photographs of all the murdered people who had lived here before. They watched her pass with slack faces, withholding judgement.

Up two flights, into the dark hallway. Her office was down there. The footsteps clearly came out of Hilde's office, originated there. Here they were dark and serious, downstairs just hints. A paintbrush that hasn't been dipped recently enough to leave a good impression.

I can see in the dark.

And I don't want to see, especially not when I wake up.

Those weren't rational thoughts so she let them slide off her mind. She just floated down the hall, leaving no prints of her own, turned into Hilde's room.

Blood on the floor, wet and sticky. A pool of it radiating out from her chair, the chair she had bought herself as a graduation present. The chair was on its side in the pool of blood and Hilde was sort of splashed across the rug like a vase of flowers knocked from a trestle table.

Too much horror. Too much stress for too long. Lisa, asleep, felt more or less nothing about the scene in front of her. *I've grown inured to it all.*

She went in the bathroom, washed her hands, wiped down the faucets and handles with a paper towel. When she glanced up at herself in the mirror, she saw Elbert in there, looking back at her. Washing his hands.

He was talking.

Eighteen

Elbert didn't remember going to sleep, but now he woke up. There was firelight behind him and he lay on one side, facing out into the night. Tall grass weakly reflected the glow.

There was someone crouched behind him, up by his head. He saw the shadow. It grew up out of his own, deformed him.

He stiffened, his mind on the thicket where a ghost had taken an unhealthy interest, on the conversations that stilled when he got close, on the way Floyd stroked that knife while watching him. On Dennis and the way he always looked but never made eye contact, like a high-school admirer too shy to do anything about it. But then the crouched figure put a hand on his shoulder, a human hand made of flesh, and stilled his panic. "She doesn't have your best interests at heart." Just a whisper, faint enough Elbert wasn't ever sure he hadn't imagined it. Then whoever it was went away. Elbert stayed still. His instinct was to whip around, grab the speaker by the collar, force sense out of them.

A whisper sounds much the same in every throat. Elbert couldn't have said who it had been. Most likely one of the men. Accented, but most of that was lost in whispering. Dennis or Osho, probably. But what had he meant?

Elbert sat up. He mouth tasted like dirt, was dry as sand. There was no-one nearby, not awake anyway. Osho across the fire, staring out into the night. Guard duty. Dennis snoring away a body-length distant. Floyd was out there someplace, stalking around the camp so the fire wouldn't wreck his night vision. The women were just two humps in the dark.

In the distance, the sky lit up in a series of flashes. Lightning or falling mortar rounds or flares dropped from a plane, Elbert couldn't have said. *War is hell.*

As if his quiet thoughts were beating drums, Wilcox sat up and looked Elbert's way. Firelight played over her face, making her sympathetic in this flicker and accusing in the next. But she said nothing, only stalked away from the camp into some tall grass to make her toilet.

Dennis chuckled. Returned to snoring.

When Wilcox returned, she set water on the fire to boil and commenced her strange exercises. Elbert joined her, bending flexing, stretching, because if he didn't do so of his own accord she'd only command him to. And if he refused that, she might melt his will with her gaze as she had the British officer, and the young man at Visiting Officers' Quarters.

Then Elbert drank bitter tea while the others started rising, making their ablutions. "Why do you drink that crap?" Dana asked him, near sunrise.

"Getting used to it, I suppose," he said.

"Smith," Wilcox demanded. "Come with me."

"Got to go," she said to Elbert. "She'll want me to bandage her chest. Don't save me any tea."

"I know," he said. "She made me do it our first morning out. Weirded me out."

But she was already out of earshot. When Wilcox called, it paid to jump and jump like a frog.

The march got started soon after. Elbert got point for a while. He walked slow, with his head down, scanning for reflective surfaces or straight lines or other things that didn't belong in the tall grass. The terrain was grass hills, jungle falling away now behind them: great for laying traps.

Dennis grabbed his shoulder about an hour in. He halted mid-step. "What's up?"

"Three more steps. Trouble."

"Spook?" Elbert said, remembering the cold feeling of something touching him, the warm trickle of urine down his leg.

"No. Box snare."

He breathed out in relief. Dropped to hands and knees, crawled forward a pace, two. Finally, with the tips of his fingers, he felt the edge of a steep hole, a box carved down into the soil.

It was completely invisible.

"How did you see it?" he asked.

Dennis shrugged and lit up one more spliff. "Been out here a long time, me. You get a sixth sense for this stuff."

"Maybe I shouldn't be on the point," Elbert said.

"Then how you ever get the sense? Here, don't be a drag, man. Take a drag."

"I told you I don't do that." Elbert had his hand down in the box. He pulled up an axle with spikes all around it. Someone's foot would go down there, stick on the spikes, turn the axle, stick in more spikes. Tissue damage, maybe a fracture, certainly a trapped foot. And if you survived all that, the wooden stakes were smeared with feces. He tossed the contraption to one side, crawled over the hole. He didn't feel any more holes, stakes, wires.

"There's no more, man," Dennis said.

Wilcox called out from the flank, "We good to go, Elbert?"

"I'm not sure," he said. "Dennis says yes but I want to feel around a little more."

"Your call," she said.

He found something. A straw-covered hole, right in Osho's path. Just plain old pongee sticks down in that one. "Sixth sense my ass," he muttered. "Got another one here. You'll have to just step over it.

Osho grabbed Elbert's shoulder on the way by, a silent thanks.

Elbert wanted to talk to Dana. Wilcox let him off point after another hour, put Floyd on it. So Elbert got close to Dana when he could. "All that stuff with the thing in the woods," he said. "Close your eyes, ears, mouth. Ass hole. What was that all about?"

"Thing? You mean the ghost?"

"My mama didn't raise no fools," Elbert said. "You say ghost, I say there's lots of shit it could have been."

"Fair enough," Dana said. "The 'thing,' if it conforms to spiritualist doctrine – and at this time they seem to have the best grasp of the phenomenon – it gets in through your openings. It wants to possess you, so it goes in through your eyes, ears, et cetera. When we start getting into the real haunts, the spiritual epicenter, we're all going to have to take certain precautions."

"Like what? Walk in a line with our thumbs up each other's butts?"

Dana laughed. "We'd look like an elephants' parade at the circus, but it would get the job done. Tampons should do it, though."

Elbert's eyebrows made for his hairline. "You want me to stuff lady-cotton up my ass?"

"Or would you prefer a vengeful spirit lodge itself in there?"

"Smoke ahead," Osho said, quiet and flat. The thump of mortar rounds punctuated his statement. And, far away, the rattle of machine-gun fire. He touched that necklace, the gesture seeming automatic.

"It's a fetish," Dana said, seeing where Elbert was looking.

"Like what, a sex thing?"

"No, no. An instrument of power. Magic, if you want to call it that, but really it helps him stay sensitive. To the spirit world."

"Not our problem," Wilcox said. "Two points off of course."

"Are we still soldiers at all?" Elbert said. "I'm happy either way, just want to know where I stand. Where we stand."

"We should take a look-see," said Dennis. "Make sure your safe-passage is holding."

"If something happens to us..." Wilcox looked doubtful. She looked to Elbert as though he had some authority here.

"Just point me where to march," he said.

Floyd nodded at Dennis, who nodded at Wilcox. Osho shook his head the merest fraction but nobody paid him any mind. Dana and Elbert just waited.

"All right," Wilcox said. "If we're going in, we're doing it fast and hard. Those are our shells landing in there. Weapons ready, fast-creep until you smell smoke, then we take the perimeter at double-time. Ready? Move out."

Elbert got low. The other men got lower and Wilcox was like a jaguar stalking in fast-motion. If anyone hostile had been watching, Dana would have got her ass shot off for sure: she crouched, but more like a mom trying not to wake the baby on a Tuesday night. The uniform never looked more incongruous on her.

A couple hundred yards went by underfoot. Mortars *thump*ed again and the world turned to smoke. It rolled over them. Elbert stifled a cough, knowing the smoke was cover. Even Dana could hide in it.

But she choked and hacked and fell out, and Elbert had to grab her under one arm and drag her forwards.

"Thanks," Dana said, and leaned on Elbert maybe a little more than she needed to.

Through the smoke, across another hundred yards of heart-pounding ground, and Elbert saw a small town, just a village really. There was one concrete building with four or five floors – Elbert didn't stop to count, only checked all the windows for muzzle-flashes. There were fifty or so little houses, ranging from mud huts to wooden structures with red tile roofs. A couple of temples. A low wall, three feet or so, all around the outside.

Floyd got there first. He threw himself down, popped up with just his eyes over the wall. Dennis arrived next, stayed low. They had guns to hand. Osho kept running, another fifty yards or so along the wall, then he Dennis arrived next, stayed low. They had guns to hand. Osho kept running, another fifty yards or so along the wall, then he did like Floyd, Elbert behind him. Wilcox and Dana jogged around to leap-frog past them, take up a new station.

There were bodies everywhere.

Women and children predominated. They were spread all over the ground, smoking and bleeding. A child cried up against a broken wall, sheltering behind a trough for watering animals. Her legs were gone, and most of her abdomen.

Dana started in her direction but Wilcox grabbed her, shoved her back on track around the village at a run. "She's dead," Wilcox said. "Soon she will stop crying. When she realizes."

Dana fell out. Wilcox tried to shove her back into motion but the smaller woman heaved up her guts. Field rations not much worsened by stomach acid and time splashed into the grass.

Dennis and Floyd ran past, scanned and covered, then Elbert and Osho. In their path, a roof collapsed over the wall. Dennis and Floyd danced away but Osho was caught in the tumble of slate, burning wood and cinders. Wilcox let go of Dana. She and Elbert rushed up to where Osho lay, half-buried in burning crud. A huge wooden beam lay across his chest.

Elbert took a side, braced his legs. But nobody else moved to help. Dana heaved and sobbed somewhere behind them. Wilcox stood over Osho, watching his face. Dennis and Floyd watched her watch him. They all had the same expression. Slightly sad, slightly satisfied.

Like viewers at an execution.

Osho gurgled, choked, couldn't quite cough. Somewhere under the rubble his life squeezed out.

Elbert tried to lift the joist on his own and it was just impossible. Soon it took enough heat from the wood burning around it that it grew too hot to touch, but he kept on trying.

Finally, Wilcox set down her machine gun and grabbed the far end of the joist, furthest from the wall and closest to Osho. She lifted it with one hand, with hardly a thought. Elbert dodged as she shoved it away, towards him, showering him with sparks and ashes. "Get his weapons," she said.

"You could have saved him?" Elbert said.

"No. He was like the little girl: he only needed a minute to understand he was dead. Get his weapons."

"What was all that about honoring your enemies? We blew up the children, Wilcox, and you let Osho die under this rubble, for nothing. Was it all bullshit?"

"Get his weapons," Wilcox repeated.

Then something fell into place, a realization. "You set this up," Elbert said.

"How, MacAvoy?" Wilcox said, making eye contact for the first time. "How did I set this up? I said this could happen, we should stay away from here. And what did I do, force him to run this way, pull down the wall on him? Get his weapons. Now."

"Or what?" Elbert said, slowly moving his rifle so he could snap it up and get off a shot if he had to. "Are you going to give me the spook look and melt my spine?"

Wilcox turned red to her hairline and all her muscles tensed. Elbert thought he was dead. But she took a deep breath instead. "We're down a man. I don't know if we can do what we have to do without him. He didn't look like much but he was a big-time spook-shuffler where he came from. Elbert, I don't know if we can win now, but I know for sure we can't without you. One more loss and we're over before we start. So please, for the love of Christ and anything else you hold sacred, pick up his mother-fucking weapons and get the fuck in formation."

He hadn't seen her move, but that giant Browning was in her hands again. Pointed off to one side, sure, but there. Elbert ducked down, snatched a rifle, a pistol, a belt knife, Osho's bandolier. Wilcox wasn't really looking at him now, eyes pointed on down the road, so he also grabbed Osho's grisly trophies. Those got stuffed in a leg pocket.

"I see your point," he said when he was on his feet again. "Let's do the thing with his dog-tag."

"What thing?" said Floyd, like he hadn't been in-country long enough to know.

"Stick it between his teeth, boot it in real good," said Elbert, about to reach down and get started.

"Don't bother," Wilcox said. "It doesn't say anything. Osho wasn't his real name, and the dog-tag is blank. Just leave it. He was nobody and has returned to nowhere."

Elbert checked, doubting everything and especially doubting Wilcox. But it was as she said. "Shit. Nothing for it but to move on, then."

Dana staggered up, looked away from the corpse with tears in her eyes. But Wilcox shouted over anything she might have to say. "You heard the man. Move out, you pasty maggots." They were running hard when she continued, "Take a good look at that place. This fucking world might not be worth saving but it sure as shit won't save itself. You don't want to live in a world like this, you got two choices. One of them is dying. The other is making sure there's still a world to change."

Dennis giggled.

***

Lisa could hear him giggling. Dennis. Like she was there with him, in that pestilential jungle half a world away.

Her body hurt. The concrete was cold and hard and her hips, shoulders, one knee jammed against it under her weight. There was a pool of spit under her face, on her arm, where she'd drooled in her sleep.

Am I awake now?

It was hard to say. The room was so dark, just the least hint of gray light around the frame of a door fitted too tight to really let in light. She might have been anyplace, any time.

"You're awake," said Elbert from the next cell.

"Elbert? I dreamed you were talking."

"I was talking. Only way to get your Pappy to shut up for a minute. Did you rest?"

"Barely. What are we doing in here, Elbert? They opening this unit back up?"

She heard him shift around, maybe sitting up on the steel bed. "Not likely, Doctor Lisa. Not very likely. We've been shuffled off into here to shuffle it off."

"The mortal coil, you mean?"

"Yes."

She ached to her feet. One leg was almost dead asleep and she shook it out, tried to stamp life back into it. Then she sat on the edge of the bed, its tubular frame under the backs of her knees, feet brushing the concrete.

"Is it all true, Elbert? The stuff I was dreaming, was it all true?"

"Yes."

"All that Vietnam shit, did that really happen?"

"Just the way I told you."

She imagined he was sitting just as she was. Not many other options. She tried to picture it, could only picture a room as dark as this one: nothing to see. "Why did you kill her?"

"Who?"

"My therapist. Hilde. I dreamed you were in her bathroom, washing your hands, wiping down the counters."

"Not me," he said. "I was there. But look at me. I'm not strong enough to do what you saw. She's not what I came for."

"What did you come for, Elbert?"

"You've got one on you."

She shifted, her backside already starting to protest the hard, flat surface. "I think I can see that now."

"You don't, still, but you will. By the time it's all over, you will. You'll see more than you want to."

"I've already seen more than I want to, Elbert. I think you should go on with your story. Keep telling it. At least I'll die knowing it's over. Maybe I can understand why all this is happening. Do you know why it's happening?"

"Yes, Ma'am," Elbert said. "Yes I do. And all that is at the end of the story. I think we have time for another run at it." And he went on.

***

It crawled back out of the ashes, as it ever did. This time, there was nobody watching or failing to watch: the survivors had gone back to their temples and their homes disheartened, demoralized.

It crawled out of the ashes of this bonfire, here across this roadside. But also across the river. By a lakeside. Under the forecourt of a temple that had stood longer than Vietnam had been a country. From ashes in front of a city ruined by falling bombs and yet still vital with life, with people struggling to make some kind of a living. Next to an airstrip where soldiers in green uniforms burned it with jet fuel, day after week after month.

It grew up from all these places, scuttled into the dawn. Each instance of the scarred, burned thing turned its feet south and started to walk.

A hundred people saw it go, a thousand people in a hundred places. Some just gaped while others shuddered and made old signs to ward off evil.

***

Osho's corpse sat under the ruins of the wall, under broken slate and burned out beams. His blood soaked slowly into the soil, enriching it with iron and carbon.

Two soldiers crept around the wall much as Osho had. "Nothing in there but corpses," one said.

"Never be too careful," said the other. "Not where Charlie is concerned."

"You know she don't like when we call them slopes and Gooks and Charlie and stuff like that."

"She ain't around. Keep your voice down. That him?"

"Yeah, seems to be. Name tape's all fucked up with blood and ashes and shit. And he don't got that necklace like she said. With the ears. That ain't GI, keeping ears."

"Well, get his tag." The soldier was nervous, kept his gun on the smoking remains of the town. Kept his eyes moving back and forth over it, up and down. "We're way out of pocket here, Davy. Make it quick, will you?"

"Tag just says Nones, Hobie. Name: None. Rank: None. Like that. What the fuck is this?"

"A shitty job of camouflage is what it is," Hobie said. "You want to make a guy anonymous, you say his name is John Smith and he's a sergeant of no distinction and he goes to Protestant services. It's the cue ball that stands out on the table."

"And the eight ball."

"Whatever. He dead?"

"As a tuna sandwich," Davy said. "I'm with you. Let's bug out of here. Place gives me the creeps."

"No," Hobie said. "One more thing to do. The Bitch said we got to chop him up fine. Steal his power."

"I don't want his power."

"Me neither – look what it got him. But she needs him not to have it."

"He don't look to me like he got no power left, Hobie. Let's just go."

"She'll know, Davy. You know she will."

"Yeah."

They got out their knives and field hatchets and set to work.

Later, when they were good and bloody, Davy felt around in his shirt for a cigarette. "Shit," he said, "All I got left's this blunt. I was saving it for a better day."

"Ain't gonna be any better days, shithead. We're the fuck in the middle of fucking Vietnam. You might could get your ass shot off tomorrow. Smoke 'em if you got 'em."

"Yeah. You might got a point there." He lit it with an old metal lighter rubbed with boot polish so it wouldn't catch any light. "Ah, feel better already. Don't seem right doing this to one of ours."

"I hear that," Hobie said. "But it's him or us, you know what I mean?"

"I guess." Davy blew out grayish smoke with his words.

Hobie startled, jumped back. "You see that?"

"See what?"

"Looked like someone walked through that smoke you just blew."

"Don't be an asshole, Hobie. This is creepy enough already. Look, I almost got his spleen. Get back in here and let's get this done?"

They went back to work. Neither of them had enough of the sight to see the things that watched them. One from the trees: a burnt, ashen thing with cracked and blistered skin. Another from behind them, maybe potent enough to do them harm but fading as they cut apart its body.

Nineteen

"Is that true?"

"You keep asking me," Elbert said. "I never said anything to you that isn't true, Doctor Lisa."

"How come I can hear you so clearly? I thought these cells were pretty soundproof."

"You know better than that," Elbert said. "You listened to enough guys screaming in their cells. Hour after hour, day after day until they finally lost their voices – like you did – or lost their will to go on screaming, like I did."

"I'm sorry, Elbert."

"I used to say that. Back in basic. I'd say 'I'm sorry, Drill Sergeant.' And he'd say, 'I know that, boy, and we're here to change all that.'"

"I want to laugh," Lisa said, "but I can't. I can barely talk."

"It's nearly over now, Doctor Lisa. I told you time was short and now it's about done run its course."

"Is there any way out of here?" Lisa said, laying back on the bed. She was so tired it was almost comfortable, except there was no way to keep warm.

"Why are you asking me that? I'm not your keeper."

"Sorry."

"I'll just go on then, shall I?"

She grunted, a noise neither of approval nor dismay, acceptance nor rejection. She threw one arm over her eyes to block out the darkness and another under her head as a weak pillow and settled in to listen some more.

***

Back into the jungle.

Elbert saw it from miles away. Sweat prickled along his back, the sun so hot it seemed to have weight, but not even the promise of shade made him look forward to going back in there.

Dana marched on the other side of Wilcox from him. He wanted to pick her brains but didn't dare to. And she was starting to look like a weak link, someone who needed to be carried through danger.

"Something's wrong," Wilcox said.

Everybody stopped. Dennis reached for his shirt pocket but Wilcox stayed his hand with one of hers, still looking into the jungle ahead.

"You won't need that," she said.

Dennis looked disappointed, but also relieved. His eyes were bloodshot and bleary. Then he thought some more. "Hey, that means it's either a human sort of problem, or something bad enough that mundanes can see it."

Wilcox nodded slowly. "Ahead. In the jungle, waiting in the shadows. It stands astride our path."

Elbert scratched as his ankles. Fleas had taken up residence in his socks. *Stands astride?* he thought. *Who talks like that?*

"What kind of thing?" Dana said.

"Not a spirit. Maybe what they are running from," Wilcox said. "Something big, and angry. I can feel it from here."

"I don't feel anything," Elbert said.

"That," said Wilcox, "is your special gift. Stay close to Smith. She'll keep you out of trouble with the spooks. Only one thing to do: we got to go that way, and it's in the way. Let's go see what it's made of."

Elbert sidled closer to Dana. "Wasn't no accident," he whispered.

"No," she agreed. "But stay on mission. You're about to see some stuff no American has ever witnessed. You'll be present at a great event, a momentous one. A revelation, like out of the Old Testament."

"You ever read the Old Testament?" Elbert hissed.

"Yes."

"Then you know no sane man would want to be anywhere near anything that happens in it. You crazy white people can't have your revelations without dragging me along?"

But he kept marching, stepped into the shadows cast by twisty trees. Vines and creepers and noise all around and the smell of stagnant water and growing things all told him this was the jungle. It was almost like going home. If you didn't like home a lot.

Ten minutes, then fifteen. The heat grew and grew. Elbert was soaked in sweat. Floyd had big dark circles under his armpits. Dana looked like she'd taken a shower in her uniform. She had the sleeves rolled up and her hair had that wispy, flyaway look fine hair gets in humidity.

"Jesus Christ," Dennis said. "Christ, there it is."

Elbert looked where Dennis was looking, saw vines and underbrush. An emerald green snake coiled around a high branch. Bugs.

"The Wendigo," Dana said, and grabbed Elbert's arm. "I'm actually seeing it, with my own eyes. Shit – my camera!" She unshouldered her bag like to dig through it.

"Use a gun," Elbert said. "Photograph the corpse." He unslung his M-16, held it waist-high. There was nothing to shoot, though. Blood racketed through his head like the elevated train in Chicago. He gasped for breath.

Wilcox had that giant Browning in her hands. She thumbed off the safety, took a stance. It was too big to shoulder and in any case had no stock, so she had it below her waist. "Come on, then," she shouted. "Step up or get the fuck out of my way."

Elbert heard a noise then, like wasps. Ten wasps. A thousand. As the noise grew, something took shape ahead. A big thing, man-shaped but as tall as a house, made of smoke. It stepped forward and the ground boomed through his feet. It dropped its long arms down low and wide, screamed with a voice like a landslide. It reached out for Wilcox. As it reached out it became more than smoke, less than flesh.

Wilcox pulled the trigger.

Nothing makes noise like a rotating fifty-caliber Browning machine gun. It was like a sewing machine amplified twenty times. Bullets jetted out at an absurd rate, jagged through the smoky thing. That thing recoiled, stepped back.

"That won't stop it," Dana said. "It isn't made of..."

Whatever else she said was lost in the hollow booming noise of a grenade. Floyd shot it from behind Elbert, then stepped up with his M60 poised. Dennis was muttering something as he pulled his belt knife. The smoke-thing shambled back a step, then lurched forward again. It reached out for Dennis, then recoiled.

He kept muttering, held up his knife like it was a sword and he was a gladiator.

Elbert had his rifle ready but he didn't see how bullets were going to be very helpful. He tried to keep Dana behind him. Wilcox had said Dana was supposed to keep *him* safe but that didn't particularly add up in the moment.

Then there was a flash of light and a whirring noise.

Everything went still. Dana wound the next frame in her camera – *crunch, crunch*. Snapped another picture, made another flash of light.

The thing's rough head turned her way. It came on fast now, leaped, went horizontal right at Elbert with Dana behind him. Now he did fire his weapon. Nothing else to do but that. It sounded like coins pouring into a coffee can.

The smoke-beast was on him, yards away, feet away, an eye-blink. But it never touched him. It broke apart into twenty smaller shadows that faded from sight, none strong enough to intrude on his consciousness. Gone.

"Where is it?" Elbert said, turning around and around, rifle pointed everywhere. "Did I get it?"

"Not you," said Dennis. "The one behind you."

"Can it," Wilcox said. "It's gone, who cares why? Let's move on before it makes another try. Something like that can't really hurt you anyway, only frighten us off. Are you frightened?"

Elbert changed out his magazine for a fresh one, set to reloading the old one. "Only shitless," he said. To Dana: "Did you really stop it?"

"Me? No, I don't know what he meant. I only took its picture. If these come out, it'll be a sensation."

"I just want to live to still have sensations," Elbert said. But Wilcox was moving, Floyd and Dennis just behind on either flank. No more time for chatter. *I got to get away from these freaks. But to where? Prison back home and a bullet or a POW camp in the North.*

Shit.

***

"It wasn't a Wendigo though, right?" Lisa said, stretching and standing. "It was the sixties, almost the seventies. You believed in all that stuff, all that nonsense. Bigfoot and space aliens and metaphysical horse-apples. But it wasn't a Wendigo."

"No," Elbert said through the wall, audible like he was on the bed next to her.

"So what was it?"

"Still don't know. But I know she's got it. She's got it now. It goes where the thing goes."

"What thing?" Lisa said.

"We're coming to that part."

"Why can't you just tell me what the hell is happening, Elbert?"

"Isn't time yet," he said. The time will be right soon enough. Don't try to hurry it. You aren't going to like it when it comes."

"I don't like it now," Lisa said, and now she did laugh. It hurt her throat, and that was funny too, so she laughed again. "I'm locked up in here waiting to die horribly. My dead father wants to avenge himself on me, and my only company is one of my patients who I'm pretty sure murdered my therapist. What else is not to like?"

It was Elbert's turn to grunt. She didn't know what he meant by it.

"Just keep talking then," she said. And he did.

***

"Maybe it was the light? The flashes?" Elbert said.

"I don't think so," Dana said, sipping water. They were companionably close, on a log with a thin rill of water by their feet. Elbert noticed her body against his in a way that was more than companionable.

He stuffed the thought down. "Can it do more than just scare us? I mean, what if it touches you, for real?"

"Something like that?" Dana said. "Maybe all it needs is to frighten. Maybe you're right about Floyd, and that's why this stuff leaves him alone and comes for you. They turn their fear into something else. But you, it can get a rise out of."

Floyd and Dennis were a few yards away with their backs to Elbert. They talked low and this time in a language Elbert didn't know. Wilcox came out of the woods into the little clearing and sat down on Elbert's other side, curing him instantly of any thoughts of romance.

"Who cares?" she said again. "It's gone and that's that."

"It will come back," Elbert said. "Whatever you're chasing, something wants to get in our way. The English, some kind of ghosts, and this whatever-you-call-it. Maybe we should think about listening. And if we aren't going to be deterred, maybe we should think about ways to kill it."

"You want me to talk straight?" Wilcox said.

"I sure would appreciate it."

"That thing is what we came for. It's the Wendigo, the skin-changer. It can do a lot more than scare. It can take people, make them its own. Use them to hunt. You know what a serial-killer is, Elbert?"

"Like what, Jack the Ripper?"

"Yeah. You ever wonder what would make a man go that way?"

"Bad?" he said. "Don't need no fairy-tale monsters for that, Colonel. Not down to Alabama way, no-sir. People come bad enough already. You trying to say killers is all these monsters, these shadow-things?"

"Not all of them, no. But maybe some. This thing, it's been around a long time. And a place and time like this one, this war... This is its natural habitat. That town made you sick, didn't it, Captain Smith? Well, it made me sick, too. But the Wendigo, it doesn't get sick when it sees human suffering, when it sees us at our worst. No, the worst of us are the best parts of it."

"A psychic projection?" Dana said. She stooped, let the stream run into her canteen.

"Whatever you want," Wilcox said. "Doesn't matter. You can't kill it and you can't control it. You can only be stronger, better, braver."

"So what the fuck are we doing out here?" Elbert said.

"I'm going to catch it." Then she stood, stretched, settled her gun on its strap over one shoulder. "Rest is for the wicked," she said. "The righteous march on."

Elbert groaned; Dana touched his arm in sympathy. Dennis and Floyd rose like they were on strings, nearly as tireless as their boss. As they fell in, Floyd shot Elbert a look over one shoulder.

Elbert shuddered, checked the pistol in his holster. "Dana."

"Huh?"

"How come that guy smoking weed can see them and I can't?" Elbert said.

"Opens up the mind. Hallucinations aren't always of false things," Dana said.

"So if I did it..."

"You wouldn't see a thing," she said. "They're not real in any accepted sense of the word. Just... projections. Ripples, from a dimension just slightly out of step with our own. Intrusions. Like that. Dennis has his focus, Osho has his fetish. You'd need something a lot stronger."

"What do I have?" Elbert said, his mind on the string of ears in his pocket.

"A chance in hell," Dana said. She touched his arm again, friendly, then moved off into her place in the formation.

"Of what?" he said, but nobody heard him.

Twenty

"Elbert?"

Time had gone by since he stopped talking. Lisa had slept fitfully, dreamed badly of nothing, woken with a question in her mind.

Elbert didn't answer, so she said his name again. She heard him shift, slide, roll over. "Yes, Doctor Lisa?"

"Elbert, why were you staring at the camera? In the common room, with the younger men. Why were you all staring at the camera?"

"Watching," he said. "Waiting. For the right time. For her to show herself. Those men were all killers. Did you know that? This is a place full of killers, perfect for her."

"I guess it's too much to ask for your answers to make any sense."

He grunted in the dark. "She's ready now, you know. She'll come down here soon enough."

"She. You mean Wilcox?"

"Who else?" he said, and his voice echoed through the room in a way Lisa's could not. She hadn't recovered from screaming, and hunger and dehydration were settling in now.

Her bladder hurt from holding in her water. Once she started to pee in here, though, it was a short, steep ride out of humanity and into plain animal. She listened to Elbert stand and walk around his cell. It was hard to tell where he was because the noises echoed around, bounced around the room like out-of-control two year olds.

Then she heard the tinkling of water. Because it was on her mind, she knew right away what he was doing.

"Elbert. Is it really that hopeless?"

"Hopeless?" he said. "Yes, it's hopeless. Our situation. But I haven't given up. What you do is this: since you got to piss anyhow, you do it in front of the door. Nothing to do about the smell except get used to it, endure it. Show them how much you can suffer. But that don't mean you got to piss in the corner like an animal. When it's the only weapon you got, you got to use it."

"Weapon?" she said, sitting up.

"Wet the floor. If they're dumb enough to come in after us instead of just letting us die, maybe they'll slip in it. Even if they don't, they'll have to walk in it. The tiniest revenge, the smallest spite, but it's still the act of a person. A person decides to survive and do whatever it takes."

"I see your point," she said, and remembered a patient a few months back doing exactly this: peeing in front of the door. Then he started smashing his head against the metal bed so staff would have to come in, slipping through wet urine on smooth concrete, to physically engage with him. Ben went home with a broken wrist and Carl got a black eye, a loosened tooth.

So Lisa slid off the bed. It made a drumming sound in her absence, no longer held still by her weight. She stepped to the door, lowered her pants. Then she thought about them touching the floor while she made a puddle, decided to strip them off completely. She set her clothes on the bed, covering her pubic area as though Elbert could see through the wall, and squatted by the door to do her business.

Her water tinkled on the cold, hard floor. Urine pooled around her bare feet, warm and stinking. She cried a little, noiselessly and soft but, when she was done, she felt better. "I'm going to live," she said.

"That's the spirit," said Elbert.

"Keep talking," Lisa said. "As long as you can. Soon your mouth will go totally dry and your throat, too, and you won't be able to talk any more. But if we're going to die in here anyway, there's no sense trying to stretch it out."

"What happened to 'I'm going to live?'"

"I'm going to live while I'm alive. And that includes seeing if I can outsmart the men who built this room, and all the men who were locked up in here and couldn't get out over the last century."

"All right, Doctor Lisa," Elbert said. "All right."

***

Another night in the jungle. Getting close to civilization now, to the towns and cities that the North Vietnamese didn't want soldiers getting close to. They'd walked well into the darkest part of the night, only Wilcox really able to move around with any degree of safety. The cough of a tiger nearby finally convinced her to call a halt.

Elbert drew a watch. He sat about twenty feet high in a tree where he could get a good view over about three-quarters of a circle while being nearly invisible himself, just a vague shape in the dark in a twisted landscape of vague shapes.

Everyone else was sleeping, or passing for it. Wilcox didn't seem to need rest but she was down there sawing logs with the rest of them.

I could slip away, Elbert thought. *I could go now, head back the way we came.* But this deep into the North, he doubted he'd have a way back. They hadn't made contact with any of the enemy, but he'd been sure they dogged every step. The feeling of being constantly under hostile eyes only faded after dark, and then not completely.

Elbert settled for checking his weapons again. Oiled his M16. Broke down and cleaned his sidearm. Oiled and sharpened his knife. Checked the straps on his field pack, resorted its contents to sit just right – and wrapped Osho's fetish in an old sock, hid it deep inside the pack.

Down below, someone got up from their bedroll and wandered off into the brush with a casual wave. Elbert assumed they needed to pee. He stood up for an extra-vigilant watch. It was hard to hear anything out here. With the noise of insects, big cats in rut, boar pigs crashing through the underbrush, and shells falling in some distant battle, the whole Viet Kong army could be feet away and totally unheard.

Whoever had stood came back a minute later. He went around the camp, put his face next to each of the sleepers. Apparently satisfied they were all really down, he came to the base of the tree Elbert occupied. "Catch," came a whisper, and he tossed something up.

If it hadn't come right in front of Elbert's eyes and caught a glint of starlight, he'd never have seen it. But he did, and years in theater had sharpened his reflexes. He caught it like a showoff kid catches a ball, one handed, snatching it at the top of its arc. "What is it?" It felt like a pill bottle. He'd handled plenty of those.

"Osho had more than ears," the whisperer whispered. Then he went back to his bedroll.

It was completely futile to investigate the object beyond listening (it rattled like a dozen or so tiny pills in a plastic container) and taking off the top to smell it (the contents were odorless). He put it in his pack next to the string of ears.

But now he knew who had warned him the other night. Not poor dead Osho after all, but Dennis. Dennis had the skill to pick pockets.

Elbert sat back down on the branch, nestled against the trunk of the tree. It bark was soft but also sharp, giving and rough. He let his eyes drift from darkness to darkness, shadow to shadow watching for movement more than for shape.

It was dull work. The dullest. Sleep scratched at the back of his eyes, pushed out a yawn. He stood again for a while, stretched, yawned. *Another ten minutes,* he told himself. *Ten more minutes and then I'll wake Wilcox.* He sat again.

His eyes slipped shut.

The world lurched sideways, then forwards.

Elbert grabbed reflexively for the tree trunk, arrested his fall. How long had he slept? An inexcusable lapse no matter how short or long. Fear was only good for so long and then the body took what it needed.

The sky gave just enough light now to see how dark the jungle was. Elbert's eyes darted around, checking for threats or movements.

There.

A large shape. Had it been there before? Fifty yards out from camp, darker than the trees around it. Still. Shaped at the top like a head and shoulders, at the bottom maybe like legs but too dark to make out. Twenty feet tall.

The thing from before, what Wilcox and Dana called the Wendigo?

Dread tickled the top of Elbert's stomach, like ice water administered directly to the duodenum. His heart started to thump in his throat, his ears, and only then did he realize the jungle had fallen silent. Like a mortuary when the lights are out and the pathologist has gone home.

"Dana," he tried to say, but his voice had dried up. "Wilcox. Floyd." Croaks only, the dry rasping of locust wings. He stood, cleared his throat with a sound more moan than cough. "Dennis." Now his voice made a sound like a man's, only a register higher than usual. "Alert. Wake up!"

Wilcox heard. She roused the others with the toe of her boot. Then she came to stand under Elbert's perch, looked where he seemed to be looking. "What is it?"

"Not sure," he said. "I think I drifted off. Shouldn't have happened. Can't have been out for ten seconds. Then there was a shape in the dark I didn't remember. Dead ahead, fifty yards."

"Can't see shit from down here," said Dennis, joining Wilcox. He grabbed hold of a branch, started to pull himself up to Elbert's position.

When he got to that branch the weight was too much. The branch flexed, Elbert wobbled and grabbed the trunk for support, looked at Dennis to tell him to get his own spot. And when he looked back, the shape was gone. "Shit."

"What?" said Wilcox.

"It's gone. It was there, and I looked away for a second, and it's gone."

Floyd joined the group, machine gun over one arm. "Bad dream," he said. "Shit like we been seeing, do it to anyone. Shapes in the dark..."

Wilcox never looked at him. Just said, "Check the perimeter. Take Dennis with you."

Floyd moved. Dennis jumped down from his new perch above Elbert, joined Floyd. They moved out into the dark.

"Think I was seeing things?" Elbert asked.

He hadn't seen or heard Dana arrive, but it was her who answered. "The question is, is what you were really seeing real? Hallucinations aren't always of things that aren't really there, remember? And sometimes the monsters in your nightmares are real."

Wilcox offered, "The crazy one is sometimes the sanest person in the room. Elbert, go catch forty winks. If there's trouble, you'll know about it."

***

"Are you making any progress over there?" Elbert said. His voice sounded hoarse now, ragged.

"There are bolts on the legs. They go into the floor. The floor is concrete. Old concrete. They keep it dry in here, keep up the roof, but it's still old. There is paint over the bolt. I could maybe peel it away with my nails then work on the bolts but I don't think so. If the bolts won't turn, though, I can try to break up the concrete."

"Hence the pounding."

"Hence," she agreed. Lisa was on her backside, back to the wall farthest from the door, legs out in front of her. She kicked the nearest leg of the bed. Not as hard as she could, but forcefully, and repeatedly. The bed vibrated, gonged, boomed. Vibrations through the leg into the flat sheet of metal made that boom. Lisa hoped those same vibrations went down through the leg, into the bolts in the concrete. She resisted the urge to stop and check, to feel if the leg had any give in it yet. She just kept kicking.

"It's no good," her father said. "You know they'll just come for you."

"Yeah. That's what I'm hoping, Daddy. I don't think they can hear us but if they do, if they come to check, we'll have a chance. At least we can die fighting instead of eating our own fingers."

"You can't fight."

"Say something helpful or shut up," she said, and kept kicking.

"Why do people hear voices in their heads?" said Elbert.

"Is it in my head? You don't hear him, right?"

"That's neither here nor there, Doctor Lisa. Just tell me why your patients hear voices."

"Unreconciled inner thoughts," she said. "Disowned mentations that appear in the temporal lobe as heard sounds. The person thinks they're real. Can't tell the inner voice from the outer voice any longer."

"How do you fix it?" Elbert said.

"Fix it? Sometimes it goes away on its own. Sometimes drugs help. About a third of the time, nothing does any good. But drugs are the first line treatment for voices. Change neurotransmitter levels."

"You ever notice the voices almost always say bad things to people? Tell them to kill themselves, that they're worthless, that there isn't any hope? To kill?"

"What are you saying, Elbert? That peoples' voices are ghosts, like my damned father? That medications don't work because people have a spiritual problem, a murder problem?" She was kicking harder now, sweating.

"No, Doctor Lisa. No, not that at all. Forget I mentioned it."

"You're going to die anyway," her father chimed in. "When you die, I finally get to rest."

She ignored him.

There had been a patient, a big black man from Louisiana. When his voices had gotten too loud, he'd take himself into the toilet and yell into the mirror. Curse them out, really work the voices over. The first time he'd done that everyone had gone scared and quiet. But he said that worked, at least for a while. He got two or three quiet hours out of such eruptions.

He never hurt anyone. They just got used to him going off on himself from time to time.

"Remember him, Daddy? You want me to do you like that?"

Her father was silent on the issue.

She kicked the bed again and now the noise was not the same as before. There was a buzz to it, barely but perceptibly a buzz to it. "I think it's working."

Elbert said, "I think I can go on a little more. If you want."

"Yes," Lisa said.

Twenty One

Elbert surprised himself by sleeping. He was gone the minute he was horizontal.

The dreams were on seconds later.

He was back with his old unit. Kilgore and Rice were still alive. Rice handed him a foil packet, just a few inches long and seeming to weigh nothing.

"How much you take out?" Elbert asked him.

"I wouldn't short you," Rice said. "Come on, man, how long we been doing this?"

"Ten months, and you done shorted me every time," Elbert said. Rice was black but that didn't make him any more trustworthy in Elbert's opinion. "What say I check in your socks? Bet you got an ounce or two of my stuff right around your ankles." That was one of the easy ways of moving stuff. Pills you had to be careful: they could slowly soak through your skin. But weed didn't mind the humidity too much.

"Whatever. Call it taxes, then, if you want."

Elbert handed over a small roll of bills.

"What the fuck?" Rice said, counting. "You're short about ten percent."

"Taxes, call it," Elbert said. "Package was supposed to be fourteen ounces. This is only twelve."

Rice opened his mouth to reply and Elbert wondered, as he always did in this dream, as he did six times a day when he remembered the incident, just exactly what Rice had been about to say. Whatever it was, it was lost forever. Because that's when Daniels stepped into their clearing.

Vines dripped water into murky brown puddles all around. Some creeper like ivy rustled in the barest of breezes. A piece of bark chose that second to drop with a plop off the side of a rotting log. And Daniels said, "I finally caught you black bastards."

Elbert didn't see much point in denying anything. He had the reefer right in his hands. "Guess you did, Captain," he said. "I always figured you knew and didn't really give a damn. Lots worse going on out here than some medicinal herbs changing hands."

Daniels laughed and Elbert thought he might be able to pull something off here. "If you'd have cut me in up front like is good manners in a top-down organization, no, I probably wouldn't give two shits about you boys poisoning each other to death. Don't try and tell me you don't move anything stronger than a little Mary-Jane from time to time, either."

"You just want a cut?" Elbert said. Maybe this could be easier than he thought.

"No, you dumb fuck," Daniels said then. He still smiled but there was something behind his eyes that wasn't just jolly. It was full of hilarity, manic joy. "I've always wanted to kill me some American boys. You just got elected."

Elbert reached, but he was too slow. Daniels had his service piece out like it was a bouquet of flowers at a magic show.

"Scene's perfect as it is," Daniels said. "Yeah, go ahead and draw that pistol. Perfect. Caught smuggling drugs, tried to kill the witness, got plugged. I get to murder you and walk away a war hero. They'll give me a medal for drinking your blood."

It was all crystal clear. Elbert couldn't stop any of it, couldn't unsee any of it. In life it had been fast, flash-fire fast, but the dream dragged on and on up to that moment, the one second that had changed everything.

He said, "Not so fast, Cap. Ain't nobody a hero out here. You been watching me, I been watching you back. Like I said, I always figured you knew. Let me give you a cut. Call it taxes, like. Walk away with some extra money in your pocket, sure, and know I'll be looking anywhere but at you next time some villager brings you a tribute."

"A what?"

Elbert watched Rice without watching. Rice was sliding slowly, so slowly to one side, putting distance between himself and Elbert. His hands were up, but only just, and getting lower all the time. "A tribute, a bribe, protection money, call it whatever you want. I know how stuff works though, Cap. And I know there ain't no money out here, not really. A few greasy dollars that go from hand to hand, some drugs, some black-market smokes. And a lot of native girls. That's what they bring you. Their mothers bring you their daughters. You promise not to shoot up their villages so long as you get to rape enough little girls."

Daniels should have spluttered in outrage. Should have shouted, denied, waved his gun in a rage.

But he didn't.

That gleeful thing behind his eyes just danced, a sick look of misplaced joy. "I'm glad," he said. "I'm pleased as shit we understand each other." Then he straightened his gun arm, pointed it right at Elbert's face.

Elbert had won. He'd talked just long enough, kept Daniels' attention off Rice. And Rice was there to exploit the opening. He drew fast, like a gunslinger. His gun was an old revolver, a black-market piece out of Belarus. The hammer kicked back, fell, as Daniels pulled the trigger on his shiny, chromed automatic. The first bullet hit, right in the meaty part of Daniels' shoulder. It disintegrated. Flesh dissolved in a fine spray and Elbert saw the joint where his arm bone met his shoulder.

Daniels spun around, still pulling his trigger. The bullet meant for Elbert's face went wild. And of all the places it might have been diverted, of all the things he could have hit while missing Elbert, he caught Rice in the sternum.

Rice dropped on the spot, heart pierced.

Both men bled the same color of red.

Elbert tried to gather his thoughts and found he had eternity in which to do it. Dreams are like that.

Daniels howled in agony, all the joy gone off his sick face. He tried to grab the gun with his other hand from where he had fallen in the dirt and muck. The pistol was half in a stagnant pool, mosquitos hatching around it. Elbert kicked the gun and it slid the rest of the way into the water. "Stop," he said.

Daniels looked up at him. "I'm still going to murder you. I got to your friend first, but you're still going to be next. I'm going to do better than killing you myself, though. I'm going to make the government hang you for a traitor. You like that?"

"Ain't no need for that," Elbert said. "I know what you are, you know what I am. We still can walk away from this.

And look: you're hurt like a motherfucker. Your ass is going home. Smart guy like you, you got to know how to look out for number one. It's a shitty gift, but take it, man."

Daniels fell forward on his face then, snarl fixed on his mouth. Blood loss, shock. Elbert had seen men die of less severe wounds. He started shouting for help.

This is where I wake up, he thought.

***

He didn't know if awake was an improvement on asleep. It all blurred together. Melted and merged and swirled around, water in a toilet bowl.

First thing I'm doing if I get home, he thought, *is taking a long, leisurely shit in a real toilet.* But that thought was just a delay, pushing aside the inevitable confrontation. He let himself remember where he was and why and what new horrors the day might hold.

It *was* day. No monster made of ghosts had eaten him in the night, and no screams had wakened him. That was a good start.

Wilcox stood over him. His now-open eyes started at her shins, traced her short, squat body up to her face. *Talk about new horrors.* "What?" He said.

"You squared away?"

"Not hardly, but I feel like I got two hours sleep in a row."

"Come with me." She marched off into the undergrowth. Elbert followed, thinking mostly about his bladder. But his left hand loosened his pistol in its holster.

They went right to the spot he'd been staring at in the night. And it was obvious why.

"Elbert found it," Wilcox said. "Obvious even in the dark."

"That's..."

"A baby's skull, yeah," she said. "Clean and bright. Couldn't say how old. Or how..."

"Old?"

"Right."

"Coincidence?" Elbert said.

"You like coincidences?"

"Maybe not." But that left a lot of unpleasant alternatives to consider. "I saw something, then. Not just a freaked-out half dream. Any more bones?"

"You see any?"

"No." Elbert scratched at his head, pushing back his cap the way he'd seen his Dad do a hundred times. Out in the pasture, looking at a dead chicken or something, trying to figure how he was supposed to feel as much as what he was supposed to do next. The tiny skull had its eyes pointed straight at the camp. There was a tree trunk behind it, a plausible explanation for the shape he'd thought he saw. But not really the right shape. "What should we do with it?"

"Dennis says leave it alone. Dana agrees. We don't know what it means. Doing anything could be words in a language we don't know. Can't predict the consequences."

"Silence is a statement too, though, right?"

Wilcox didn't answer.

Guess that means 'yes,' Elbert thought. He walked back to camp, packed up as quick as he could. Took a second, when he thought nobody was looking, and examined the pill bottle Dennis had tossed him in the night. There was no label. *Not medicinal, then.* Plain white bottle. Plain white tabs. Too small for aspirin, too ordinary for LSD. That usually came in stamps and such, not little pills. Mescaline, maybe? He hadn't seen mescaline before but he knew about it. Peyote extract, the molecule that made it send you on trips.

If Osho had been from the Americas, maybe somewhere South of Mexico, for sure he might have carried the substance. Spiritual purposes, medicine in the old sense. He did what he had to do with the pills.

Before he was done, the smell of pot stole through the air. Dennis giggled. Elbert hurried, stuffed the pill bottle back in his bag just as someone came into view.

"Time to move." Wilcox. "We'll be at the site later today. Some open country, a little south of Hanoi."

Everyone but Dana tensed up at that name. Bad place, in the lore of soldiers. If the Cong caught you, that's where they'd take you for torture or brainwashing or worse.

Elbert shouldered his gear, got moving. Dennis fell in step with him.

"You got to be careful," he said.

"I heard that. Five by five."

"I didn't just find a skull out there, buddy," Dennis said. "You got to be careful. New spirit, not like the old ones in the trees, man. She still had her face, her race, hadn't faded into hate and longing like the old ones do. She got shot up. Last year, year before, who can say? She tell me she was a sniper. Too young to be a sniper. But ghosts, they don't lie, you know? Well, only the old ones, the worst ones. The really evil ones. And they lie only until you let them in."

"Are you ever not high?" Elbert said. But he was creeped out, a feeling that was more or less of a permanent state now. Last night he'd only known he was about to fall because he wasn't always about to fall; but his life was one of fear and dislocation so constant he didn't know what it would feel like to not feel that way.

"You think I want to see the things I see? It's what you call occupational, not recreational."

"Where's that accent from?" Elbert asked, suddenly suspicious. Those were big words for a second-language speaker of English.

"Don't change the subject. They're watching you. We tried to tell you before: your attitude is getting attention. You got to decide to believe or not believe. You stand halfway, one foot in each place, they notice you. They notice you, they see you're a doorway. From there, in fiction, to here, in the real place."

"You're confusing me. You're saying they aren't real after all? That thing seemed pretty real to me, like it was going to rip of my head."

"You are a smart guy," Dennis said. "But they didn't never give you no books to read, did they? Just the Bible. Keep you ignorant, out of trouble."

That wasn't true, not exactly, but it was close enough Elbert just stayed quiet.

"Alam al mithal," Dennis said.

"That Arabic?"

"Shut up and listen." It was hard to march and talk and the terrain wasn't helpful. Dennis stopped talking a minute to gasp and splutter his way over a deadfall. "It's the realm of ideas and abstractions. Like Plato's realm of perfect forms, but only it includes the things about us that are permanent so long as we are remembered. They don't exist, but yes, they do exist."

"Lost me, chum," Elbert said, but he had a glimmering of what the man meant.

"A square. Is it real?"

"Yes."

"No, this square or that square might be things, but a square is just the word we use for the form it seems to take. But what is a square?"

"A shape with four side the same length, four angles ninety degrees."

Dennis giggled, turned his eyes to one side as if trying not to see something the other way. Stopped walking, relit his toke. "Exactly the same length, exactly ninety. Can two side be exactly the same? Down to the inch, the sixteenth, the milimeter? The micron? Smaller? Can you draw that with a pencil and a ruler and say it's a *perfect square*?"

"So there's something perfect about us that can't live in an imperfect world?"

"You starting to get it. And you're staring that world in the face, thinking about perfect squares and spirits and history instead of the trees around you, the sky above, the mud between your toes. The woman, her, that bit of flesh. She'd fuck you if you asked her, you know? And they see you, turning away from that but towards them. And like you was at a train station, you look at somebody, and they got to look back, you know? Like, is that somebody I know? Only they don't stop at wondering. They think, that's someone I should get to know. Like a girl looks at you, the way Smith do, and you can't help but look back. And you go over and you say Hi."

Elbert thought as they walked. He thought hard. "Those aren't quite the right words, are they?" he said, after a while.

"Now you starting to catch on, man." The accent was thicker than ever now. "The right words, they're there up in the Alam al mithal. We stuck here making noise with tongues too big, lips too heavy."

"Yeah." For the first time, Elbert wanted a toke of what Dennis was holding.

"So, decide. Do you believe, or do you don't believe? Neither way makes this all go away, but either way, they stop being so interested in you, you know? You, you're the girl you ask to go with you and she says *maybe*. That shit drives you crazy. She says yes, she says no, it's good. She says *maybe*, then you got to chase. She could be not so pretty, not so smart, not the right girl for you. But *maybe*, she says, and you can't think of nothing else, day and night, until you get her to say yes."

"I don't believe it, any of it," Elbert said.

And Dennis didn't call him a liar, just sucked in rancid smoke, held it, blew it out again, and giggled.

Please help me live long enough to have nightmares about that giggle.

***

Someone was giggling in the dark. It echoed around the room: hard ceiling, hard walls, hard, flat floor, bed like a big steel drum. Lisa tried to catch it, catch the sound, isolate it.

"Dennis?" she said. "Is that you?"

"He's dead," Elbert said from the next cell. "Long time ago."

"Then who is giggling?"

"Nobody," Elbert said, voice flat and husky. He was down to a whisper now. "That's you. Sobbing."

"Oh." It made sense now. Why she couldn't catch the sound: she stopped sobbing to listen for the noise, gave up and started sobbing again. "Why am I crying, Elbert?"

"I thought I heard the bed come apart," he said. "Maybe it was relief."

She felt around with her hands. Her foot hurt, and her shin. Concrete was a lot sterner than her body. But the floor around the bed post was cracked, powdery. The leg had indeed come free of the floor. She pushed on it and it gave, wiggled.

About a centimeter.

Because it was still attached to the frame – part of the frame, hard-welded. It was a piece of tubular steel that stretched from one corner, up to the bed, along the short edge, and back down to the floor. It was welded all along that short edge to the flat base, the part she slept on. She had bruised up her foot and given herself a shin splint to free one foot from the floor. And the freed foot of the bed profited her nothing at all.

How many hours? No way to know. The air in the room tasted of copper, of sweat and urine, of the feces she had deposited by the door in a pool of her own liquid waste. Of fear.

"There's nothing to do, Elbert, except the futile thing. I've freed one leg from the floor. Now I have to go on with the next one. And then hope I can free that leg from the bed itself. And then hope I can use that leg to somehow open the door, or weaken it, or dig through the concrete or something. Something."

"Yes," he said, and she heard him lie down.

"I'll get us out of here," she said.

"No you won't."

She didn't know if that voice was Elbert or her father. She didn't care, only went back to kicking the bed.

Twenty Two

"Daddy, can you get me out of here?"

The second leg was almost free, almost free. One bolt still clung to the concrete but when she kicked the leg it didn't vibrate. The other two bolts were free and the whole leg could shiver and shake without really moving that last bolt at all.

"Daddy, I need you now. I'm sorry I yelled at you. I'm sorry I killed you. Don't let me die in here. Can't you go and get help? Go and tell someone..."

"Nobody cares about you," he said, and she knew it was him and not Elbert because Elbert couldn't talk at all now. He could only whine through a dry throat. Her own voice was not much better. Breathing hurt, and her legs felt like pulp. Her stomach was the worst.

"Someone does, Daddy. Someone does care about me. Hilde cares about me."

"She's dead, remember? Murdered. Elbert did it."

"The detective, then. I hired him. He'll have to come for me sooner or later. Can't you tell him where to find me? Please, Daddy."

"Hanrahan," he said.

"Yeah. Hanrahan, Daddy. Go find him. You don't want to watch me die in here. You love me. That's what daddies do: they love their daughters, even when their daughters hurt them. I loved you the best I could. Go on. Forgive me. Save me."

"I can't," he said, and then he was silent. So was she.

***

Her finger was bloody. She sucked at it, tried not to lose any precious water into the hole, but she had to stick it back in there. The pain... It hurt, but she was becoming slowly inured to hurt.

As the flesh wore away from the tip of her finger it became a more efficient digging tool.

The bolt wouldn't rattle enough to break down the concrete, so she picked at the floor itself. Dig-dig-dig, suck. Dig-dig-dig, suck. Scratching, poking, prying, scraping. Tiny particles came away, worried away.

It seemed like the bolt went down forever. Like she was following it down into hell, through the crust of the Earth into eternity.

I could use a different finger.

But then she'd have two ruined fingers. This one was almost down to bone. Her right index finger would never look normal again. She might go get her nails done and she'd get a discount because she only had nine. In the future. *Survive into that future.*

It was a new moment. She'd survived one more.

I'm thirsty.

That thought she pushed away, sucked at more of her own blood.

Dig-dig-dig, suck.

The bolt came away from the floor. It pinged, cast up a tiny rain of concrete turned to dust and grit, and came away.

Half the bed was now free from the floor.

I did it.

She smiled in the dark, nobody to see it. Stood up. Shouted, like an animal shouts in the forest over a kill. *I'm here, I'm alive, this is mine.*

Next, she started on the leg assembly, the squared-off, upside down U shape that ran from the floor, along the bed, back to the floor. She'd been kicking it for... a long time. Hours, maybe days. She'd slept twice, dreamed of what Elbert was saying. Maybe the weld was weak.

It wasn't, though.

She took hold of one leg, back to the far wall, and pulled. Over and over again she pulled, tugged. Short, repeated pressure. Loosen the weld like she'd loosened the concrete. She was exhausted already and it hurt to stand, hurt to breathe, hurt to keep on living. But she kept doing it.

It came away with a loud clang, a ripping noise, and she fell over backwards. Smacked her head against the wall. She didn't have the voice left to cry out in surprise or triumph or pain so she just stood back up, dusted herself off, sucked a little more blood from her wounded finger.

This wine you drink, remember always that it is my blood.

She laughed voicelessly. Bent to feel out her success.

The leg was still attached to the bed. Her hand bumped it, expecting to find it laying on the floor and instead finding it just where it had been, eighteen inches high, but closer now.

The leg had not come away at all – she'd free the other two legs from the concrete.

Shit, shit shit.

Without those legs bolted down, there was no more leverage to try to pull off the leg.

I've lost. It was all for nothing.

"It was always for nothing."

She didn't have any voice to tell her father to shut his mouth.

"It was always futile. Don't you get it? Everything was always futile. You're going to die. You knew that when you started, that there was no chance. That's why I gave up. Because there was no chance of winning. I made a choice and so did you."

You're right, she thought. *You're exactly right.*

Sometimes you can tell the right thing to do, because it's the futile thing to do.

I made my choice: to die fighting.

She couldn't hear Elbert anymore. Not talking, not breathing, not moving around. Not for a long time. She assumed he was dead in there. He'd been nearly eighty, not fit to be on the tough unit, not fit to be down here starving. He'd died laying down on his back, his business here incomplete, story unfinished.

Not me.

She licked her finger, trying to keep the wound clean, assuming a life after this cell. Infection could cost her the hand, her arm, her life. And she was going to live. A discount for one finger would beat a discount for all five.

She surveyed the room, the black, utterly black room, using her mind rather than her eyes. Low ceiling, but a short bed. Leverage was the problem.

The bed coming free had not made the leverage problem but solved it.

The bed was heavy. It was steel, every part of it steel. Tubular steel, so the weight was moveable, liftable. Lisa got to one end, lifted, pushed it up over her tired head. Stood the bed on end. The screws holding the other feet down could not bear any such strain; they scratched and cracked and popped out of the concrete. There was just enough clearance to the ceiling that she could take hold of one leg, hold on with both hands, put all her weight on it.

Hanging there was exhausting and her tank was empty. She imagined her body eating up the last of her fat reserves, starting to work on the muscles. Eating itself from the inside just as she sipped at her own blood from the outside.

And hanging wasn't enough. She had to bounce, which meant pulling herself up as much as she could, letting her weight drop, catching herself with the strength in her hands. The ebbing strength in her hands.

Over and over again.

The tube was too big to grip comfortably, designed that way. And it was slick with her blood. But she kept at it.

For ten minutes? An hour? Two?

The dark yielded no information about time.

But, eventually, the leg came off. Lisa spilled onto the floor, landed on the bolts that had held the bed down. They poked into her back, started her bleeding again, and the leg landed on her face. She heard her nose break, saw light for the first time in maybe days as the blow sent a starburst of pain through her vision.

"Fuck."

Ah, voice. Her voice was back enough for one word, one exclamation. The pain said she was alive and her voice was able to proclaim it.

She held the tubular steel across her chest like it was a blanket, or a child just saved from a potential danger, and lay there. Her face bled and her back bled and her finger bled but there was nothing she could do about it, nothing she wanted to do about it.

Survival had left her mind. Nothing but the battle with the steel bed had mattered. And she'd won.

I won.

Lisa rolled onto one side and slept. Lightly, troubled, alert for starvation, dehydration death, more a state of conserving energy than really resting, but sleep.

***

Dennis' number came up.

The jungle was, once more, in the proverbial rear-view mirror. A vague path led between fields full of some vegetable Elbert didn't recognize. Lisa looked around, apparently startled to find herself here. But she wasn't here, just dreaming Elbert's dreams.

Just be me for a little while, Elbert thought. *It's almost over now.*

All right, Lisa thought, and Lisa was Elbert.

Ahead, three men in bright clothing sat on the road.

Behind them were the remains of an old and repeated bonfire, ashes so dark they drank the mid-day sun.

One of the men stood when they were in shouting distance. He held up his hands, open: a sign of non-confrontation. The others stayed sitting, backs turned. The guy was old. Hard to tell with these Vietnamese. Back home white people said they thought he was younger than he was, but that's just because whites and blacks didn't socialize. Same problem here: he hadn't spent enough time with enough Vietnamese to really tell. The guy could have been sixty or eighty, same difference.

He chattered for a while but nobody understood what he was saying. Soon they were close enough to stand chest to chest. The other two guys never moved. Wilcox stopped about four inches from the little guy's face, glared down at him. Then she talked back in his same language and Elbert's jaw dropped.

"You got the lingo?"

"Enough," she said. "He's telling us not to go on. It's a trap, he says. But we're going on. Right over him if we have to."

"I don't like it," Dennis said.

"Me neither," said Dana.

The guy jabbered some more. Elbert couldn't even tell where the words began and ended. Wilcox talked back, pointed past the guy, started walking.

"I wouldn't do that," Dennis said.

Wilcox stopped. Turned. Looked Dennis right in the eye. She didn't have to ask *why*. Her face and posture said it all.

"Up ahead. Dudes with guns. They got a watch on for us. And worse than that. Those two other guys, they ain't guys at all. They're dead men."

Wilcox turned back to the guy in the orange robes. Spoke in short, choppy sentences, pointed at the seated figures. She didn't seem to like his answer. "He says they didn't watch the ashes well enough and it got away. And when it came back it was tired of playing... hide and seek... So it took their eyes and made sure they could never watch the fire again. He seated them like this so their spirits could do what their bodies had failed to."

Dana said, "Can I touch them?"

Elbert said, "I thought you'd lost your enthusiasm once things got real."

She didn't look at him, only at Dennis. "You could," he said. "They're right there, like the man said. Watching the ashes. They've been here about two days, about as fresh as they come."

A smell worked its way into Elbert's nose. The stench of corruption, of death in the sunlight. He hadn't noticed at first because it was always kind of there: cooked meat and jungle and rot.

"None of this matters," Wilcox said. She pushed past the little man, forcing him to side-step to keep his balance.

When he was steady he came up with a gun from somewhere. Inside his robes, maybe. Elbert never saw. He didn't know where his own gun came from, only that it was in his hands and pointed at the little guy. "Put it down," he said, voice shaking. This wasn't how it was supposed to go down. No death for him. The man's pistol looked like it was forty years old, a slender barrel on a boxy frame, five shot revolver.

"It's not for you," Wilcox said, not breaking stride.

And it wasn't. The guy didn't point the gun at any of them. He put it under his own chin. Pulled the trigger.

Nothing. The first shell was dry.

The second wasn't.

Dana had figured out what was up after the first and decided to have no part in it. She could have tried to stop him, Elbert thought. But she didn't. Just strode forward between clicks, drifted along in Wilcox' shadow. Elbert followed suit, didn't even react when the gun snapped off its shot, a sound more like a branch breaking than the hollow boom they put in movie soundtracks.

Elbert had stepped up to knock the gun away, but too late. Too late. He looked down at the dead guy. *Nothing more to do here.* He left the man laying between his two companions, forever to stare at the night sky and wonder, perhaps, what it all meant.

"How far?" Wilcox said as Elbert caught up.

"Quarter mile," Dennis said. "You'll see them in a minute."

They did. The men weren't hiding. They stood across the dirt path. Their rifles were slung behind them, and nobody made a grab for a weapon. Looked like a patrol waiting to check paperwork, something like that.

"You got paperwork?" Elbert asked.

"No." Wilcox just kept walking.

"You want to go around?"

"No more time for going around," she said. "Straight up the middle."

Once again, when they were in hailing distance, one of the men raised his hands in a show of openness. He started to talk.

"You're right," Wilcox said. "He wants to know who we are. It will be pretty plain when we get close. They'll harass us a little for sake of form then send us on our way."

But Dennis moaned. "It's coming."

"What's coming?" said Dana, grabbing for her camera.

"The ghost, the thing from the ashes. It's hungry."

"Where?" Wilcox said.

"Right there, right in front of us. It's... It isn't coming, it's going. For the one who talked to you."

"Shoot it," Wilcox said.

"Won't do no good," Dennis moaned, lips wobbling.

Floyd punched him on the arm. "Straighten up. Think of something."

"Get out of its way," Dennis said. "Go around."

"No," said Wilcox, and strode forward. She yelled back at the patrol in their language. They suddenly looked panicked.

Then the leader, the talker, grabbed at his face. Quick, panicked, tearing at something only Dennis could see. The other soldiers had their guns out now, looking all around for a threat. Wilcox held her gun overhead with both hands and the others followed suit, not wanting to become targets. The leader dropped to the ground, blood all over his face.

"It's still hungry," Dennis said. "It could eat a thousand men. I can't take any more. I want to go home, forget all about this. Such things did not haunt me at my home. Never did I see them."

"Get ahold of yourself," Floyd said. "I got to whack you again?"

"Won't help," said Dennis. "It doesn't want fear, not any more. It wants more than that. It wants despair. You have to feed it."

"So feed it," Wilcox said. And she looked at him. Right at Dennis, right in the eyes.

Dennis shook his head, slow, then fast, but his eyes never left hers. They couldn't. He started to cry. Then he laughed, and cried again. "OK," he said. "OK, I'll do it. But you remember me. You goddamned remember be, OK?" Then he lowered his gun from over his head, pointed it at the patrol. They were still deciding what to aim at and he presented the perfect scapegoat. Wilcox lowered her weapon, too, and pointed it at Dennis. Telling a story, and no words needed.

"Do it," she said.

Floyd took aim at Dennis. Elbert and Dana stayed in the surrender position, she not comprehending, he not participating.

Dennis looked daggers at Wilcox. But he turned his head, lowered it, started to charge the patrol.

They shot him to death. Both sides. Wilcox' oversized .50 caliber tore off his legs. A dozen other wounds punched through his body from four discrete trajectories.

Then Wilcox shouted something at the patrol. They packed up their guns and came to inspect their kill. Wilcox led her unit past them, another man short. A few hundred yards past, she grabbed Elbert by the collar while they marched, pulled him close.

"Remember him, like he said," she told him, almost whispering. Her breath was hot on the side of his face. "But he didn't mean you any good. Remember *that*."

Elbert staggered on, nothing else to do but march.

***

March.

Nothing else to do but march. Lisa thought she was awake again, but there was no way to be sure. The cell was cold after the jungle, blessedly cool and cold as hell. There was a big steel pipe in her hands, a crude tool, a base weapon.

What did I want it for?

Nothing to do but march, and noplace to go but through the walls. Maybe her father could go through walls. He was touching her even now, scratching at the back of her neck with spectral hands made of hate and frost, trying to get in. And her back was against a wall, no room back there, so he had to be in the wall itself.

Maybe Elbert could go through walls. Time-travel, teleport. He'd gotten out somehow before. But he was dead now. Walls and confinement meant nothing to dead people.

She couldn't go through walls, but there was nowhere else to march.

She stood up, hefted the big curved pipe in her hands. Awkward weapon, too heavy, too big. But it was all she had. So she marched to the door.

Not enough space up there to swing. Steel frame all around the door. That was the only way that lead to anything but more disused, locked rooms, though.

So Lisa started to pound the floor, splashing through urine, mashing up her sad little pile of feces.

It would take exactly forever to tunnel out under the door, longer than she had left to live. She could feel herself dying now, going dizzy with the effort of lifting the pipe a few inches and letting it fall. Breathing shallow, tongue too swollen to let out her grunts of exertion even had she the voice to make them.

I'll die on my feet. Thank you, Daddy, for showing me how to be brave by being a coward.

Nothing else to do, so she marched. Her father's corpse stood behind her, trying to get into her body, clawing at her wounds. Elbert's corpse lay in the next room, perhaps rotting gently. And her corpse pounded at the floor, trying to speed up erosion by a factor of thousands.

Twenty Three

Corpses.

It was a dream of corpses that woke him. He hiked through jungle, not feeling the heat, the sweat on his face and chest, not feeling the leaves as they splayed across his exposed skin.

The jungle was abstract.

The dead were concrete.

He hiked, muscles laboring, boots crunching over bones like ashes. Ahead was jungles: vines, creepers, leaves fine and gross. But behind was just corpses.

They stank. Some had flesh, others were just bones. Elbert looked forwards, pressed ever forwards, but he could still see behind himself. Fresh dead lay at his heels, rotten things further back along his trail, and nothing but bones behind them. Piles of bones, great heaped stacks, enough dead to choke any mortuary, all the mortuaries and graveyards and ossuaries on Earth.

Consciousness freed him from the dream but the smell did not recede. The stench of death lingered like the jungle was made of it.

But there was no jungle. That was far behind.

He remembered. Dennis' death, his sacrifice. Leaving his corpse in the hands of the enemy. A day of silent marching. Falling down into the dirt to sleep.

The stench came from a durian plantation off to the east. A big green fruit the size of a melon, it gave off a stink meant to discourage living things from eating it. Elbert was discouraged. Wilcox was awake, heating nasty meat in cans. Elbert wanted none of it. She looked at him, he looked at her. Nothing passed between them.

Dana woke, too. She touched Elbert on the back, familiar, on her way to find a bush.

Floyd stayed down. He snored, the sound like boars rutting.

"Today," Wilcox said. "This is the last day."

Elbert grunted, hitched up his pants. His rifle wanted cleaning so he did that while the others ate, no more conversation attempted. Then they got up, moved on. Not so much marching any more as trudging, defeated.

Sun beat on Elbert's neck and he found himself recalling the first night with Wilcox, sleeping in a hammock under a gentle rain. *Funny what passes for a good day out here.*

There was a compound ahead. Wire fence with bamboo posts, signs in Vietnam's alien script. Small men with guns stood around a gate. They had white helmets with blue symbols on them, Chinese rifles slung over their shoulders so that bayonettes stood in a ragged forest behind them. The fence seemed to stretch around a hole in the ground, a pit.

"What is it?" Elbert said.

"Crater," said Wilcox. "U2 photos make it half a mile across. Old enough to have a forest inside it."

As they approached the gate, a group of the guards came out to meet them. One of them had shiny insignia on his collar, seemed to be in charge. He surprised Elbert by speaking English. "Once you go in there, you go no further," he said. "What you want is in there. If you still want it."

"I want it," Wilcox said, "and I'll get it. Once it's in hand, you probably want to back off the goon squad. We're walking back out of here because it's the only way. I expect safe passage to hold as far as the frontier."

"No promises," said the man. "They find out what you have, all hands will turn against you. I will be going now, and these men with me. We don't want any incidents. Avoid all contact. With everyone. I will help as I can – from a distance. We saw Japanese on the coast this morning, and Germans parachuting in where they thought we could not see them, and the hated French coming through China."

"I'll take my chances." Wilcox waited until the Vietnamese man moved out of her way. He looked like he was going to salute or bow or something, but he only stood aside, turned, walked off. His men followed and soon Elbert, Dana, Floyd and Wilcox were alone at a chain-link gate. There was a padlock but it was open, the chain rusted. Wilcox grabbed it, pulled. The chain slid with a sound like silver coins piling in Judas' hands then clattered to the ground.

She led the way through the gate.

Elbert used trees to keep from going too fast. The hill was steep but shallowed the further they went. Like a hemisphere cut from the ground. The trees were stunted, twisted, tortured. They had leaves with too many lobes, too many veins. The dirt itself was a loamy black but full of squirming white shapes.

"Maggots?" he said.

Nobody answered.

Down into the crater, the horizon close and rising all around him, Elbert became aware of the dread that was always with him now, the fear so close he wouldn't know what to do if it went away. His hackles rose, the skin on the backs of his arms and neck. His scrotum tried to climb back into his body.

Something bad is down there.

He heard his drill instructor's voice in his head: *This is Vietnam, boy. Something bad everywhere. Nothing but goddamn bad. You see something out here that ain't bad you let me know and I'll start on your section fucking eight.*

He was off in his head examining his fear, and that's how she surprised him.

Wilcox had been ahead of him, and then she wasn't, and he didn't notice until she popped out from a tree to his right. She punched him in the chest and he thought his heart stopped. All the breath busted out of him and he dropped.

"What did he give you?" she said.

Elbert couldn't talk, couldn't breathe. He tried to gasp out, "What?"

"Dennis gave you something. I want it."

"Bag," he panted. He doubted the word was intelligible.

Wilcox stripped the pack off his bag, dumped everything out into that crawling, fetid soil. Not much worth having anymore: some boot black, a few ammo boxes, a book of matches. Worn socks and skivvies. Tins of food a dog wouldn't eat. A pill bottle.

She seized on it, snatched it up. Flipped off the lid with one blunt thumb. It was empty.

"What was in it?" she said.

"Don't... know..." He had almost enough wind back to speak like a human. He stood, rubbed his chest. "You could have just asked..."

"What was in it?"

"I don't know, it was empty. I don't know what he was trying to say. He was high all the damn time. Maybe he saw something in there that wasn't."

"What was in it?"

"I don't know what else to tell you," Elbert said.

She tossed it into the trees. Then she grabbed Elbert's shoulder and pushed him ahead. "You aren't getting away from me," she said. "Osho couldn't help you and Dennis couldn't help you."

Elbert struggled to stay on his feet down the steep grade, settled into a shambling half-run until the bottom started to flatten out. He tripped, sprawled, rolled, came up half on his feet. Out of the corner of his eye he saw Dana with her back up against a tree on the downhill side. He stayed crouched longer than he had to, looking anywhere but at her, got up as Wilcox closed in.

"On your feet," she said.

Then Dana hit her from behind. Elbert ducked down again so Wilcox tripped over his back, dropped into the dirt. Elbert kicked her in the top of the head, as hard as he could, like punting a football. It was like kicking a tree trunk, but she yelled and covered her head and rolled over into a defensive ball.

"Run," Dana said.

"No place to run," Elbert said. He unlaced a boot, working fast. Dana pulled a pistol from somewhere, pointed it at the bigger woman. Elbert had one boot off now, and stripped down the sock. Just above the ankle was a ring of surgical tape. He peeled it back, revealing another layer of tape with pills stashed between the two layers. Elbert peeled three off the tape and stuck them in his mouth. "Noplace to run, but at least I can see what I'm running from."

Dana nodded.

Then she died.

Her chest exploded in a gout of blood, a horizontal volcano. Then the sound hit: the boom of an M-60.

Floyd.

Wilcox got up, stared at Elbert. The stare. Elbert just stared back. Her eyes tried to bore into him but something else was trying to bore out. Colors stood out too sharp, the greens and browns all around multiplying like rabbits in a hutch. Wilcox' eyes moved farther and farther apart, a whole universe springing up between them.

"I can see," Elbert said, then he laughed.

***

He saw more than he wanted to.

Everything melted. Wilcox dissolved into a mass of sprouting fungus that split into new fungi and again and again, a meaningless squirming mass of growth and regrowth. The air became spiraling flowers in violet and magenta, lime green and pastel pink. Elbert receded inside his own skull, aware of the shape of his face, his nose usually so familiar a part of his view of the world that it was forgotten but now an intrusion. His eyes could not unify their disparate views and became two individual scopes on the world.

"Get it together."

That was Dennis' voice, but Dennis was dead. He'd died yesterday. Or was it before?

"You're tripping. Stupid shit, you were supposed to do this earlier. Can't help you now, man."

"Shut up, Dennis," Elbert said.

Then Dana stood up. Her corpse stayed on the ground where it had fallen, but she stood there in front of him, and Elbert saw how that could make sense. She said, "Don't listen to him. He's dead. He can't help you now."

"You're not dead?"

"Yes, I am. But I can help you. You have to block up your orifaces."

Wilcox rose up and shook off her mushroom shroud, strode down the hill through flowers that had biting teeth, unperturbed. Floyd followed like a dog that had been kicked once too often. They laughed and it sounded like razor blades falling on tinfoil. "Too late," Wilcox said. "I almost have it, then there's no going back."

"I can't stop them," Elbert said. "I don't even know what I'm supposed to stop them from doing. I just wanted to get away."

"Close your eyes," Dana said. "Stick a tampon in your anus. Cover your ears. He's coming for you."

"If I do all that I can't see. Or hear. I can't fight when She comes back for me. I can't get away."

"You have to," Dana said.

"She is right," said Dennis. "He's right behind you. He has always been right behind you."

Elbert turned, slowly.

Captain Daniels was there, his chest shot out, bare-chested and heaving. He had a sick smile over his face. "I always wanted to kill me some black boys," he said. "I'm gonna do worse than that now, though. I'm gonna rape your mind and steal your body. You like that, boy?"

Elbert didn't know why he thought of it then, but he did. His hand crept as though of its own accord down into the big pocket on his leg. When it came back up between him and Daniels, it had Osho's necklace wrapped around its fingers. "You can't touch me," he said.

Daniels looked pissed. He was all teeth, then, bloody teeth in a gnashing jaw. He attacked.

Dennis got in his way, pushed him off.

Elbert saw who else was behind him, then. A line of them, twelve Vietnamese men. They were shadowy and confused, not clear and bright like Dennis. They barely had faces, the last one in line hardly more than smoke. But he knew all of them. He'd shot them. Looked into their faces and gunned them down. That they were trying to do him the same way didn't count for nothing, not when he dreamed of them some nights.

He looked where Wilcox had stalked off, and behind her was a ragged line of dead men, and some dead women. They marched behind her, down into the crater, stretching back up towards the gate and maybe beyond.

"Oh, god," Elbert said.

"There isn't one," Dana said, "And that's for sure. He wouldn't allow any of this. But there's a devil and Wilcox almost has it."

"Is that why you saved me from her?"

"Don't be stupid," she said. "I just wanted it for myself."

Dennis was losing. Daniels came closer, his fingers brushing Elbert's chest. It felt like ice and pain. He swatted at the spirit with the hand holding the fetish and Daniels recoiled but did not desist.

Down the hill, Wilcox screamed in triumph. "I have it. It's mine! I have it!"

Daniels grew more hideous, sprouting teeth all over, mouths full of dogs' teeth and sharks'. Dennis grew thinner, wispier. Elbert laughed but he didn't feel like laughing. "I'm tripping so hard..." And Daniels took command of the ghosts behind him, marshalled them, sent them against what was left of Dennis.

"I'll have you," he said. "Maybe I'll take your body home and make you watch while I rape your mother with it."

He ate the last of Dennis. With his hands and stomach and face he ate him.

I'm going to die, Elbert thought. *I can win if I die.* He dragged his pistol out of its holster.

"No," Dana said. "No, that's what she wants. She promised Daniels a body, that he could share what she found. He taught her how to... well, you'll see her again in a second, what she did to herself. And he was going to get your body. After you shot him, he couldn't come here himself anymore."

Daniels came a step closer. "She's right. Put down those ears. They aren't yours. They can't help you. Nobody can. Come on, boy, let's get this on." He lurched forward.

Elbert put his gun under his chin. When he pulled the trigger, nothing happened.

Oh god...

Daniels had ahold of him now, started to force his way in.

Let me die. Don't let him have me.

The other spirits, just shadows now, whirled around him. He felt his mind being pushed away, into the back of his skull, away from the influence of the mescaline. Out of physical space where such things mattered. He couldn't resist.

Then Dana hit Daniels just as she'd hit Wilcox minutes before, drove him back. She changed as she charged, becoming not a slender woman but a black stooping thing, all whirling dark full of claws.

"She thought I wasn't bad enough for this," Dana said. "She thought I was naive and she could take me." Elbert didn't know how she was talking. She had no mouth or anything human to speak with. And she grappled with the darkness that was Daniels. "But I fooled her. I'm as bad as she is. As bad as Daniels was, the murderer-cultist. Nearly as bad as you, Elbert."

She laughed and hacked, and soon the only unreal things he could see were the things lined up behind Wilcox.

No, no, that wasn't true. Not entirely. There was the beast herself, coming back up the hill, the marching line now extending back down behind her. Floyd by her side had his own line of Dead.

And neither of them was human.

Voices in the hall, waking her up.

She was asleep in her own filth, mixed in with the concrete she had turned to gravel and powder. A little concavity, an inch or two deep and three feet across by two wide.

I must have collapsed.

The voices were closer. "She said it was a clanging noise, from inside this place?"

"They hear noises in her sometimes. Haunted."

"I'd believe it. Some of the shit I've seen go on."

Two voices, men. Footsteps and clatter came with them – keys and flashlights hanging from belts.

"I don't see anything."

They went past the door, turned and went the other way.

"Help," Lisa said. Or tried to say. Her voice was beyond broken: wrecked, destroyed, desiccated. Her lips oozed something that wasn't blood, a thick syrup that tasted of illness. She tried to lick her lips with a swollen tongue dry as newspaper, tried to cough.

All she could do was lay there.

"Well, we should check out the patient rooms just in case, but I think it's their imagination."

"Or raccoons."

"Or ghosts."

The two voices laughed.

It's a ghost, all right, Lisa thought. She tried again to speak, to shout, to wiggle her finger, but there was nothing left in her. Nothing at all.

Twenty Four

I'm dying.

"I said you would." Dad.

No, really, I'm going to die. Soon.

Silence.

In the dark, she couldn't tell if her eyes were open or not. She'd forgotten about light. The merest tickle of it glimmered from under the door and it was a sunrise.

In her other mind, it was different. Maybe she was dreaming but she didn't know. She only knew she was Elbert at the same time she was herself.

***

Elbert didn't feel good.

His mouth was dry as old newspaper in the sun. His head hurt, a wicked hangover. His teeth ached and his eyes, though squeezed shut in pain and denial, said the room was full of light too bright.

Room?

Someone spoke. Vietnamese. Someone else replied in kind.

I thought they split? Or are these the men I killed?

Someone levered him up so he was sitting rather than laying. There was just dirt under him, no bench or cot. Cold water arrived at his lips in something battered and metal, and he drank it. It tasted like iron, copper, dirt. Like Heaven. He tried to gulp it but it was snatched away before he could get his fill.

"Where am I?"

He thought they only asked that on television, laughed at himself. He tried to crack open an eye but got no cooperation. And no answers. Two men talked over him, more Vietnamese. One tossed a bucket of water over him and only then did he become aware of the stench, of blood and feces and long-soured sweat, of rotted flesh.

Is that me?

And when they tossed linen rags on him, he knew he was naked.

The men went away. Elbert was too weak to dress himself, or complain, or beg for more water. He went to sleep.

I can't be asleep if I went to sleep. Who dreams of sleeping? Is this what it's like to die? I wish I could wake up and die conscious. The last great adventure.

Those were Lisa's thoughts, but Lisa wasn't there to have them. She was Elbert.

She was there in the dream, a triumph of evil. In one hand she had a bit of rock. It looked like any random piece of stone, if said stone had been dipped in chrome. Although that hand hung by her side, her face announced it as though she'd held it over her head: a trophy.

Floyd was there with her. Spectral things gnawed at his neck, hung from his spine. They infested his rifle. One form like an attenuated women stretched from the trigger to his crotch and it was moving, sliding... His face was impassive, joyless.

Floyd was bad; Wilcox was worse.

There wasn't much left of her. His drug-opened eyes saw her spare frame, much like Dana's. Under her skin crawled things of spectral smoke. Her muscles were wasted, shriveled, but they had hold of the long bones. Under her skin was not anatomy but murder.

How many men did she kill, and enslave to her body this way?

Her chest was made of enslaved spirits, and her arms and legs and broad back. She wasn't real, almost none of her was real.

The scar across Wilcox' face hosted a dark thing that leeched and sucked. He could see through it like it wasn't there, but could also see it like it was solid. It was splotchy green and gray, and it heaved and tossed as it fed on whatever was inside Wilcox.

Floyd saw Elbert was still alive. He smiled, then, but there was still no joy. His face might as well have stayed blank. "Kill him?" he said.

"Daniels didn't take him. Stupid bastard. Always too much talk and gloating." Wilcox didn't even look Elbert's way, but he couldn't miss the way she directed her triumph his was. "Just leave him. He's no good to anyone, now."

Elbert still had his own gun out, pointed under his own chin. But it was dry.

***

Now I understand, Elbert. I get it now.

I've seen that stone before, that chrome-dipped piece of rock.

That's what you came here for. Because where that thing goes, so does madness. So does your Alice Wilcox.

She opened her eyes, knew they were open. There was enough light under the door to see faintly by, and Lisa wondered how she could ever have thought it was completely dark.

She levered herself up to her feet. Slowly, achingly; a night passed out in a pool of fluid in the cold had done little good to her joints. She felt like an old woman.

I'm ready now. I know what I'm dealing with. It's time to get out of here.

She picked up the bed part. Smashed it against the door. She would never, ever dig her way out of here, but someone would hear. And this time she would make noise as they passed by.

***

They came. She guessed it took an hour, but they came.

She heard keys in the lock of the main door. Footsteps, running now as she kept up her racket. The deadbolt slid and chunked and then the big steel door opened away from her. She fell out of the cell, into the cold hallway, naked and wet and filthy.

"Holy shit."

She rolled over to see who was talking. A guard. Not a safety officer but one of the security guards from the office wing. She might have seen him before.

"Lady, how long have you been in there?"

She gurgled something up at him. Tried to stand.

"Forget it, Jeff. I don't think she's in any shape to talk. Go in the cabinet back there, see if they left any blankets. Or go across to Children's and get some. I'll call an ambulance." He talked into a radio clipped to his epaulet.

Lisa got to her knees, braced hands on the wall, almost stood.

Then she fell.

Strong hands reached under her knees, her back, and lifted her off the cold tiles. Hanrahan. Hanrahan had come for her, after all.

"I had a dream about you," he said. "No, don't try and talk. It was your father, all dressed up in a bus driver uniform or something. Medals and stuff. Do bus drivers get medals?" He carried her towards the door. Some threw a blanket over her, tucked it in around her. She could hear sirens in the distance. "He said he loved you and you were in trouble."

He hates me. Don't trust him.

She wanted to stop being afraid. Here it was: liberation. Wilcox had failed. It was over, Lisa was out, free.

But it wasn't done. Not yet.

***

"Her blood pressure is total shit, Jim."

Jim? No, not her Jim. Common name. This guy was young, Hispanic.

"Totally dehydrated. Surprised she's alive," Jim said. "Check her QT interval when you get a chance. I'll start an emergency IV. No good if she checks out on us now."

They worked on her like she wasn't there, like it was just her body. That was all right. She was leaving, anyway. Elbert needed her.

***

Something splashed into the dirt near his feet. Drops bounced and hit his toes. Warmish. It smelled almost like food. Or dishwater left in a sink overnight.

Elbert rolled off his back, onto one side, and shuddered. Too weak. He was still naked, but now he was naked in the dark. One eye creaked open, all but audibly. Then the other.

He was in a hole in the ground. Above, bamboo bars prevented him from leaving – or standing all the way up, if he thought he could stand. He had just enough room to lay without bending his knees, and half that room in the other direction. Down there by his feet was a metal pot as big as his fist with a puddle vaguely near it.

He lay and contemplated the new dimensions of his universe, tired of sleeping but hardly capable of movement. Time went by but how much of it he could not have said. Then a guard came by overhead, just a shadow in flickering torchlight (Elbert shivered, became gooseflesh). The guard stopped over his pit, dunked a dipper into a bucket of water, and poured the water into what passed for a cell. Again he was somewhat close to the tin cup down there.

Someone screamed. Near, far, Elbert had no idea. There was a world beyond the bars but it was unreal. Only the dirt under his face was really real. The screaming went on for a long time, almost until sunrise. It took that long for Elbert to understand the game:

If I want to eat, I have to catch broth in my bowl. If I want to drink water, I have to drink the soup fast, then catch water in the bowl. And they will not say when those things are coming. So, if I want to eat or drink, I can't sleep.

As the torchlight was subsumed in the growing light of day, Elbert contemplated whether he wanted to eat or drink.

If I die, will I be tied to this place forever, until I'm worn too ragged? Or will I be slaved to some person, doomed to follow around a murderer all the days of their life? Are there still things behind me, following me because I killed their bodies? Not Floyd, please not dead-ass, fish-eyed Floyd. Would dying set them all free?

Would it set me *free?*

The sun got high in the sky, high enough that its rays came directly through the bamboo bars and landed on Elbert's skin. He cooked slowly in the light, sweated. Soon the heat became painful. Finally, Elbert found the motivation to move, to roll onto his back. The linen rags re-entered awareness as he rolled onto them. He moved around, crawled into the clothing. It helped with the sun a little, what little it covered.

Then he investigate the puddles down by his cup.

They had dried up and smelled unappetizing. Maggots squirmed in the soil there (The dirt itself was a loamy black but full of squirming white shapes), drawn to the few scraps of meat in the broth, the hints of protein. He wondered if maggots were edible. He'd heard stories, about people stuck in these pits. The Hanoi Hilton, they called this place, all these places. Eventually, they said, you ate the maggots or spiders or worms or whatever else you could find in the dirt.

Above, screaming started up again. And whimpering.

Came night again, after an eternity of screaming, and a guard walked by with a bucket. This time, Elbert had his cup ready. He caught some of the weak broth, a chunk of something green he hoped was a vegetable.

He'd found something inside as he listened to the man screaming above. He'd found hate. *I'm going to make her scream like that*, he thought. *I'm going to find that bitch, whatever she is, wherever she is, and I'm going to make her scream. Just... like...*

***

I'm free now but he's still trapped.

"You aren't free yet," her father said. "Look. You're handcuffed to the bed right here."

Handcuffed?

He was right. Both her hands were chained to bed rails. There were tubes in her right arm, bandages all over – white and hard and sterile. Her finger ached more than anything else. Morphine in a drip bag kept her consciousness sketchy and the pain bearable.

"She's awake."

Two cops by the bedside, visible only when she looked right at them. A man and a woman, both stocky. Bullet-proof vests. Behind them only darkness, the darkness of the seclusion room, the abandoned unit.

"We need some information," the female asked. Lisa couldn't read her name tag. "Where were you the night of the eighth?"

She couldn't talk. Lisa had no voice at all and less will to try it.

"You could wait for a lawyer," the male said. "In fact, I'd advise it. It would look bad for you, though. And this is mostly a formality. You have to look at it from our perspective."^t

She stayed quiet, unable to do anything more.

The woman took up the narrative. "Locked in an abandoned building, covered in blood and excrement, and you were the last living person to see her alive."

To see who?

"I'm not sure she's really with us yet," the male said.

"Or she's playing dumb. Murder your therapist, abduct a patient, lock yourself into a cell like that. Pretty crazy."

"That's not what the private guy said."

"Whatever. Those old retired guys, like to think they know everything."

The male again: "Well, the nurse at her work did say she was into the psych meds."

"Crazy bitch. Well, when she wakes up for real, we'll nail her ass to the wall."

"See?" said her father. "You aren't free. You won't ever be free. You'll wish you had died in there. Look what you fought so hard for. A cell in a hospital to escape your cell in the hospital. And I'll always be here behind you."

Yeah. Yes, you'll always be there behind me. But you won't be in me. That's what Elbert was trying to say. The spirits that follow you, they want to possess you, to take you over. Using your guilt and shame, they want to become you. Look out through your eyes.

But her father was outside. Could have climbed in through her wounds, but he never did.

Because of Elbert, Elbert protecting her. Elbert had climbed in but had not taken over. That's why she had his dreams.

Elbert needs me. He isn't free yet. I can't be free until Elbert is.

***

The gun hadn't fired. It was dry, a dry round.

He could still get them to do the job though. He turned the pistol, pointed it right at Floyd. Wilcox had dumped her machine-gun someplace, the thing in her hand a more potent weapon maybe. So he'd threaten Floyd and get Floyd to cap him. And if that sent him to hell or bound him to Floyd forever, well, didn't he deserve it? And could it be worse than this?

So he pointed, pulled the trigger while Floyd raised his own weapon. He was so surprised when this pistol fired that he fumbled it, juggled it, dropped it. While he was bobbling the gun, Floyd died. The bullet went through his neck and he fell down, dead before gravity was done with him. When Elbert looked up, Floyd's blood pressure had equalized and he soaked out into the soil, all the drama missed in a distraction.

The things all over him, they detached slowly, turned to face Elbert. Not all of them had faces, but they had hungry smiles. Wicked smiles. Like guys in prison who just realized one of them is the cop who busted them.

Wilcox just laughed. "Saves me the trouble," she said. Then she looked at Floyd's corpse, and all the monsters around it sort of faded. They didn't disappear or go away, but they just thinned, like a blanket washed one time too many. "I'll be seeing you around, Elbert." She walked past him, up the hill, out of the crater.

By the time he thought to check if he had any rounds left, she was gone.

Then the dream morphed. He got drugs again from Rice, watched him shoot Daniels. Then he went back, back to basic training. Drills sergeants. He was asleep in the barracks with two dozen other guys, and the drill sergeant came through banging trash can lids, only there were MPs with him. They were coming to arrest him.

They cuffed him, pushed him along a path towards a bridge. The Edmund Pettus Bridge. Four thousand black folk massed on this side, ready to cross. The MPs shoved him ahead, made him stagger into the group, then they backed off. He didn't want to cross, not like this. He knew what was waiting on the other side: a bunch of rednecks with guns and billy-clubs. Hoses, pipes, ropes.

The group started walking and he walked with them, drawn along by the mass of people like a planet is drawn along behind a star. When the violence got going, it all happened by the script. He'd read the papers. No TV news out here, but the papers were grim enough.

The cops, they didn't try to get him. He was a ghost on that bridge on that day, just a bad spirit. They beat everyone they could reach, whoever didn't run fast enough. Blood everywhere. And he ran up to one of the cops, said, *do it, beat me. I deserve it.*

The cop said, "Not you, MacAvoy. You're on our side."

When he woke up, he knew.

"You're a black one," she'd said – but she hadn't meant his skin. She'd known, seen into him, even then.

"Turns out I was right. You're exactly the man I need."

The kind of man who would do cold-blooded murder, evil enough to drag along an evil spirit through miles and miles of jungle. *Wilcox was bad*, he thought. *And Dana, and Floyd, Dennis, even Osha. Daniels was evil from top to bottom. But me, I've been the worst of us.*

"I know what's being sacrificed," she had said. He thought he had known, too, but he hadn't.

He woke up, and, awake, he knew.

***

"I know," he said. Outside was dark again, torches holding back the mosquitos more than the dark. "I understand. I'm ready now."

Groans from all around, other men down in holes, waiting their turn to be tortured. Wishing they could sleep.

Quieter now, he said, "She didn't want us to call you names. Gooks or slopes or the Cong, even. Because she wanted us to know what we were doing. Those white guys with billy-clubs, even they were better than me. Because they convinced themselves we were animals, that we deserved it.

"But me... I killed people I knew were people. Boys, only, some of them. For what? To keep myself alive? I could have just gone to jail, man. I could have said no, and just gotten locked up.

"I've been a coward, a weak man. I knew about Daniels and I did nothing – I knew they were little girls, someone's little girls, and I let it happen so I'd have leverage."

"Shut up," someone shouted from nearby.

"I did it all," Elbert said. "I'm guilty of all of it. I am the sinner, the original sinner, who does bad and keeps doing bad and worse. None of you did worse than I did. I thought it was just the drugs..."

"Shut up," said another voice.

A soldier came and stood over him. Elbert grabbed the bars, levered himself into a crouch. "Take me next," he said. "You have to torture someone, torture me. I'm guilty of all of it. Everything they did, I did, and I meant it. I knew what I was doing. Let me take their place."

The soldier unlaced his pants, pulled out his pizzle, and pissed down into the hole. It splashed, hot and fragrant, on Elbert's face. In his eyes and hair, all over the linen shirt they'd given him. He gagged and jumped back.

When the guard walked off, chuckling, Elbert sat in the corner, half-defeated. Stripped off the shirt, used it to wipe himself off as best he could. Then he thought, tried to hold onto ideas that wanted to scamper away as he considered them.

Twenty Five

Lisa woke up again, glanced around the room with bleary eyes. She wanted to rub them but she couldn't: her hands were still chained to the bedrails.

There was a man overflowing the blue vinyl chair standard to hospital rooms. He had on a wrinkled suit coat the size of a circus tent.

"Hanrahan?"

"You sound like crap, Doctor Jayne."

"I do." But she sounded like something, which was a net gain in her book. "Why am I chained down?"

"Well, probably you'd best talk to a lawyer about that, Ma'am."

"A lawyer?"

"I'm not qualified to discuss the facts of the case with you. Or, um, anything. I'm sorry, though. For your loss."

"My loss?" She tried to sit up, couldn't work up the strength or the leverage.

Hanrahan picked up a controller from her bedside and pushed a button. The bed lifted at the head, eased her into an inclined position. But she was too low for it to be comfortable, bending at the chest instead of the waist. "I guess I shouldn't say any more. I'm sorry. I thought you knew."

"Hilde?"

"That was her name, yeah."

"I dreamed Elbert killed her. Help me sit up. Properly, not like this."

Hanrahan stood up, mountainous, put his hands on her sides and slid her higher up in the bed. Then his giant hands slid up to her chest where they groped and squeezed.

Lisa scrambled back, held in place by the cuffs as well as weakness. "What the fuck are you doing?"

"You know I was a cop once, right?" His hands moved down her body, over her hips, to her thighs. "Back in ninety-two, a bust went bad. Should've been routine, you know? Slap the cuffs on him, get him safely in the car. Drugs were on him, everything was a go."

"Get your hands off me, Hanrahan."

"Wish you'd call me Pete," he said, hands moving to her crotch now. "I got the guy out of the car, no problem, hands on the hood, cuffs in my hand." He found what he wanted, touched gently. Lisa tried to recoil, thrashed, squeezed her legs together, but he was four times her size. "But another guy came around the corner. Had a gun in his hand. Nothing I could do. They had the drop on me. I got shot in the shoulder, but the wrong shoulder. Pulled out my revolver, put both guys down.

"Anyway, I got a psycho discharge after that. Went private."

"Get the fuck off me, Hanrahan. Peter. Stop it, get off me."

"Shh. If you make too much noise a nurse will come, then I'll have to kill her."

"What the fuck are you doing?" Lisa said, almost shouted, through gritted teeth.

"She said I could have what was left when she was done with you. But I don't think there's going to be much left. Not enough to have any fun with." He took his hands away, put them under his nose and inhaled deeply. "Shame. But I killed those men. That's how she gets in – through the guilt. Through the dead ones you drag around with you. That's how she'll get into you."

Tears stung Lisa's eyes and her face burned, her neck. She wanted to throw up but there was nothing inside her, nothing at all. "I liked you, Peter," she said.

"That's what she said." He reached out to touch her again and she spat on him, weak, foamy spit from a mouth dry as a sponge that's been left too long on the counter. His hand stopped where it was, deviated course for the handcuff on her right hand. Across her body from him. He grabbed hold of the chain and pulled upwards. The hardened steel chain came apart in his hand like it was made of spun sugar.

She used her suddenly free hand to claw at Peter's face, surging for his eye and missing. She got his cheek, left it welted. He ignored her, snapped the other chain. She slapped, punched, kicked at him, and he just absorbed it all. Lifted her from the bed like a grown man lifts a child. She just wasn't strong enough to do so much as inconvenience him.

Weeping and sobbing, she put her hands around his neck and squeezed for all she was worth.

"I wish you were stronger," Hanrahan said. "I really do. I deserve every bit of it, Doctor Jayne, every last bit. If you only knew me..."

He opened the door with the hand under her knees, stepped out into an empty hallway. No cops, no guards, no nurses. The hallway was empty, the nursing station was empty. The elevator opened with an electric hum and slid quietly shut as they stepped in. It was empty, too. As was the lobby, the garage.

Cars were parked in the stinking, soggy dark, filling up all the spaces between the white lines. Only one moved, though: a big black Lincoln SUV. The weak overhead lights gleamed in its rich paint as it rumbled closer, stopped alongside Hanrahan. He opened the back door, put Lisa gently on the back seat, climbed in next to her. Even the roomy truck was a tight fit for him. His stubbly hair brushed the ceiling.

Lisa kicked at him, struggled for the door handle on her side, but the locks thunked into place and the truck started rolling ahead.

***

Lisa sat up, tried to get the paper gown she was wearing to cover more of her body. Peter ogled her from the other seat and shame heated her skin. There were two people in the front seats. From her position she could see Killroy on the passenger side, dressed in his usual checked suit and bowtie. The driver was visible only where his body extended around the oversized seat.

He wasn't as tall as Hanrahan or as well-rounded, but he was big. Body-builder big, with leathery brown skin marked by dozens of scars. She could see the edges of his shoulders and the backs of his triceps and they looked like an anatomy lesson, or a relief map of Mars.

"You're going to straight up fry for this, Jim," Lisa said. She wanted to sound angry, strong, confident, but she just about squeaked.

"Oh, I know, Lisa." Killroy stared straight ahead. He had that metal thing in his left hand, the thing that looked like a meteorite dipped in chrome. "And I think I shall still come out of this better than you shall. I'm so sorry. I think it's time you met the architect of all this mayhem, dear."

"I have the same training as you, Jim. You know what my answer to that has to be."

"Refusal to participate until we start acting sane? Perhaps pull over and let you out? Quite right, dear, exactly correct. Except we're not demanding anything of you. Just revealing to you some truths." He turned his head now, not towards Lisa but towards the driver of the vehicle. "This, dear, is Alice."

Lisa's mind went blank. She searched for a reason for that name to make sense. For a way to square the feminine name with the masculine physique she could see.

"Alice? Like as in Wonderland?" she said, groping for meaning.

"As in Wilcox," the driver said. "Colonel Wilcox, United States Army." Her voice was guttural, female but unfeminine.

"No, you're dead. You evil fucking bitch, you're dead."

Wilcox laughed. "Call me a ghost, then. If you want to believe in things like ghosts. This here old fellow is my murderer."

"Ativan following a restraint episode," Killroy said. "I knew it was risky, but there weren't many other choices."

Hanrahan turned his head to follow the conversation, looking now at the back of Killroy's head. Lisa watched him watching. "So she's dead, like my father. My father talks to me sometimes, but he can't drive a Navigator."

"Your father," Wilcox said, "doesn't have the grumlet. Or the will to use it. I've heard him talk, knew his kind. When the going gets tough, some men are just quitters. But I have the will. I went out there and found it, found the grumlet, had the knowledge and the spirit to use it. I've been waiting, and now I'm back."

"Waiting for what?" Lisa said.

"For someone depraved enough but guilty enough, with just the right body. So that I can be them. Old Killjoy here is on his last legs. Cancer. Did he tell you that? I never wanted to be a man anyway, always distracted by that bit of dangling flesh between his legs. But I have the right candidate now."

"Who?" Lisa said, but she knew the answer. She shifted around, slowly, put her back to the door. With one hand behind her back, she fumbled for the lock.

"I think you know that," Wilcox said.

"I want Jim to tell me. Tell me, Jim. How can you help her do this?"

"How can I resist her?" Killroy said and, as he spoke, Hanrahan's head turned to follow the conversation.

As he looked away, Lisa popped the lock on the door – it thunked open. She grabbed the handle, pulled up, pushed out. Used her feet against Hanrahan, lurched out into the brightly-lit morning, head first towards the pavement.

But a hand on her leg stopped her movement.

Hanrahan dragged her back inside. "I'm sorry, Doctor Jayne. You should have squeezed harder. If only you had squeezed harder."

***

It was dark in the back of the truck. The windows were tinted down so far Lisa had trouble seeing where they were going. Since her escape attempt, Hanrahan had her wrapped up against his body with one flabby-strong arm, her feet extended across the back seats. They almost touched the door on that side. She thought about using her foot to try and hook the door handle, mostly to distract herself from Hanrahan's giant hand squeezing her right breast.

Shame and disgust fought for dominance of her stomach, but they both wanted to make her puke.

Then she recognized a building, a parking lot. They went around the hospital to the rear, the loading docks. "There'll be people. Someone will see, and they'll come get me out again."

Wilcox grunted. "You know better than that by now. Elbert tried to tell you. Time is ambiguous around us. We can slip in between normal events, slip out again. I've been slipped out for a decade. And if you aren't very, very good, I'll let your meaty friend there do his own kind of slipping in."

Lisa thought about struggling. She wasn't an athlete, though. Not strong of body. And soft self-defense techniques weren't getting her out of this, the therapeutic holds and evasions meant to prevent harm to and from patients.

"Why here?" she said.

"This place? I like it," Wilcox said. "This is where we warehouse the worst humanity has to offer."

"The patients? They're just mad."

"Them, some. Madness doesn't prevent guilt but is a product of it. I mean you, though."

"Me?"

"The doctors, nurses. The people who should help but control instead. Medications, electro-convulsive therapy, restraint rooms. Might as well be a Chinese brain-washing camp. Some of you are much sicker than them."

Lisa shut her eyes. "I'm not ashamed of trying to help."

"No," Wilcox said. "No, and that's your depravity talking. But you are ashamed of failing. Day in and day out, the same people in through the revolving doors. Drugs and failures and more drugs and restraints and more drugs." She laughed then, delighted. "But I'll show you how to take control. Really take it. You aren't going to like that."

The truck bumped over a curve, into the shadow of the loading dock. Killroy and Wilcox got out. Both came around to Hanrahan's side. Wilcox opened the door. Lisa made a last-ditch, desperate effort to pull free of Hanrahan, to slide out towards the other door. He just ignored her, dragged her out onto her feet.

Lisa bit his forearm as hard as she could, kneed him in the crotch, spent the last of her energy trying to break away.

Even at full strength, though, it would have been totally hopeless.

He pulled her along like a man handles a tantrumming child, stowing her under one arm. A piece of luggage. They went in through the loading dock, along abandoned hallways rich in institutional paint and fluorescent light, back to the abandoned unit.

The cell stank. Broken concrete and the broken bed lay just as she had left them. Wilcox didn't even bother taking away the bent bed part Lisa had stripped down as a weapon, a tool, just had Hanrahan toss her in there.

She listened to the bolt shoot home. It was a final sort of sound, like a gavel.

Lisa rushed forward, pounded on the door, screamed and kicked. Just like the first time. And, like that time, it was totally and completely futile.

***

"You might as well do it," her father said.

She had a flake of concrete in her hand. It was too brittle to make an effective cutting tool. Suicide by flaked concrete could be very messy and take a really long time.

"What else is there to do?" he said. "I would step in for you, take you over. I would do your suffering for you. Only you've got that soldier in there protecting you."

"You don't want to protect me," she said.

"Not exclusively for your own good, no," her father said. "Even the dead are selfish."

"What do you want?"

"To exist. To live. To be."

"My body is the only way for you to do that?"

"Yes," he said. "I am real to nobody else."

"Elbert heard your voice."

"Don't think about him."

That was her clue, really. Daddy said only unhelpful things. In essence, he was the door guard who always lied. If he said stop, she should go; if he said black, she knew the answer was white.

So, Elbert.

Are you there, Elbert? Inside somewhere?

The dark stayed dark and the silence stayed silent. Her father scratched and clawed at her back but she ignored him; at least it wasn't Hanrahan groping her absently.

Elbert, I need you.

"Selfish bitch," her father said. "So selfish. You didn't give me those drugs to help me die with dignity, but to let you witness my death with dignity. You couldn't handle it. The blood, the bloody vomit, the weakness and starvation. You couldn't handle seeing me that way again, starved, sweating, exhausted."

She thought about it. When he had come home from the war, he'd been thin as a willow switch. He was only young then but there were deep lines around his eyes, deep as wounds. He slept on the couch, couldn't handle her mother's touch. And he woke up screaming two nights out of three.

"They hurt you," she said. "They tried to take something away from you."

"No."

"Meaning yes. And you didn't want to let cancer take it from you again. For years I thought it meant you didn't love me, didn't love life. But I understand now. Maybe." She leaned back against the wall, tossed the bit of concrete away from herself. If pinged off the bed with a resonating note. "You loved life. Enough to suffer for it. But what life offered you was unlife. A hopeless life. Needless suffering.

"Daddy, I love you. And you wanted me to do it. You needed me to do it. Because you could take it. You took it in the Gulf, and you could take it from cancer. But you knew I couldn't. Not after Mama. You didn't kill yourself for you."

"I did. Just for me."

"Liar."

He stayed quiet. Lisa stood, moved around the room a little – carefully, carefully.

"You're right," she said. Time had passed but, here in the never-changing dark, time was ambiguous. It might have been tomorrow or yesterday or nineteen sixty-eight. "I'm being selfish. A selfish bitch."

"Sometimes the truth lies," he said.

"And sometimes there is truth in a lie."

"Don't do it."

"Now I know I have to," she said. "Thank you, Daddy. Thank you for everything. I love you. I would have suffered for you, you know."

"That's why I had to go. That's why I have to go now."

"Goodbye, Daddy."

Nothing. And nothing and nothing. Lisa stood alone in the dark amidst the wreckage she had made of the place, the unseen turmoil and chaos, and sobbed.

When she was done, later, she turned her voice inwards again.

Elbert. Elbert, you need me.

Twenty Six

Mornings came and went, days and nights behind them. Elbert sat in dirt, mud when it rained. He collected water when the guards dispensed it, soup when they poured that down into the cell. Wiped himself with disintegrating linen rags when they pissed on him, and dug a trench against one wall to contain his own wastes.

Outside, men screamed.

Every day a new voice. He didn't know how many men were kept here, how many neighbors he had. He couldn't tell if any of the voices were repeated. They almost never said any words, and that was the worst: it meant no questions were asked, and pain was given for its own sake. He knew only that tomorrow's voice would not be the same as today, and today was not the same as yesterday.

Rain fell. Sun shone. Weight sloughed off Elbert's body.

Let me be next. Take me next.

The guards never came for him. Elbert just rotted slowly in his hole in the ground, prematurely buried in a hole they hadn't even bothered to fill in properly.

One day, there was a change.

When he woke up, his face full of sun, the sky was plain and open. No bars cast shadows across his eyes. Elbert stood just for the novelty of doing so, his back creaking and cracking into position.

His view might have been of hell.

Open pits stretched away for hundreds of yards. Each had a bamboo cage standing open. Some of the grates stood vertical, pointing at the cloudless sky; others lay half across other pits. Padlocks littered the ground. And all around, men stood in their holes, peering about like subterranean animals afraid of the sky.

They had short hair and long, smooth faces and beards, tans and pallor. What they had in common was a haunted look a gauntness that was nothing to do with privations of these pits.

They were all afraid to move. "It's a trick," one man whispered, and it sounded loud as the crack of a rifle in the night. "It's a trick. They're watching. They'll punish us."

He was one of the bearded ones, with flyaway hair across his face.

They never even took me, Elbert thought. *My number never came up.*

"She should have killed me," he said out loud. Whisper-quiet, gunshot loud. All faces turned to him, regarded him the way that thing had, the thing under the tree. He hadn't seen it, not then, but he'd felt its touch and dreamed of its face, its teeth. The cold, the dread, the hunger: all in their faces. Behind their withered lips and cracked eyes.

"I'm guilty," he said now. "I'm guilty for all of you. For all of them, too. I accept it. I'm guilty."

"Not for me," one man said.

"It's mine," said another. "It's mine and you can't take it."

"Yeah." A third man. "It's all I got left, man."

"I'm guilty," Elbert repeated. "I'm guilty for you and you're guilty for me. All of us, together. We're guilty."

"Let's just get out of here," said the first one.

"They'll know," said another.

"So what?" said Elbert. "We're all guilty. Let them punish us. But they can't keep me from wanting it. From wanting to be free, to live in the sun. The door is open and I'm leaving until they stop me. They can't make me want to stay here."

"I'm guilty," one man said, and Elbert couldn't keep track anymore of who was talking. Two more people said it, then another and another, and then they were all saying it. Climbing out of their holes in the Earth, struggling upwards, gaining their feet like toddlers. Staggering, all in one direction by unspoken agreement. "I'm guilty. I'm guilty."

Elbert was the freshest of them, the strongest. He led the way. Along a path between bamboo stands, over a rise, through an abandoned village made of mud and sticks and thatch. Past a concrete tower with machine-guns roped to a ceiling joist. Nobody was there to cut him down.

Nobody was anywhere.

He was alone. All his companions had fallen behind, fallen. They were gone. He was alone in the world.

The place got dark, the early sun moving backwards, setting, making the world a tunnel. A tunnel, groping-dark, with a door at the end.

A big steel door with a dead-bolt as thick as his thumb. It stank of shit and sour sweat.

Don't we all? He thought.

He reached out for the door.

***

The door opened. It squeaked a little, came to rest against the wall.

Whoever had come had brought no light. Lisa waited quietly against the back wall, relaxed. Sanguine, almost.

"Time is ambiguous down here," she said. "In the dark. You can't tell what time it is. How much has passed."

"Are you ready, then?" Wilcox said. Lisa heard her crunch across broken concrete, shuffle around the busted bed.

"Yes. I'm ready for you."

Wilcox grabbed her by the front of her shirt, hoisted her up to her feet. Lisa could feel the rock in one of Wilcox' hands, bundled up with shirt and fingers all against her chest. "I'm going to take you now. Hanrahan was right to get what he could while he could. I'm not going to leave him anything."

"He's dead anyway, isn't he?"

"Of course he is. I was done with them. You know, he tried to stop it. I let the big dumb bastard frag the old man, then I knocked him over and kicked him in the teeth so hard they'll never identify him through his dental records."

"I forgive you," Lisa said. She was crying and smiling at the same time, terrified but also completely sure. *Maybe this is the end, maybe I'm going to die now or something worse. But I can handle it.* "I forgive you."

"What?"

"I forgive you. You poor mad thing, just driven crazy. War is hell, as they say, and that's where you live. I'm as guilty as you are, though. Because we're the same thing, in the end, aren't we? I'm you and you're me."

"In a few minutes, yes," Wilcox said. She pulled Lisa up closer, face to face, rank breath spilling across Lisa's teeth. "And your forgiveness won't change anything. It's not my guilt that makes this work, you idiot. It's yours."

"Oh, I know," Lisa said. "I know that, Alice. Poor Alice. I forgive you anyway."

"I don't care."

"Doesn't matter, dear. I forgive you, but he doesn't."

"What?"

That's when Elbert hit her with the pipe, the tubular steel bed support. It made a noise like an axe into a hollow log. Wilcox' face smashed into Lisa's, whose head hit the wall behind her, and the two went down in a chaos of limbs and torsos to rival the wreckage already present. One sound was lost in the noise, an important sound.

Elbert stepped around behind them, hit Wilcox again. Right between neck and shoulder. The pipe dented with the effort, the strain. He hit her once more.

Then she stood up, slow, stable, inexorable. He hit her twice more as she rose and turned around. Another swing, and she caught the pipe in one hand. It came loose from Elbert's grip like nothing at all. Wilcox tossed it aside, contempt invisible on her face in the dark but felt by everyone. The pipe clattered and clanged into the corner, spent.

"I've been waiting for you, Elbert," Wilcox said.

"Have you?"

"Yes. What else do you think this was all for? I missed you in 'Nam. You ruined everything. Those fucking gooks interfered, took you away before I was ready. You killed her, Dana Smith. She was going to be my ride out of there. But now you're here, I'll take you."

"Language," Elbert said. "What happened to honored enemies?"

"You figured that all out forever ago, didn't you?"

"Yes," he said. "So let's get on with it."

Lisa spoke from behind her. "Hey. Hey, you forgot something."

Wilcox turned in the dark. "What?"

"This."

And light crept into the room, illuminating first Lisa's hand, then her arm and body, and then Wilcox. Elbert was lost in the shadow behind her, and other shadows grew around the walls, thrown by the busted bed, the bodies.

"You dropped it," Lisa said. "When Elbert hit you. You dropped it on the floor and I picked it up."

"Give it back."

"Take it."

Wilcox reached out a hand, tentative, almost shy. "Why is it doing that?"

"Glowing?"

"Yes."

"It never glowed for you, did it?" Lisa said.

"No." She reached more, almost brushed it with her fingertips.

"They're all here," Lisa said. "I can see them. Sometimes hallucinations are of real things. They're all around. Osho. Dennis. Floyd. Dana and Elbert. My Daddy. Oh, those men – I don't know their names, but there's a lot of them, the ones from the jungle. Whoever got in your way, or Elbert's, or anyone's."

Wilcox withdrew her hand an inch, two. Glanced around the room. The strewn, empty room. "They can't hurt me."

"They couldn't. So long as you had this thing."

Wilcox started to panic, snatched for the thing, the rock. The bit of chrome dipped in light. Lisa let her take it. It shone out from between her fingers, still bright. Brighter. Blinding now, painful. So much light the walls around them disappeared in it. They were washed away into bright, brilliant sunshine.

All around, now, were dead people. Men, women, all wounded. Faces lost, arms or legs lost, chests open and sucking, skin torn like clothing after Biblical mourning. They pressed closer and closer, twenty of them, sixty, a hundred. A world full of them.

"But I have it. I have it, all its power. Its mine. You're all mine." Wilcox turned in a staggering circle, brandishing the thing at them.

"No," Lisa said. "No, you never had it. It always had you. See, I worked it all out. It isn't my shame that binds me and makes me obedient. It's yours."

"I'm guilty," Elbert said, just a face now in the crowd. "I'm guilty for all you have done. I participated, I knew, I failed to forgive. I'm guilty. They never took me. I'm guilty."

And another. "I did it. I did it all."

Floyd. "You made me do it, you made me rape him, but I wanted to. I'm guilty."

Dennis. "I did it. I skinned that man. I killed that staff sergeant. I'm guilty."

A chorus of men, dead men, dead women. I'm guilty. I did it. I share the blame. It's mine, and it's all I have left. You can't take it from me.

"She lies," Elbert said. "The living always lie, the dead only tell the truth. It's all we got, man. She lied. I forgive you. And you lied, too, because you forgot you were dead."

"No," Wilcox said, shrinking, growing frail and deflated, gray and haggard. "No, I meant it."

"Doesn't matter," Elbert told her. Dana told her. A Vietnamese man told her. A child told her. "Doesn't matter that you meant it, it's still a lie. It does matter. We forgive you, and that does matter. We forgive you because we're guilty, and only the guilty can forgive."

"I forgive you," Lisa said, lost somewhere in the sea of corpses.

And then she was alone again.

*****

Time is ambiguous, down here in the dark.

The door was open, she knew that. The place stank like corpses, and shit, and the door was open. There was a way out. Through the corpses and filth, across the disaster that was this broken room.

"I'm afraid."

Nobody answered her.

She was alone. Elbert was gone, Wilcox was gone. How long? Sixty years, or just sixty seconds?

What's the difference?

And still, no answer. No voices in the dark.

After a while, she got up from the floor. She was sticky with blood and worse, fragrant with grass cuts, mosquito bites, sunshine and darkness. But she got up, picked her way cross the room to the door. Terrified it would be shut, locked, barred. She reached out for where it would be, solid and cold and made of steel.

Her fingertips brushed the metal. Her heart, empty of hope, sank down into her stomach as she sank down to her knees.

She rested her head against the door.

And it swung open.

Unbolted, unlatched.

I can leave whenever I want, she thought.

In the common room, light spilled in around the blinds, cold winter light or maybe spring in the morning, or maybe a rainy June afternoon. The blinds obscured all but the fact of the light, white, cold.

I can leave whenever I want to.

Other Titles by Jason Dias:

Fiction:

The Girlfriend Project
For Love of Their Children (Part 1 of Because of Her
Shadow)
Half-Lives
What Hope Wrought

Non-Fiction:

Values of Pain

https://www.amazon.com/-/e/B00K2EQQIY

Turn the page for a preview of For Love of Their
Children.

Prologue of For Love of Their Children

Children surrounded her. None of them were hers, but she loved them all the same. She strode past two boys who could be twins, brown and lean, with dark hair and downcast eyes. They chiseled at a rock that would outlast them by thousands of years. They were old enough for clothes, just sack cloth tied around their waists with tufts of hemp. When her eyes left them, she heard them sigh, just the barest wisp of breath, a secret relief.

It did not do to attract the attention of the Masters.

Dirt, sand and gravel slid and crunched under her sandals. The Master let her fingers trail along one of the orange blocks, the one to her right. It would eventually be part of a magnificent tomb. The Great Ones would find their immortality beneath such stones. For the children, though, there were only shallow mass graves, anonymity in dust.

The blocks made a valley, a place of cool shade. More of the older, stronger children were here, working with chisels or antlers to square off blocks that got more complete the farther she walked. At the end of this lane, naked children worked in the full harshness of the sun with sticks and cloths to polish away the last imperfections, to make the blocks immaculate. Nothing less would do for the chosen of the Gods, those who would ascend after their deaths.

The Master turned left at the end of the row, around the corner and out of the stone valley. On this side, the sun raged against the side of the quarried blocks and the weaker children, the expendable ones, worked with inferior tools. These were the ones not born to be slaves, the ones captured in the outlands and sold for profit. She loved them, too. She loved them all. Hordes of them labored here and the noise was clangorous, a riot, though their mouths were silent.

Here was a small boy of indeterminate age, with dark skin and broken nails. He looked at the Master as she approached, looked her in the eye. And he held up his broken tool, an antler gone blunt and passed down from the coolness of the valley where the strong ones worked, finally snapped and useless.

Like many of these children.

The Master held a tiny crop, a symbol of her rank. She pointed it at the insolent boy and an Underseer rushed out of a canvas lean-to. His crop was not a symbol but a tool, and he whipped the boy across the face with it once, hard but not hard enough to break his teeth. The face for insolence, and then the back for sloth. The boy's back received harsher treatment. After the first blow he cried out, by the third he screamed and tried to squirm away, and by the fifth he only sobbed in prostration.

This is how the weak ones were spent. Only a few of these would grow strong, adapt to their lives. Building the tombs was a war against time, against the impermanence of the Kings who were Gods. Soldiers died in wars, the Master knew that. Only the strong would survive, and she loved the strong ones into their strength, the weak into the mercy of death.

It was cool in the ground where the weak were buried.

"I am tired," said one of the girls. One of the weakest of them all. Always tired, always slow, back scarred with almost hourly reminders to keep up her pace. Tall for eleven, scrawny, skin that said she came from the North – far from this place of God-Kings. The sun was not kind to these blonde-haired ones, with eyes like the sky nearest the sun.

The Master pointed her crop, and an Underseer came. "If your stone is not cut there is no rest," the Master said amiably.

"No," the girl said.

The Master raised an eyebrow. 'No' was not a word allowed to the children. Her name was Mithodroxes, the Master recalled — and if she knew the name of a child it was because the child frequently required her attention. None too bright, then, this one. But the Underseer would know what to do with her. She would lose a tooth today, or worse.

"No," Mithodroxes repeated, and the Master heard something other than defiance - maybe fear. "I'm not tired, I don't feel well. I feel... dizzy, and the rocks are glowing, and there is a gray band surrounding you only it's gold at the same time."

"An aura?" The Master lurched, the crop forgotten. She waved off the Underseer before the first blow could land. "You're sure? You had best not be lying to me, girl." A girl who could see auras would be worth more alive than spent under the quarry sun, worth more than a thousand such children, more than a brick of gold. And if it was more than merely auras, if the aura presaged a vision... The Master shuddered, licked her dry lips.

Mithodroxes was not looking at the Master any more, or the stones; her eyes shut and her body started to shake. The stone adz dropped from her hand as forgotten as the Master's crop. Her bare feet twitched in the hot red sand of the quarry, and she dropped down into that sand, started to shake from head to heel among the rocks. Her fingers and toes were impregnated with quarry dust and glittered as she twitched. Where her skin had not merged with the dust, it reflected the red stones and red dirt and was red with too much sun for too long, poor fair skin that would always burn and peel and burn again and never tan.

The stones stood over her, some rounded and striated and rough, some squared, about to be freed from the ground to be hauled away and made part of some human construction. A thousand boys and girls labored over the rocks, swarming them with ropes and wires and adzes made of stone or bronze or horn, each playing their part in the liberation of the blocks. The powder-blue sky overhead was the seat of a brutal yellow sun whose heat was like a great fist.

"Take her to the cooling shed," the master said, and Underseers rushed to obey. "Tell the Great Overseer. No, he will beat you for speaking to him. I will tell him myself." At the end of the row, in front of a piece of leather stretched over sticks to provide shade, a messenger-boy awaited. "I treat you fairly, do I not?" she asked him.

"Yes, Great One," the boy said, dropping to his hands and knees and staring at the sand in front of her feet.

"Do I only beat you when it is proper to do so?"

"Yes, Great One."

"Do this thing for me. Go to the cooling shed, by an unseen way, and listen at the walls. Come back and tell me what you hear. If you do this, tomorrow you may go inside the shed and drink the cool water at the hottest time of the day. Of course I will have to beat you for spying, but I will have Thud do it." Thud had the lightest hand of all the Underseers.

"Yes, Great One," the boy said, and scrambled off through the sand, running before he was even upright.

He is a good boy, the Master thought. Perhaps he could join the priesthood, just as a slave to begin: carrying water and cleaning the temple. But in time he might be taught to read. He was of old Hitaian stock, smart and nimble. When the Great Ones had come to this place, they had found it already populated with great tombs, roads, writings. The boy's blood came from the people who had done all that, built all those things, before the Great Ones had taken them.

The Master strode through the quarry. It took a thousand or more steps to reach the tent where the Great Overseer sat in his gilded chair, reviewing plans scratched on parchments.

"Great One," she said, pressing herself into the dirt just as the messenger boy had done for her. Two large women with bronze kilts stepped behind her, flanking her. She could hear their feet in the gravelly sand, see their shadows. The Overseer's punishers, the ones with enough rank to punish the Masters. The shadows had sword hilts poking over their shoulders.

The Great Overseer did not see fit to notice her for longer than it had taken her to walk her thousand steps. He shuffled his parchments, issued orders to messengers, drank cool wine from a cup of hammered bronze. At last, when he had attention to spare for her, he said, "Speak." His voice was hoary, like the sound of a broken antler scraping against granite.

"One of the slaves has seen an aura," she said into the dirt. "And her body went into the spirit-dance, like a fallen dervish. I am much too lowly to judge such a one, Great One. I sent her to the cooling shed."

"Yes," he said, as if the word were an effort. "The cooling shed. It will be an interesting day."

"Yes, Great One," she said, not understanding.

"Go."

"Yes, Great One." She retraced her steps, grateful to leave the presence of the Great Overseer unmolested.

Back at her quarter of the quarry, the children had slowed their work. Without Underseers to remind them, their pace slackened, and without the eyes of the Master they lost all pride in their efforts. In the shade, her good ones still did at least fair work. In the sunshine, though, it was necessary to point her lash. The Underseers returning from the errands she had set appeared to enforce her will.

The cries of children in pain always set her nerves on edge, burdened her with sadness. But time wore ever onwards. These ones would be crushed and she pitied them.

Later, when the children were working once again at capacity, the messenger boy returned to his post before his small shade. The Master went to him and he prostrated himself.

"What did you hear, boy?" she said.

"A strange tale, Great One. The child, the slave, she slept in the shade for some time. The Great Overseer never came. Another person was inside, one of high rank, and all of the Underseers fled his presence as quickly as they could."

"His?"

"Yes, Great One, from his voice that I heard later. A voice I never heard before. The girl woke and she spoke to the darkness. She said, 'I saw through closed eyes, saw myself lying in the red sand, saw the children at their labors (but were they moving slowly, so slowly they were not moving at all?), saw the Master standing over me with hands on hips, shouting something I could not hear. Saw all the Masters and their Underseers and their whips held static while I whirled out above them, higher and higher, the quarry shrinking beneath her. It was a red patch in a sere brown desert. A dusty road stretched away to the city of Hitai that is also the kingdom of Hitai, and that was just a patch of ground beneath me too, and I saw the great mass of land that housed the city, saw my home far to the Northeast where I had lived with my mother and my brothers when just a small child, and all the places, all the lands of the world, and the world receded into darkness. It was a map on a black wall, then an orb hung in darkness, then just a point of light that whirled away into the nothingness around me.'"

The boy paused for breath, licked his lips with a dry tongue. "Did she say more?" the Master demanded.

"Yes," he breathed.

"Then speak it."

"Now she was among the gods, little white points of light glaring at her unblinking. Under the sky they twinkled and winked but here in the dark they probed her with a constant stare. She saw the world that had swept away from her was just one of many worlds in thrall to the yellow sun (cooler but more brutal out there in the dark), sweeping through the night amongst the gods. Farther away, past two more such worlds, through a staggeringly huge herd of tumbling stones of all sizes from sand to mountain, most of them the size of the rocks she quarried. More of them than all the water buffalo in all the world, all the greatest herds come together in one place to cross an infinite river - if only her slave mind had words for the concept of infinity."

Yes, the priesthood for certain, the Master thought. *Messenger boys should not contemplate the universe, only their instructions.* "Go on," she said.

"You will not beat me? For speech so high above my station?"

"If it is fair to do so, I will," she said. A scowl crept across her mouth, there and then gone, like a breeze in springtime.

"Yes, Great One.... And out past this, where the sun was impossible to tell from the other gods, just a tiny point of remote light, there was a ball of rock and cold and fear. Cobalt blue in the darkness, it crept through space impossibly slowly, as the boys and girls had been moving at their work as she left the world. It was not round, not even solid, a collection of things held together by mutual attraction. She could not see it moving but she knew it turned, turned, always turned about itself. How large it was she could not say: she was beyond knowing about the size of things now. Bigger than her body, smaller than her soul. And it was made of fear.

"Off in the further darkness, beyond what she could see with or without her eyes, something else moved. Something more massive, not bound to her yellow sun. And as it moved, the space near this blue thing moved, rippled like the water near shore when a bug lands in the center of the pond. It was enough, though, to set the blue fear on a new course. She watched it for a thousand thousand years, moving and not moving, drifting across the paths of other things. It skimmed above the herd of stones, wobbling through the rippling space that was their wakes, left the field in a new direction. She watched her world growing in its path, bigger and bluer and greener by the moment, each moment a thousand years. It whipped past, growing a great white tail behind it, nipped into the outer clothing of the sun and around, and then shot back towards the world so fast she could nearly see its motion."

The Master felt gnawing worry, chewing at the bottom of her stomach. Was this boy, too, a prophet? He would not do for the priesthoods after all. So much education, lucidity, was a danger. He would have to be murdered. *Strangled, I think. A mercy killing.* And all the while his strange words grew in her mind, painted a picture she could almost see. It was right there, just beyond her comprehension.

"And then what happened?" she said.

"Then I heard the other voice," he said. "The voice of the Great One. A dry voice in the dark. 'You bit your tongue. You are dry and need water, hot and need cooling. The fair ones die in droves in this place. They should reserve you for indoor labors, but you are so expendable. The Kings care little how many die to make their tombs, only that the tombs are beautiful and impress the people.'"

"The one in the shed said so?"

"Yes, Great One," the boy said. "I know you must have me thrashed for repeating such things."

"Yes. I will do it myself."

"Too great an honor," the boy said.

"Go on. What next?"

"'I was in the sky,'" the girl said. "'The blue fear is coming.'" The Great One told her to be quiet, to drink cool water. It was silent for a time – perhaps the girl went to sleep again. I heard the Great One tend to her, wiping her skin with a cloth. Then he said, "Lud. I need you."

"His name?" the Master said, her voice low, secret. "He used the name of the Great Overseer?"

"I did not know," said the boy. He dropped lower to his ground, scraped his forehead in the sand. "I am too humble for such a name to cross my lips – I did not know."

He would certainly need to be strangled now, and had provided the perfect excuse. "You are forgiven, child," she said. "Only, continue. The Great Overseer came, yes?"

"Yes," the boy said, lifting his head fractionally from the sand. "The Great Overseer wondered how he might serve. The Great One told him, 'Have this girl taken to my palace. When I see her next, she is to be clothed in green silk and samite, anointed with rosewater, with gold at her wrists and ankles. See that it is so.'"

"He said that?" the Master whispered.

"Yes, Great One," the boy said.

There was no color in her face when she caught his shoulders, dragged his to his feet. "What are you, boy? What kind of devil?"

"Only a messenger," he said, and his face was split in a smile. White teeth in a dusty bronze face, dark eyes like polished jewels, mirth like sadness.

"The Gods have smiled on you," the Master told him. "I had marked you for strangling. I was going to do it myself. Remember that. Remember my mercy."

"If there are gods," he said, "this is their mercy, not yours. Look. They are coming for you now. Best to not be seen handling a slave."

She let go of him, turned around.

Lud stalked out of his work section into the dusty quarry proper, squinted into the brightness of the day until his eyes found her. He strode across the yard, slow steps seeming to take eternity to cross the thousand steps between him and her. At last he was close enough to make himself heard. "Xand," said the Great Overseer.

The little woman seemed huge to the children, she knew that, a monolithic figure whose face beamed down to them from the sky. But she groveled before Lud, as befit her station. "Tell me how to serve," she begged. Later it might occur to one so humbled to resent being demeaned before her charges, but not now. Before Lud she was meekness itself.

"That child. Whence did she come?"

Formal language was not a good sign, and she replied in kind to try to mitigate the damage that must be coming. "From Sorub, Great one, by way of the caravans. That day you in your wisdom bought the whole shipment of slaves to speed the quarry, else she might have become a bed slave or a house slave, but she most fortunately came to work for us and learn the great speech of Hitai."

"She never showed any signs of the sight before today?"

"No, Great One. Never anything, else my eyes are blind."

"Not yet," he said, and Xand's heart beat faster. "Your King took her, marked her for greatness. Is your King wrong? Is she a slave to be bought and sold, scourged with whips, worked as an ass from the desert? Or is she a Great One to be dressed in samite and bathed in rosewater? Shall she have dust on her wrists and elbows, or bands of gold?"

It was a trap she could not avoid. She did her best not to whimper. "The King is correct, Great One. I should have seen her greatness but I am stupid and unworthy. I must be punished accordingly."

"Yes," said Lud, and made the tiniest of gestures with his index finger, the one bearing his ring. Three Underseers appeared as if from the air to enact his will. Two restrained Xand while the third drew a long curved knife from her waistband and slashed out her eyes. "You are banished," Lud said next, and waved vaguely, unseen, at the Western wall of the excavation, facing the desert.

To her credit, Xand did not cry out or beg. It would be useless and might result in further punishment. She refused to be dragged away, walked under her own power although the ruins of her eyes drove nearly everything from her mind except pain and panic. Tears and blood mixed to wash her face in gore, wasting precious water. The Underseers led her, one at each hand, almost kindly but denied any overt expression of kindness. At the gates the Underseers made to cast her to the sand, but Lud shook his head ever so slightly and they backed away, leaving her on her feet.

"You are blind and stupid," he said loudly. And more softly - for her ears alone - "but a loyal and devoted servant of the King. Go in His grace." Lud tossed his own waterskin, half full, at her feet. Xand heard the sound, knew it for a day of life, snatched it up.

"Thank you," she said simply, and turned away. She walked with all the dignity she could muster from the quarry out into the sand, into the full embrace of the sun. Only when she heard the gate clang closed behind her did she allow herself to collapse in pain and despair, as ruined in her person as in her eyes.

From the wall behind her, above the gate, the messenger boy watched her go. His teeth caught the sun, a smile making him seem half a god.